Don Pendleton's Mack Bolan®

Apocalypse Ark

A GOLD EAGLE BOOK FROM

WORLDWIDE®

TORONTO • NEW YORK • LONDON
AMSTERDAM • PARIS • SYDNEY • HAMBURG
STOCKHOLM • ATHENS • TOKYO • MILAN
MADRID • WARSAW • BUDAPEST • AUCKLAND

Recycling programs
for this product may
not exist in your area.

First edition June 2013

ISBN-13: 978-0-373-61561-2

Special thanks and acknowledgment to
Michael Newton for his contribution to this work.

APOCALYPSE ARK

Printed in U.S.A.

"You're after the Ark of the Covenant."

Bolan paused and studied the cleric. "You take that seriously?"

"I hate to think the Ethiopian Orthodox Tewahedo Church would perpetrate a fraud, mounting armed guards over nothing," Halloran said, "but stranger things have happened."

"And you were sent to check it out," Bolan prodded.

"I submit to discipline and go where I am ordered. Where I can be useful."

"Well, you earned your pay tonight. I didn't even know the Vatican had soldiers."

"Sometimes," Halloran said, "the issues we confront are...extreme."

"Like an attack on the Vatican. Do you really think they've got some superweapon from the days of Moses?"

"Even without it, zealots pose a threat to the faithful everywhere," Halloran replied.

"Bishop Astatke? I shot him," Bolan said, "when he pulled a piece."

"A true believer—" the cleric nodded "—willing to kill and die for his faith."

"I'm not big on faith these days," the Executioner replied, "but I've got the killing down."

Theological religion is the source of all imaginable follies and disturbances; it is the parent of fanaticism and civil discord; it is the enemy of mankind.

—Voltaire
Philosophical Dictionary

I don't judge any man according to his faith. They judge themselves when faith becomes their reason for persecuting and destroying others.

—Mack Bolan

For Lance Corporal Scott Olsen, USMC, Ret.

PROLOGUE

Axum, Ethiopia

Claudio Branca checked his watch, confirming that the midnight hour had struck. He spoke a single word into the slim stalk microphone attached to the small wireless headset he wore beneath a black knit stocking cap: *"Procedere!"*

Proceed.

No voices answered through the earpiece. All the members of his team were sworn to silence short of dire emergency, but Branca knew they would be moving in, as he and his companions were already moving through the darkness toward their target. Toward the goal that had obsessed them for the past twelve months and more.

The Chapel of the Tablet stood adjacent to an older, larger structure, the Church of Our Lady Mary of Zion, erected by Ezana, the first Christian emperor of Ethiopia, around AD 340, renovated and rebuilt over the centuries as time and damage from the nation's endless wars required. The Chapel of the Tablet, Branca's target, was a relatively modern structure from the 1950s, built specifically to house an object of such power that the older church couldn't contain it.

Branca and his soldiers meant to steal that power for themselves—and for the higher cause they served.

They'd come prepared, all dressed in black, with lightweight body armor underneath the trench coats that concealed their weapons. Each man on the team carried a Spectre M-4 submachine gun fitted with a sound suppressor, loaded with quad-column casket magazines containing fifty 9 mm Parabellum rounds. The Spectre's double-action trigger let them leave their safeties disengaged with no fear of an accidental discharge. Extra magazines filled pouches on the belts that each man wore.

Each member of the raiding party also wore a silenced Glock 17 pistol in shoulder rigging tailored for the individual, accommodating right- or left-hand shooters. As with the selection of their submachine guns, firepower and silence were the prime considerations. Nothing that could be planned out had been left to chance.

Aside from weapons, each man also carried certain tools: bolt cutters, pry bars, hammers, drills, a battery-powered rotary saw with titanium blades. Unable to determine what exactly they would find inside the Chapel of the Tablet, they had come prepared for anything except failure.

Five vehicles were standing by within a thousand yards of the target. Three sedans were disguised as squad cars of the Ethiopian Federal Police, with uniformed drivers. The fourth was a heavy-duty pickup truck, complete with ramming bumpers and a small electric forklift riding in its bed, designed to lift a half ton if required. The fifth, a long-body cargo van with reinforced springs and shock absorbers, would carry the team and their prize to safety.

Unless they were killed this night. In which case, another attempt would be made. And another, until success was finally achieved.

But Branca didn't plan to fail. He and the fourteen men he led, drivers included, had come prepared to sacrifice themselves for victory, and likewise, anyone who barred their way.

The Chapel of the Tablet was a domed square with an ornate cross surmounting it, built out of granite blocks, with two tall windows in each wall, and one door at the front. Its grounds, modest in size, were surrounded by a wrought-iron fence with outward-curving spikes on top. Its only gate was chained and guarded constantly by members of the church armed with the same AKM assault rifles issued to infantrymen of the Ethiopian National Defense Force.

No sound suppressors on those guns, meaning Branca and his men would have to drop the guards before they had a chance to fire or call for reinforcements. Four more guards were stationed inside the chapel proper, for rotation on the night shift, but they wouldn't really be expecting any danger. Who in his right mind would try to storm the Chapel of the Tablet in the heart of Axum, after all?

Nearing the gate, Claudio Branca clutched the Spectre underneath his coat, thinking, I would.

IT WAS AN honor to be chosen as sentry for the Chapel of the Tablet, Mamo Dego realized. A sacred trust, in fact. But it was boring, too. Despite his nation's troubled history of war and rebellion, going back to the 1970s, no serious assault had been directed at the chapel. Even members of the far-left Ethiopian People's Revolutionary Democratic Front had respected the church enough to leave its holiest of holies undisturbed, for fear of rousing public wrath.

Why should this night be any different?

Dego and Marcus Hersi were together on the gate for one more hour, watching cars pass by at ten- or fifteen-minute intervals, none of the midnight drivers slowing on Highway 3 to ogle the structure or adjoining church, much less pull in and stop. Their great excitement of the evening, so far, had come when three police cars passed, eastbound, and disappeared in the direction of Axum's main market, a half mile farther on.

Dego stifled a yawn, wished he could light a cigarette, but it was ruled unseemly for the chapel's watchmen to be smoking in the public eye. What public? You could never tell when someone from the church might happen by—or be deliberately sent by the bishop to spy on the guards and report back any infractions observed.

"What's this?" Hersi asked, peering into darkness on the far side of the highway.

Dego turned, followed his comrade's gaze and saw a man emerging from the shadows, crossing toward the chapel. Seconds later, two more figures fell in step behind him, all three dressed identically in black knit caps and unbuttoned knee-length coats, black clothing underneath. Something about their faces struck him as peculiar. They were dark enough to pass inspection at a glance, but still…

Could they be white men with their faces painted black?

Dego rolled one shoulder to release his rifle from its slung position, cradling it and releasing the safety, wishing he had cocked it when he went on duty, so that there would be a live round in the chamber. There had been an incident some years before, however, where a shot was fired by accident. Now protocol dictated that no chapel guard could bear a weapon cocked and locked unless a threat was imminent.

And Dego was worried that he might have lost his chance.

The foremost of the three approaching men surprised the guard by calling out in Amharic, the official language of the nation, "What time does the chapel open, please?"

A foolish question, since the Chapel of the Table *never* opened to outsiders, but the stranger's tone was courteous enough. Dego opened his mouth to answer, then froze as he saw a weapon rising from beneath the trench coat, its muzzle bulky with the fat extension of a silencer.

You never hear the shot that kills you.

Mamo Dego had to have heard that said a hundred times, at least, during his military service.

Now, with nearly silent bullets ripping through his chest, he found that it was almost true.

TWO SENTRIES DOWN, and Branca watched the front door of the chapel while Fontana used his bolt cutters to clip the chain securing the wrought-iron gate. The fallen guards had dropped without a sound, besides the clatter of their weapons onto pavement, and a few more seconds would see Branca's team inside the fence. Already, reinforcements were approaching, nine in all, their blackened faces stoic, weapons at the ready.

As the severed chain rattled to the ground, Branca announced into his microphone that they were through the gate, the message alerting his drivers to be ready with their vehicles. The pickup wouldn't have to ram the fence, but they might still require its forklift if the item they were seeking proved too heavy. The counterfeit patrol cars were prepared to intercept and deal with any actual police who turned up on the scene. The van would wait its turn to carry them away, arriving on command.

Branca led his strike team toward the chapel, proudly taking point for the assault. They'd learned that guards required no key to enter or exit the building. Its door was left unlocked, the chapel's custodians trusting the fence, the sentries and the wrath of God to keep its contents safe. But none of those would help this night.

A guard was seated in the chapel's narthex, startled to his feet as Branca entered, then collapsing as the Spectre M-4 whispered death into his ear and turned the beige wall crimson. The other three watchmen, huddled in the nave, had been conversing in hushed tones, and were responding to the clatter of their comrade's dying in the narthex when Branca and company surprised them.

With no quarter asked or given, Branca shot the nearest of them as the guard reached for his weapon. Other muted SMGs cut down the rest in seconds flat. No clamoring alarms betrayed them to the world outside.

So far, so good.

The chapel's vault lay dead ahead of them, beyond the chancel, apse and altar. This was where the plan risked breaking down, since neither Branca, his superiors, nor anyone he'd managed to suborn along the way had ever seen the object they were sent to claim. It might be the size of a trunk or a small compact car. It could weigh fifty pounds or twenty times as much.

Branca *did* know about the vault, its door secured by an older-model combination lock. One of his soldiers, Franco Arieti, was an expert cracksman, well equipped this night with fifteen years' experience, a stethoscope, Semtex plastique with detonators, and a thermal lance for use if all else failed. As fate would have it, though, his basic talents were enough to crack the aged box.

It was Branca's honor to open the heavy door, his thrill to be the first man from his team inside the vault. He was prepared for anything, somewhat surprised by the reality of what confronted him. After an awestruck moment, Branca turned to face his men.

"Michele, you're with me," he said. "The rest of you, let's find out what it weighs."

Four men for each of two short poles designed to aid in moving what they'd come for, built along the pattern of an old-fashioned sedan chair. Branca watched them grip the poles, then put their backs into it, raising the object six inches, then a full foot from its concrete base.

Perfect!

"Rocco, stand down," Branca said, speaking through his stalk mike to the night outside. "The forklift won't be needed. Enzo, bring the van. The rest of you, routine patrol in the vicinity. Be ready for intruders."

Orders given, Branca focused on his soldiers and their burden, smiling for the first time that he could remember during recent weeks. Eight pairs of eyes watched him expectantly.

"Come on," he said at last. "It's time to go and meet our destiny."

CHAPTER ONE

Bole International Airport, Addis Ababa, Ethiopia

Bole Airport ranked among the busiest in Africa, logging flights for nearly four million passengers yearly, while moving two and a half million tons of cargo. Its single runway was the continent's longest, at 15,502 feet, and the airport's relatively new passenger terminal, opened in January 2003, was fully air-conditioned for travelers' comfort, boasting numerous duty-free shops, restaurants, even banking facilities.

None of that mattered to Mack Bolan as he deplaned from his British Midland International flight at 2:15 p.m. local time. He traveled light, a midsized carry-on his only bag, and cleared customs without a hitch. The officer who stamped his passport welcomed Matthew Cooper to Ethiopia with the approximation of a smile and waved him on.

Why not? The passport was legit in all respects, except for Bolan's travel name. The home address existed, in the form of a Manhattan mail drop, where the bills for Matt Cooper's credit cards arrived, were forwarded and always paid on time. Cooper's credit history was excellent.

From customs, Bolan found a currency exchange, trading dollars for Ethiopian birr, then walked on to the Avis booth, to claim the rental car he had reserved before departing the States. The smile he got this time was slightly more sincere, but still reserved. He was a stranger to this land, marked by his nationality, his accent and the pigment of his skin. What should a white American arriving in the capital of Ethiopia expect?

His rental car was a black four-door Holland Tekeze hatchback, locally produced by Ethiopia's first auto assembly plant. As in the States, the car and roads were left-hand drive, so no mental change-up was necessary as he slid behind the wheel, turned the ignition key and exited the Avis section of the parking lot.

Leaving the airport, Bolan picked up Bole Drive and followed it northwestward, staying with the flow of traffic when it changed names to become Africa Avenue. Most of the major streets he crossed in transit to the downtown area were named for other nations on the continent, or for the men who'd left their mark on Africa: Kenya's Jomo Kenyatta; General Reginald Wingate, one-time British administrator of Egypt and the Sudan; and Ethiopia's own General Ras Makonnen, father of Emperor Hailie Selassie I. It seemed peculiar at a glance, collecting names from so many disparate sources, but Bolan guessed that Ethiopia's turbulent history explained the choices.

His first destination in Addis Ababa was a second-hand shop on Senegal Street, three blocks west of the Jan Meda Race Ground. The shop was called Blomkamp's, after owner Pieter Blomkamp, a South African of Boer descent who'd traveled twenty-five hundred miles from home to make a killing in used furniture, old books, estate items—and guns.

The latter trade was dicey and illegal. Ethiopia, while not forbidding private ownership of fully automatic weapons, *did* require registration of all firearms sales and mandated licensing of handgun purchasers. The maximum penalty for possession of an unregistered gun was fifteen years in prison, yet Ethiopian law placed no specific regulations on arms dealers, and customs demanded no enduser certificates for imported weapons.

Lately, the asking price for AK-47s on the street averaged 250 U.S. dollars.

Not bad.

Bolan had cash to spare, collected from a human-trafficker in Dallas some weeks back, then supplemented by a fat donation from a D.C. numbers banker on the night before he flew from Dulles International to London Heathrow. It was dirty, sure. Blood money. But cash didn't know where it came from and didn't care where it was going. Call it Bolan's form of money laundering, spending illgotten gains to balance out the books.

Free enterprise, and then some.

Addis Ababa claimed some four million inhabitants, confined within an area of two hundred square miles. To Bolan, navigating downtown traffic, it appeared that most of them were out and on the streets that afternoon in cars and buses, perched on bicycles and scooters, many of them gambling their lives to duck and dodge through traffic on foot. Most of the signs were in Amharic, a Semitic language Bolan didn't speak or read, but many had English subtitles. In fact, as the soldier's guidebook had informed him, English was the most widely spoken foreign language in Ethiopia, used as the standard medium of teaching in the nation's secondary schools.

So he'd get by all right. And if words failed him, there were other ways to get his point across.

Like pure brute force, the language understood by human predators regardless of their race or nationality.

BLOMKAMP'S WAS NOTHING much to look at from the street, probably just the way its owner planned. Bolan parked his car a half block south and fed the meter, walked back to the shop, and entered through a glass door with a decal listing business hours. Somewhere at the back, a buzzer signaled his arrival.

Pieter Blomkamp came out of the back room, dressed as if for a safari in a khaki shirt and matching shorts with cargo pockets, ginger hair cut short above his fleshy, florid face. He approached Bolan smiling, extending a hand.

"You're a welcome surprise, I can tell you," Blomkamp said. "Not many like you come my way."

"How's that?" Bolan asked.

"White men! There's a shortage in the neighborhood, in case you hadn't noticed."

Bolan let it pass. He'd come for weapons, not political debate. Reforming bigots lay beyond his field of expertise unless a bullet was the medium of change.

"I got your name from Jack Armstrong, concerning special merchandise," he said.

"How is old Jack?" Blomkamp inquired.

"Alive and kicking," Bolan said.

So far. Under another name, of course, as chief of station for the CIA running clandestine operations in the Horn of Africa.

"Good, good. So, special merchandise it is."

Blomkamp took time to lock his shop's front door, reversed the hanging sign to indicate the place was closed, then beckoned Bolan toward the back room he'd emerged from moments earlier. Once there, he moved a sliding bookcase to reveal a padlocked hidden door, unlocked and opened it, and led Bolan into his armory.

The place was wall-to-wall in guns, with crates of ammunition, magazines and other items stacked up in the middle of the room to form a kind of island. Bolan started browsing, picking weapons that would suit his purpose without leaving any trail back to the States. His prime considerations were reliability, convenience and availability of ammo on the streets, if he ran low. With that in mind, he leaned toward weapons issued to Ethiopian soldiers as standard equipment.

His first choice was an AKMS variation of the AKM assault rifle, distinguished by its under-folding metal shoulder stock. That change aside, it was identical to its parent weapon, chambered in 7.62 mm, with an effective range of four hundred meters and a cyclic rate of six hundred rounds per minute.

Bolan's chosen backup weapon was an Uzi submachine gun, purchased by Ethiopia from Israel. His model was the standard version with a metal folding stock, chambered in 9 mm Parabellum, with its muzzle threaded to accommodate a suppressor. Bolan added that accessory as well, together with a stack of 40-round magazines.

For his sidearm, Bolan deviated from the standard-issue Makarov and Czech-made Vz-52 PSL pistols carried by Ethiopian officers and noncoms. He opted instead for a Beretta 92, renowned for its reliability, and chambered for the same 9 mm Parabellum rounds as his Uzi to avoid carting around an extra caliber. As with the Uzi, he picked a Beretta and added its sound suppressor to his shopping list.

Finally, grenades. Blomkamp had several crates of Russian RGD-5s, weighing eleven ounces each. Inside each lethal egg, 110 grams of TNT lay ready to detonate on command, expelling 350 precut metal fragments with a killing range of twenty meters. Each grenade's UZRGM fuse gave Bolan four seconds to place it on target, once he'd pulled the pin and released the safety spoon.

Blomkamp approved his choices with a smile, quoted a price, and pocketed the cash while Bolan packed his merchandise into a pair of nondescript gym bags, wearing the pistol underneath his jacket in a fast-draw shoulder rig.

As they were walking toward the exit, Blomkamp said, "You're going on safari, I suppose?"

"Something like that," Bolan replied.

"Well, bag a few for me, while you're about it, eh?"

"A few what?"

"Kaffirs, man! What else? They make the best sport, eh?"

Bolan considered decking him, decided that it wouldn't be the smartest move he'd ever made, and left the jowly racist peering after him. He made sure that Blomkamp couldn't see his car or make the license as he drove away, feeling a sudden urge to shower, or at least to wash his hands.

No time for that. They would be bloody soon enough.

BOLAN'S TARGET WAS a church of sorts on Congo Street, two blocks southeast of Addis Ababa's Amanuel Mental Hospital, near Dilachim Secondary School. The proximity of lunatics to schoolchildren bemused him, but he trusted both facilities to be secure, and neither figured in his mission of the moment. Rather, he was looking for a way inside the job at hand, and that required that Bolan go to church.

Specifically, the Temple of the Holy Covenant, presided over by one Bishop Berhanu Astatke, who'd been born in Adigrat, in Ethiopia's Tigray Region, and adopted by Swiss parents when his widowed mother died in a tuberculosis epidemic. Educated in Zurich and Rome, he'd found religion as a graduate student and returned to his native soil as an evangelist for the sect he now served as its highest-ranking officer in Ethiopia.

All perfectly legitimate on paper, and according to Astatke's flock of two hundred parishioners. Defectors told another story, and their tales had reached the U.S. embassy in Addis Ababa, where one Paul Ray—alias "Jack

Armstrong"—had passed the word along to headquarters at Langley. His report was filed there, more or less forgotten, until very recently, when circumstances had raised it from the status of a curiosity to urgent business.

As it happened, urgent business for the Executioner.

Bolan drove past the Temple of the Holy Covenant, a less-than-stately building made from cinder blocks and painted apricot, now faded by the sun to something more like antique-white. An overhead marquee identified the church and listed hours for its services throughout the week. Around the block, an alley lined with battered garbage cans permitted access to a back door fitted with a dead bolt lock, and windows of dirty frosted glass behind cages of rusty bars.

However Bolan tried to breach the place, he'd have to wait for nightfall. Daylight penetration meant witnesses on hand and probable involvement of police. Once law enforcement got involved, his options would be reduced to two: escape somehow without employing lethal force, or go to jail with no hope of assistance from the embassy or any other outside source.

Deniability was key to every mission Bolan undertook. He had accepted that from day one of his service to the government that had once pursued him as the world's most wanted fugitive. Exemption of police from deadly force was Bolan's private rule, a self-imposed restriction recognizing law-enforcement officers as "soldiers of the same side," even when they sold their badges to the highest bidder and were criminals themselves. He'd long since given up on arguing the point with any of his few surviving friends. It was a rule—a solemn vow—Bolan would live or die by, if it came to that.

The dashboard clock in his Tekeze told him it was nearly five o'clock, which left him two hours to kill before nightfall. He drove around downtown until he spied the golden arches of McDonald's, where he bought a sack of burgers at the drive-through window and consumed them as he reconnoitered neighborhoods adjacent to the Temple of the Holy Covenant, marking approaches and escape routes that could serve him after dark.

He had the layout now, but there was still much that he wouldn't know until he breached the temple. He expected guards but couldn't guess their number or surmise how they would be equipped. Smart money said they would be true believers, primed to kill or be killed for the cause, but he could test their mettle only when the action started. Until then, guesswork was worse than useless and could lead him into fatal error.

When he had finished his burgers, Bolan found a shopping mall, pulled in at the outer edge of its parking lot, with ready access to the street, and passed his time reviewing maps of the capital. He'd roughly memorized them on his long flight from the States, but there was no such thing as being too prepared. A wrong turn on a one-way street could trap him if he wasn't ready for it, and he hadn't stayed alive this long, against all odds, by skimming over small details.

By sundown he would know the battlefield as if it were his own hometown.

Whatever happened after that was up to Fate.

BISHOP BERHANU ASTATKE checked the large clock on his office wall again and saw that he still had ten minutes left before his special members gathered for the evening service. Glancing toward the closed door to his left, he opened the bottom right-hand drawer of his desk and removed the bottle of Baro Dry Gin that he kept hidden there. Whether the bottle was in fact a secret from his flock didn't concern Astatke at the moment.

Nothing in his chosen creed forbade the use of alcohol, though several passages from holy writ condemned excess in any phase of life. Bishop Astatke smiled at that, considering the course of action his superiors had chosen, nearly chuckling to himself as he unscrewed the lid and drank two swallows directly from the bottle.

The gin drowned nervous twitching in his gut, leaving the bishop more relaxed than he had been a moment earlier. With some reluctance, he recapped the bottle, tucked it out of sight and closed its drawer on the temptation to keep guzzling fire until his mind went blank.

His message for this night, delivered to an all-male audience, would call for fortitude and courage in the troubled days ahead. A prophecy of conflict that should come as no surprise to any member of the church's inner circle by this time. It might come down to all-out war, in fact, and he assumed that most of the parishioners expected at the gathering would turn up fully armed.

Soldiers of God, bless them.

Bishop Astatke only hoped that they—and he—hadn't been led astray.

The bottle whispered to him from its hiding place, but the bishop had a response on the tip of his tongue. "Get thee behind me, devils. At least for the next few hours."

In the spirit of the evening, he opened the drawer above his liquor stash and a clip-on holster for his belt. Nestled inside it was a Makarov pistol, no longer issued to Russian troops as standard equipment, but still manufactured for sale at home and abroad. The pistol's magazine was fully loaded with eight 9 mm Makarov rounds, but Astatke didn't keep a round in the chamber. Why take chances, when he'd never been proficient with guns in the first place?

Still, it was a symbol and would send the proper message to his loyal parishioners. Preparedness, a will to fight and die for their beliefs if need be. Death to infidels who stood between God's chosen people and their goal of ultimate redemption.

Bishop Astatke rose, finding it easier to clip the holster on his belt when he was standing, and had nearly managed it when angry voices focused his attention on the nearby chapel. He was halfway to the office door, phrasing an admonition in his mind, when someone yelped as if in pain, then gunshots echoed from the church's breeze block walls.

Astatke tried to draw his pistol, but brought the whole loose holster with it, cursing most unlike a clergyman as he unsnapped the leather thumb-break strap, pulled out the Makarov and let the holster fall. With trembling hands, he pumped the pistol's slide, chambered a round and reached for the doorknob.

I could hide here, he thought, but he had to find out what was happening outside his door. The church and its parishioners were his responsibility, a debt he owed to God and to his temporal superiors. Above all else, he had to stop the hellish racket coming from the chapel before someone passing on the street took notice and alerted the police.

Clutching his pistol in a death grip, tight enough to make his knuckles ache, Astatke cracked his door and peered outside. He saw nothing in the empty hallway, but recoiled as more shots reached his ears, louder without the closed door as a baffle. Muttering a hasty prayer, he crept out of the office, edged along the corridor to reach a door that stood behind the chapel's altar. Shaking like a man gripped by malaria, he hesitated there, then found his nerve and pushed on through.

Into a scene straight out of hell.

BOLAN HAD COME in from the alleyway, knowing he couldn't pick the back door's dead bolt, so letting the Spectre M-4 handle it. One nearly silent round at point-blank range was all he needed, but he heard the shattered locking mechanism clatter on a concrete floor inside before he cleared the threshold. Braced to deal with sentries double-timing to investigate, he was relieved to find himself alone inside a short, deserted corridor.

The church *was* occupied, however. On his last drive-by, he'd seen a guard on Congo Street, playing it casual, and now the sound of murmuring voices drew Bolan toward what he supposed had to be the meeting hall. He passed two doors along the way, paused long enough to listen briefly at each one, then moved on when he heard nothing on the other side. A risk, but so was dawdling in the hallway when someone might wander by at any second, going to or from the chapel.

Bolan reached another door; no doubt about the voices emanating from behind this one. It sounded like a conversation under way, rather than any kind of mass or sermon, and he took his chances, barging through into a room with seating for a hundred people, give or take. Most of the pews were empty, but he counted seven men down front before they registered a stranger's presence in their midst.

As luck would have it, Bolan's entry placed him in the chapel's apse, behind the altar, facing toward the nave. It felt like being pushed onstage before a surly audience, except that most theater patrons wouldn't have been packing guns. This group was armed to the last man, all reaching for their weapons as they realized someone stood before them with a submachine gun in his hands.

Bolan was quicker, since he didn't have to draw. He caught one of the gunmen rising, pistol raised, but still off-target when a 3-round burst spit past the altar, stitched a bloody track across the would-be shooter's chest and sat him down again. A second burst from Bolan's SMG sheared through the next grim face in line, then the survivors started to return fire, peppering the back wall of the apse with hasty shots.

Bolan fell prone behind the altar, hoping its mahogany facade would hold up long enough for him to prime one of his Russian frag grenades and let it fly. He'd hoped to find Bishop Astatke without battling through the bishop's congregation, but the fat was in the fire now, and he had no other choice. Survival was his first priority, living to fight—or to collect intelligence—another day.

The soldier had palmed one of the green RGD-5s and was about to pull its pin when someone burst in through the same door that had led him to the chapel. The belated entrant was a man older than any of the trigger-happy worshippers out front, dressed all in black except the snow-white backward collar marking him as clergy. In his hand, where casual observers might expect a crucifix or other scepter of his faith, he clutched a pistol angling Bolan's way.

This had to be Bishop Astatke, likely coming from one of the rooms that Bolan hadn't cleared in passing, and his hope of questioning the clergyman was gone. Before the bishop had a chance to use his sidearm, Bolan fired a burst that cut his legs from under him and dropped him squealing to the carpet. With the pistol spinning from his grasp, Astatke's threat was minimized, and Bolan focused on the members of his congregation, who were more enraged than ever, yelling for the interloper's blood as they poured gunfire toward the altar.

Bolan primed the frag grenade and lofted it over the altar, toward the chapel's nearest pews. Somebody saw it coming, and called a warning to the rest, but the four-second fuse gave little time for anyone on the receiving end to find cover. When the blast erupted, he heard shrapnel peppering the altar inches from his head, but none of it came through. Screams rising with the smoke from the explosion told him that he had an opportunity to move and shouldn't let it go to waste.

Another second saw him up and running toward the bishop, who was sprawled and moaning on the floor behind him. Bolan reached the man and rolled him over, and was about to pose a question when a shout from the direction of the street drew his attention to a crowd of gunmen entering the chapel, weapons drawn.

Bolan beat the storm of bullets by a heartbeat, dashing through the door he'd entered by and along the hallway toward the alley at the chapel's rear. Were other gunmen waiting for him in the darkness there?

One way to know. He hit the back door at a sprint and plunged into the night.

CHAPTER TWO

Washington, D.C., two days earlier

A handful of early-bird tourists were clustered outside the Lincoln Memorial at 9:00 a.m. Mack Bolan, aka the Executioner, watched them from a distance, mostly couples taking turns as they approached the throne of Lincoln, posing almost bashfully while their partners snapped photos to memorialize the event. Looming nineteen feet above them, Lincoln remained impassive, as he had since May 1922, staring across the National Mall toward the upthrust spire of the Washington Monument with a look of resignation.

Or could it be sadness?

Bolan didn't know what the sculptors had had in mind when they'd started carving Honest Abe from Georgia marble more than ninety years earlier. Had they been striving to depict a president well pleased by the results of catastrophic civil war? Perhaps bemused by his own murder at Ford's Theater less than a week after the rebel Army of Northern Virginia's surrender at Appomattox? As Bolan knew from high school, fighting had continued for a month after Lincoln's death, and the last sizable force of Confederate troops hadn't surrendered for another five weeks after that.

Did Lincoln, dying, even know he'd won?

Was any battle between Good and Evil ever truly won?

Spring sunshine on his face made Bolan disinclined

to chase that question in an endless circle, as he had for years, since the beginning of his one-man war against a world of human predators. In fact, he knew the answer: victory was never more than temporary. You could kill a human enemy—or hundreds of them, sure—but killing Evil was impossible. It grew like cancer in the dark corners of human hearts and minds, somehow invulnerable to the chemotherapy of education and enlightenment.

Were some people born bad, or turned into monsters by hellish childhoods?

By the time Bolan encountered them as murderous adults, what difference did it make?

He checked his watch and saw that it was 9:06. The meeting had been set for 9:15, no reason asked or offered. Maybe Hal Brognola had some paperwork to finish off at Justice, across the Mall on Pennsylvania Avenue. Most likely, he'd be walking over from his office.

A few more tourists had arrived to stare at Lincoln, climbing granite steps that rose from the Reflecting Pool toward fluted Doric columns with a frieze above them, naming all fifty states with dates when they'd entered the Union that Lincoln had fought and died to save. Bolan couldn't have said if they were properly impressed, but none were laughing, cavorting or blaring music from boom boxes.

The soldier rated that a plus.

He saw Brognola coming now, dressed for the office in a stylish charcoal suit, white shirt, a red tie adding color. The big Fed was wearing a fedora. His hangdog face, as grim or simply tired as Lincoln's, indicated that the world's weight rested on his shoulders.

So far, it appeared that he was bearing up all right.

Bolan met the man halfway, automatically checking his old friend for tails. No one was tracking him, as far as

Bolan could determine, but with the technology available these days there could have been surveillance on Brognola from the far end of the Mall—or from the depths of outer space. At least Mack couldn't spot a human stalker within killing range.

"Been waiting long?" Brognola asked, as they shook hands.

"Not very."

"I thought this would make a change of pace from Arlington," the big Fed said. "And with the heat on, I've been tethered to my desk. Getting away to Stony Man is problematical." Stony Man Farm was the site of the country's top covert counterterrorism organization, the Sensitive Operations Group. Brognola was its director.

An hour's flight or less by helicopter from the capital. Brognola had to be under the gun.

"Which heat is that?" Bolan asked, conscious that the temperature ran high in Washington, regardless of the season.

"It's weird this time," the man from Justice said.

"This time?" Bolan replied, half smiling.

"Okay, weird*er*." Brognola observed the nearby tourists for a moment, frowning at them. "We should take a walk."

They walked. When they had put a hundred yards or so between themselves and Lincoln, the big Fed slowed down and asked, "What do you know about the ark, offhand."

"Which ark is that?" Bolan asked. "Noah and the flood, you mean?"

"The other one. The Ark of the Covenant. The Ten Commandments. All that."

Bolan had to smile, then. "I saw *Raiders* years ago, on cable in some hotel room. Beyond that, nothing much. Why do you ask?"

Brognola cocked his head, peered skyward with a

squint, as if he sought the satellite that could be tracking them from somewhere out beyond the exosphere. Or was he seeking something else?

"Okay," he said at last. "Get ready for the weird. Have you ever heard of Custodes Foederis?"

"Not a whisper that I can recall," Bolan said.

"It's Latin for Covenant Keepers. A cult that popped up after Y2Kaos fizzled and left all the doomsayers dressed in their sackcloth and ashes with nowhere to go. They were pissed, if you noticed. Some big names with egg on their faces, and donations dropping like stock market prices when Standard & Poor's knocked an A off the U.S. credit rating."

"Stands to reason," Bolan said. "When prophets drop the ball, their profits suffer."

"In my opinion," Brognola replied, "it couldn't happen to a nicer bunch of con men. Rip-off artists selling misery they can't deliver to a bunch of folks who can't afford it. What the hell, don't get me started."

"Anyway," Bolan said.

"Anyway, when the dust starts to settle, there's Custodes Foederis, operating from a modest base in Rome. At first glance, you'd mistake it for a Catholic splinter group, on a par with the Latin Rite Church, the Congregation of Mary Immaculate Queen and various others."

Bolan nodded, though the names had a vague familiar ring. "But it's different?" he asked.

"In spades," Brognola said. "Turns out, for all their trappings, that the Keepers are as anti-Catholic as any outfit you could name, the Ku Klux Klan included."

"And they're based in Rome?"

"To keep a sharp eye on the Vatican," Hal said. "Or, as they like to call it in their literature, the Scarlet Whore of Babylon."

"That kind of thing still sells?" Bolan asked.

"Like ice cream in August, to the proper target audience," the big Fed said. "Turns out you've got a sizable collection of defectors from the church who've split over one grievance or another. Everything from Vatican II and masses in English to pedophile padres, you name it. Somebody doesn't like the pope's red loafers, they can find a place to bitch about it with the Keepers. They've even got a formula worked out that brands the pope as Satan, from his crown."

"Say what?"

"There's an inscription on the papal mitre," Brognola explained. "*Vicarius Filii Dei*. It translates from Latin as 'Vice-regent of the Son of God.'"

"And how do you get Satan out of that?" Bolan asked.

"Roman numerals. Throw out the letters with no numerical value, noting that the *u* in *Vicarius* looks like a *v,* and it adds up to 666. The Mark of the Beast from Revelation, that is."

"You're kidding, right?"

"I wish," Brognola said. "Of course, whoever did the math forgot that 'IV' counts as *four* in Roman numerals, not one plus five, so the actual total is 664. Try telling that to crazy people, though."

"Okay, you've taught me something," Bolan said. "But what's this got to do with me? With us?"

"Good question," Brognola replied. "As luck would have it, Custodes Foederis isn't just another bunch of kooks ranting about the papacy and Armageddon. They're convinced they had a destiny to crush the Scarlet Whore of Babylon and save the world."

"With faulty math?" Again, Bolan was forced to smile.

"If only. This is where the Ark comes in."

"How's that?"

"If you remember your Old Testament—or *Raiders,* take your pick," Brognola said, "Moses received the Ten Commandments on Mount Sinai. Twice, in fact, but that's another story. Anyway, he stashed them in a wooden chest—the Ark—along with other magic goodies, including a jar of manna from heaven, the staff he used to strike Egypt with plagues and the first Torah scroll. He covered it with cloth and goat skins, mounted it on golden poles and got a team of priests to carry it twelve hundred yards ahead of the wandering Israelites."

Bolan nodded, still waiting for the story to make sense.

"Your movie viewing may have told you that the Ark was powerful," Brognola said.

"Melts Nazis," Bolan said. "It would've come in handy on D-day."

"In fact, whoever touched it without God's express permission was supposedly struck dead. Its power allowed Joshua's trumpet players to drop the walls of Jericho, after they'd marched around the town for seven days."

"And this connects to your cult in Rome…how, again?"

"Funny that you should ask. They claim to have the Ark," Brognola stated.

"Okay. I thought you said—"

"You heard me right. There are several stories about where the Ark and its contents wound up. One version says a cave on Mount Nebo, in Jordan. Another claims it's in a cavern in the Dumghe Mountains of South Africa. Some Frenchman said the Knights Templar found it and took it to Chartres Cathedral during the Crusades. Another has it hidden at Rennes-le-Château, in southern France, then found by GIs and brought back to the States after World War II."

"So, how do the Covenant Keepers claim they bagged it?"

"From Axum, in northern Ethiopia. The Ethiopian Orthodox Tewahedo Church has claimed to have the Ark for decades, under guard. The church's head man announced its unveiling to the public in June 2009, then changed his mind the next day, telling the world to take his word that it exists."

"Must be a tough sell," Bolan said.

"Not to Custodes Foederis," Brognola replied. "They claim to have it now, extracted by a special action team sometime last week. We've verified a raid against the Chapel of the Tablet there, in Axum. Half a dozen sentries killed by shooters who escaped with something."

"That sounds like a job for Ethiopian police, or maybe Interpol," Bolan said.

"Would be," Brognola agreed, "if it was just a theft."

"What is it, then?"

"The kickoff for a new Crusade, apparently. The Keepers claim they'll use the Ark to crush the Vatican and bring on the Apocalypse."

"Don't tell me that you buy it," Bolan said.

"It's hard to swallow, I admit. The last bit, anyway. But they can raise hell trying, and the word's come down to head it off if possible."

Bolan had tackled killer cults before, and terrorists who claimed their marching orders came from the Almighty. Hoping he could spot a way inside the mission being offered to him, he told Brognola, "Okay, then. Run it down."

"Deep background's on a DVD I brought along," the big Fed said, and took a slim disk from the inside pocket of his suit coat, passing it to Bolan in a jewel case. "As for the basics, Custodes Foederis popped up out of nowhere, as far as we knew at the time, in the summer before 9/11. The founding father, or Pontifex Rex to the faithful—that's 'Patriarch King,' by the way—calls himself Janus Marcellus. Born Giovanni Capasso in Naples, June 1974."

"Why the name change?" Bolan asked.

"The Keepers are big on their Latin," Hal said. "His pick translates roughly as 'Hammer of Janus,' whom, you may recall, was the two-faced Roman god of beginnings and transitions. Also doorways, gates, endings and time."

"Two-faced," Bolan said. "Pun intended?"

"His father was a Catholic priest, defrocked and excommunicated for his opposition to Vatican II. Couldn't keep his mouth shut under orders, so they booted him."

"So, no more celibacy," Bolan said.

"His son was born six months after the excommunication," Brognola replied. "You do the math."

"And little Giovanni grows up hearing that the church his father left is everything corrupt and evil in the world."

"You got it. Giovanni's partner in the Keepers—and his wife, in fact—is known as Mania Justina, known to the sect as Reginae Matris. 'Queen Mother,' that is. On her birth certificate, she's plain old Clara Vitti, born in Palermo, October 1981."

"Mafia territory," Bolan said.

"Correct, and she's connected. One of her cousins got life for murder and extortion at the Maxi Trial in 1987. Clara was in court to hear the verdict. Six years old."

"So…what? The whole church thing's some kind of scam? A racket to extort cash from the Vatican?"

"I wish it were that simple," Brognola replied, "but no such luck. The shrinks at Quantico have been dissecting Janus and his queen since the attack at Axum. They read both players as sincere in their professed beliefs, as far as profiling can take it."

"So, sincerely crazy," Bolan said.

Brognola shrugged. "I doubt they'd qualify as legally insane, but what's the difference? We're not collecting evidence for court. It all gets shaky when you're dealing with religion, anyway. Somebody claims God told him he should run for president. Another one jumps in and says, 'No, He told *me!*' Toss in your miracles and prophecies, the so-called history that can't be verified, jihads, crusades and clinic bombings. Hey, don't get me started."

"And the job is what? Retrieve the Ark and haul it back to Ethiopia? Confirm its power as an icon or a weapon?"

"We don't even know there *is* an ark," Brognola said. "The church in Axum swears there is, and it's been taken. But remember, no one else has seen it since the middle of the thirteenth century, if then. Let's grant that they had something, and it's gone now. If Custodes Foederis can use it to stir up dissension and bloodshed, whatever it is, that makes it a weapon."

"Same question," Bolan said. "What outcome are you hoping for?"

"Job one," Brognola answered, "is to neutralize the threat by any means required. Church politics doesn't concern me when we've got lives riding on the line."

"Okay. How public is this thing?" Bolan inquired. "I have to say, this is the first I'm hearing of it."

"Chalk that up to clergy saving face," the big Fed said. "Our knowledge of the Axum raid came in through diplomatic channels, from Addis Ababa. Janus and his Keepers have been taking credit for it on the down-low, circulating word among their chapters, not admitting anything to get them in hot water with the media or Interpol."

"And you know this because…?"

"A couple of informants in the cult have passed the word along, but can't say where the prize is, much less what it is."

"And I'd be starting on the ground in Ethiopia?" Bolan asked.

"Familiar territory, more or less," Brognola said. "You had that rumble in Sudan, next door, not long ago."

"No reason to believe the Ark's still there," Bolan observed.

"Unlikely. But the Keepers have a congregation in the capital. Smart money says they must know something about heavy action in their own backyard."

"Makes sense," Bolan agreed. "I'll need a flight."

"I took the liberty of booking one," Brognola said. "In case you ran with it. You're on British Airways out of Dulles International tonight, connecting with BMI at London Heathrow down to Addis."

"Right. Connections at the other end, for gear?"

"It's on the DVD."

"In case I ran with it," Bolan said, smiling.

"If you'd rather pass it…"

"Not likely," Bolan said. "May need a hat and whip, though, so I'll measure up to what's-his-name."

THE DVD FILLED Bolan in on the strange history of Custodes Foederis. Based in Rome, as Brognola had said, the sect had twenty-three additional congregations, in Italy, Holland and France, Great Britain, Canada and the United States, Latin America, Africa and Australia. Headquarters—dubbed the Seat of Enlightenment—claimed thirty thousand followers worldwide, but verification was dicey at best. The church kept secret membership rolls, and no concerted effort had been made on any front to track its followers before the Axum incident.

Bolan read the brief police report, confirming six men dead and an assertion by the Chapel of the Tablet's rector that an "object of supreme importance" had been stolen by the unknown raiders. Add to that the summaries of statements from informers inside Custodes Foederis, claiming possession of the Ark, and Bolan granted that the case was made, at least for his limited purposes.

He took for granted that Janus Marcellus and his wife would keep their hands clean when it came to killing—at least until the time came for them to pull the trigger on the great apocalypse. He focused on the sect's chief of security and its presumed enforcer, one Ugo Troisi, known to the flock as Dextera Dei.

God's Right Hand, no less.

Troisi, like the former Clara Vitti, was Sicilian, born in April 1982 at Montedoro, in the province of Caltanissetta. He'd done time for assault and robbery before finding religion with the Keepers, and while nothing on file linked Troisi to the Mafia per se, it was impossible to grow up in Sicily without awareness of the so-called Honored Society. A candid photo of Troisi with the sect's patriarch and queen, taken in Rome, had caught him ogling the woman's ample cleavage while Janus Marcellus was signing copies of some book he'd written.

Something going on there? Bolan wondered, but he couldn't think of any way to make it work for him, off-hand. At best, a weak spot in the hierarchy. Possibly a fault line where a wedge could be applied, downrange.

The sect had soldiers of a sort, under Troisi's leadership, known collectively as Exercitus Dei: the Army of God. Officially, they were bodyguards for Janus Marcellus and Mania Justina, securing the Seat of Enlightenment and other church property against infidel opponents. Little was known of their background or training, but defectors from Custodes Foederis claimed that Troisi favored ex-military personnel, requiring pledges of allegiance to the cult and its royal couple. Estimates of total membership for Exercitus Dei started at one hundred and topped out at double that. Most of the troops were thought to hang their hats in Rome, but if they'd been involved at Axum, who could say?

When Bolan was done with the DVD, he snapped it into half a dozen pieces, pitched the fragments in a garbage bin behind a busy fast-food restaurant, and went to catch his flight at Dulles International. He traveled light—one carry-on, no weapons—and arrived two hours prior to takeoff, as recommended by Homeland Security. His British Airways flight was leaving from concourse B in the main terminal, a long walk past shops and food courts to the designated gate. Bolan kept an eye out for watchers but saw nothing to concern him.

Trouble would be waiting for him at the other end—not London, but once he arrived in Ethiopia. He knew enough about the troubled nation's past and recent history to realize that guns were plentiful and life was cheap, despite creation of a coalition government to wrest control from the Ethiopian People's Revolutionary Democratic Front in 2010, after a decade of autocratic rule. Images of drought and famine from the mid-1980s had returned in 2011, when two consecutive rainy seasons failed to materialize on schedule, and pursuit of long-term strategies for meaningful relief was still in progress, making little headway against spiteful Mother Nature.

Meanwhile, Bolan knew, cracks had developed in the hopeful coalition government, as eight member parties jockeyed for position, stepping on one another's toes. Police had jailed the leader of one party, Unity for Democracy and Justice, prompting renewed calls for rebellion that could tip the scales back toward an era of coups and repression seen at the turn of the twenty-first century. Some elements were obviously spoiling for a fight, while others hunkered down to play defense and hold their ground.

In short, the whole place was a powder keg.

And Bolan was about to light the fuse.

CHAPTER THREE

Addis Ababa, the Present

The alley had seemed wider going in, not such a narrow shooting gallery. The widely spaced security lights at each end had looked dimmer to Bolan, somehow, on his approach. Now, they seemed to glare like spotlights focused on him as he ran along the cluttered passageway, hearing the church's back door slam behind him, then crash open once again, spilling a clutch of hunters.

There was fury in their voices as they shouted after him, their feelings clear, although the words were unknown to him. Another heartbeat, and their weapons started speaking for them, hammering the alley with a hellish racket, the crack of shots and whine of ricochets. The air around him sizzled with a hiss of angry hornets in pursuit.

Bolan ducked and rolled to his left, coming to rest behind a garbage bin that reeked of rotting food, at best. A rat squeaked out from under him, and Bolan hoped it was alone. There'd be no time for rabies shots if he was nipped by vermin at the outset of his mission. No damn time for anything, in fact, if he stayed cornered where he was.

The garbage bin started taking hits, reverberating like a big, malodorous bass drum. Bolan reached out to fire a short burst from his Uzi back the way he'd come from. The muffled sounds of his shots were lost in the cacophony, but someone yelped a warning and the charging gunmen slowed, diving for cover of their own.

Stalemate.

A standoff had to work against the Executioner. Remaining where he was, pinned down, he couldn't stop his enemies from doubling back around the block to seal the alley's mouth and cut off all escape. That done, they had only to risk a cross fire to eliminate him—or hold fast until police arrived, then scatter, leaving uniforms to deal with the invader of their chapel.

All for nothing, Bolan thought, since he'd obtained precisely nothing from the man he'd come to grill. Bishop Astatke might be dead, or only wounded. In either case, the pistol-packing clergyman was lost to Bolan now.

Which wouldn't matter if he died within the next few moments, where he was.

Grenade time.

Bolan palmed the second RGD-5 that he'd carried on his house call to the church, released its pin and used blind guesswork on the placement of his targets. He figured they were spread across the alley, hiding where they could, using any cover readily available, from garbage cans to recessed doorways. He knew that he couldn't get them all—and might wound *none* of them—but he could raise the ante and disorient them long enough to sprint along the alley's final fifty feet, duck clear and try to reach his waiting car.

Maybe.

It was a gamble, sure. Like every other move that Bolan made.

But if he didn't roll the dice...

Another Uzi burst to keep their heads down, then he twisted in his crouch and lofted the grenade over the stinking bin, giving it some altitude and distance, hoping that he didn't overshoot, in fact, and drive his adversaries closer to him by mistake. Grenades were always iffy, the direction of their blasts determined by the nearest solid surface, shrapnel flying everywhere and maiming without any care for whose flesh it was shredding.

One…two…

Counting down the second until detonation, Bolan braced himself to run like hell the minute the blast gave him an opportunity. No hesitation, if he planned to make it through the night alive.

Three…four…

The explosion came half a second late, by Bolan's count, but who could really say? He bolted, running through the smoke and dust and screams, sprinting to save his life.

INSIDE THE TEMPLE of the Holy Covenant, Tamrat Gessesse crouched beside the prostrate form of Bishop Berhanu Astatke, doing what he could to stop the bleeding from Astatke's legs. One of the attacker's shots had drilled the bishop's right thigh, and it seemed that two had torn his left leg, one piercing his kneecap, though Astatke's blood-soaked pants made an assessment of the damage difficult. Gessesse's full weight on the thigh wound hadn't stanched the bleeding yet, and he had no hands free to deal with any other hemorrhages at the moment.

"Eyasu! Benjamin! Come help me, will you!"

The two armed congregants, who'd been standing back and whispering, as if afraid to touch the bishop in his worst extremity, stepped reluctantly into the spreading pool of blood, seeming dazed by what they saw before them.

"On your knees, for God's sake!" Gessesse commanded. "Never mind your pants. Put pressure on those wounds. We'll lose him if the bleeding doesn't stop."

They knelt together, did as they were told, both grimacing in their distaste—or was it sympathetic pain for what their clergyman was suffering? Gessesse didn't know and didn't care. He looked around and saw a fourth man standing well back from the action, wincing as the bishop groaned and shivered.

"Tafari, call an ambulance!"

The young man blinked at him. "But the police—"

"Are coming anyway, with all this shooting. Do it now!"

Tafari dug into a pocket for his cell phone and turned away to place the call. His voice, a murmur in the background, barely registered over the sounds the bishop made. And was he only moaning now, or was he trying to speak?

"Please save your strength," Gessesse said, half whispering. "You've been badly injured."

Astatke's face contorted with the pain he felt, the effort to talk. "Dextera Dei…warn him…enemy…the Ark…beware…."

Gessesse felt a sudden chill. "Hush, now," he said, and turned in wrath to face Tafari. "What news of the ambulance?"

"It's coming," the man said, looking as if he might be going into shock.

"Wake up!" Gessesse snapped at him. "Remove the weapons from those bodies and conceal them. Quickly! When police arrive, say only that a crazy white man came into the church and started shooting. Understand?"

"Yes, sir." Tafari turned and started lifting pistols from the bodies of their brothers who had fallen in the brief attack.

Gessesse knew his hasty plan was likely futile, but it was the only thing that he could think of. Blame the nameless gunman for disrupting worship services, and hope the law wouldn't look closely at the Temple of the Holy

Covenant. Perhaps, if they were very lucky and the Lord obliged them—

Gunfire and the *crump* of a grenade explosion from the alleyway behind the church cut off that line of wishful thinking. With a silent curse, Gessesse focused on the task of trying to preserve the bishop's life until the ambulance arrived. What happened after that was unpredictable, beyond his power to control. Perhaps he could escape in the confusion and—do what?

Obey the bishop's halting command. Warn someone higher in authority of the attack and the potential danger that it posed to Custodes Foederis. As far as personally reaching Dextera Dei in Rome, Gessesse had no clue to how he should proceed. There had to be contact numbers, maybe even email access through the church's website, but the message he'd been tasked to pass was not for open lines.

In fact, if he was careless, it could doom them all.

SOMEONE WAS FIRING through the cloud of smoke and dust raised by Bolan's frag grenade as he broke from cover, running toward the alley's mouth. Wild shots, unaimed, but stray bullets could kill as well as shots precisely targeted. He ducked and dodged, hearing the slugs strike bricks on either side of him and ricochet into the night beyond. The impulse to return fire would have slowed him. Bolan ignored it, concentrated on his goal of getting to the cross street, ducking out of range, reaching his rented car.

Then, suddenly, a muzzle-flash winked at him from the alley's opening onto that street, bullets flying at Bolan from a new direction, reaching out to swat him down. Blocking his way and cutting off escape. He dropped facedown, felt gravel digging into elbows, chest and knees as grazing automatic fire swept overhead.

A quick glance left and right revealed his choices when it came to cover. On his left, two battered garbage cans with dented lids askew; to Bolan's right, a doorway recessed far enough to let him stand upright, concealed, but still a death trap if his enemies advanced from either side.

Choices. But staying where he lay was no option at all.

Rolling, returning fire, he made it to the alcove, slammed his back against the metal door and tried the knob. Locked tight, of course, and while he might have picked the lock in other circumstances, trying now would only leave him fatally exposed to shooters flanking him on either side. Gunfire from both ends of the alley rattled past him, missing him by inches. For a second, Bolan hoped his would-be killers might take each other out, but someone shouted from the street side, the words incomprehensible, and suddenly the firing stopped.

Okay. They'd recognized each other and the risk of firing blindly back and forth. They knew that he was trapped somewhere between the side street and the back door to their temple, maybe had a fix on his position and were working up the nerve to rush him. In the sudden silence, he could picture gunmen creeping forward, pressed against the nearest wall, and he tried to listen for their footsteps in the alleyway.

Nothing so far.

Instead of being grateful for the respite, Bolan knew that every second spent in hiding, wasting time, increased the likelihood that cops would soon arrive. That spelled the end for him, whether the cultic shooters fled or not. Police would either gun him down on sight, or mob him when they realized that he wasn't about to fire on them.

And either way, it meant his death, as sure as if he pressed his own Beretta to his head.

In fact, that might be preferable to arrest, but Bolan

drew the line at suicide. Self-sacrifice in battle was an
option always on the table, but to simply waste himself…

No way in hell.

Better to go down fighting against hopeless odds before
the law arrived, if that turned out to be his only choice.
Hope someone else would be dispatched from Stony Man
to finish off the mission, where he'd failed.

But fatalism wasn't part of Bolan's makeup. Long experience had taught him there was always hope, as long as
life remained. In situations that seemed hopeless, sheer au-
dacity could sometimes shift the balance, catch an enemy
off guard and shift a slim advantage back to Bolan.

Maybe.

Switching out the Uzi's magazine to keep a full load in
the weapon, Bolan braced himself to meet his adversaries.
Rout them if he could, or go down trying.

KITAW MEHRETU'S PALMS were sweating, slipping on the
wooden stock and foregrip of his old Beretta Model 38
submachine gun as he fumbled to reload it with a fresh
30-round magazine. The gun was an antique, manufactured forty years before Mehretu's birth, but still in use
by soldiers of the Ethiopian National Defense Force. Mehretu didn't know if his had been stolen or bought off the
street, only that it functioned well enough for a weapon
of its advanced age.

And he hoped that it would save his life.

The enemy they'd cornered in the alley had already
killed no less than half a dozen of Mehretu's friends and
fellow members of the Temple of the Holy Covenant. The
white man had come out of nowhere, had left Bishop
Astatke lying in a pool of blood, perhaps already dead by
now. Honor demanded vengeance for that insult and the
other lives that he had stolen in his unprovoked assault.

But could they manage it?

The white man had an automatic weapon, hand grenades, and he was clearly desperate. Concealed within the alley, he might hold them off until police arrived, forcing Mehretu and the rest to flee before they finished him. For all Mehretu knew, the killer was in league with the police, an agent sent to punish Custodes Foederis for the recent, brilliant move in Axum. Lacking evidence, it wouldn't be the first time Ethiopian authorities resorted to their version of rough justice.

But a *white* man? That confused Mehretu and disturbed him. He could make no sense of it, and they were running out of time.

Already, in the distance, he could hear the *bing-bong* echo of the first siren approaching. They had only minutes left, at most, to root the killer out and execute him, or the opportunity would slip away. Once he was jailed— *if* he was even placed in custody—the church might lose him to the courts.

Better to end it here, but that required more courage than Kitaw Mehretu possessed. Rushing the gunman where he was, braving his gun and his grenades, was tantamount to suicide. Mehretu reckoned they had men enough to take him, but who would volunteer to lead the charge and sacrifice himself?

Not me, Mehretu thought, and felt an instant stab of shame.

His fear challenged Mehretu's faith, his very manhood. He was thankful for the mask of darkness that obscured his face.

Beside him, Ephraim Desta said, "We need to hurry."

"I know that!" Mehretu whispered in answer.

"Someone has to lead."

Mehretu nodded. "You go," he suggested.

"I'm already injured, Kitaw."

"What?" Mehretu turned to peer at his companion, looking for a wound.

"My ankle," Desta said. "I hurt it, running out here from the temple."

Faker, Mehretu thought, but he didn't speak the word aloud. His own fear kept him from reviling Desta as a coward.

"You should lead us," Desta whispered. "You have the machine gun."

"Not the only one. Mohammed and Genzebe—"

"Were both in the alley," Desta said.

Meaning that both were likely dead, Mehretu understood, since neither one was firing. They had nearly shot *him* down by accident, before the last grenade went off. How many of his comrades still remained there, in the shadows, waiting to attack if only someone led the way?

Mehretu looked past Desta, back toward Congo Street, and saw that only Ale Hanna still remained to help them if they charged the white man's hiding place. Eyes alight with fear, he held a short-barreled revolver, even less effective than the Browning semiautomatic Desta carried.

It comes down to me, Mehretu realized. I have to prove myself.

"All right," he said at last, reluctantly. "Let's go."

BROTHER JOSEPH HALLORAN had nearly seen enough. From his position on the northern side of Congo Street, he'd watched events unfold around the Temple of the Holy Covenant, first curious, and then fascinated. He had seen the stranger, clearly European or American, drive past the church, then park his car, which bore a rental sticker that he recognized from Bole Airport. Halloran had watched the man step out and lock the car, then disappear into the alley behind the church.

Before all hell broke loose.

The first shots had been muffled, coming from inside the building opposite where Halloran stood watching, but their sound was unmistakable. Then the explosion, and before he knew it, shooting from the alley, louder as it echoed unobstructed in the night. He'd drawn his own gun then, a SIG-Sauer P-226 chambered for the bottle-necked .357 SIG cartridge, and held it ready in his hand as he moved closer.

Just to see what happened next.

The solitary gunman wasn't Halloran's concern, but anything connected to the Temple of the Holy Covenant might have some bearing on his mission. If the stranger had some cause for hunting Keepers, they might share a common interest. At the very least, Halloran wished to see the outcome of what seemed to him a most uneven contest.

But should he intervene?

So far, he'd passed unnoticed, more or less, in Addis Ababa. That was the plan, of course. Collect intelligence and move only when he was ready. When the time was ripe. Intruding here might jeopardize his mission, or…

Three gunmen from the temple had the near end of the alley blocked, trapping the man somewhere in the shadows farther back. Dim lighting there showed Halloran that several more were huddled near the back door of the temple, cutting off retreat in that direction. With a siren warbling from the east and swiftly drawing nearer, logic told him that police would soon be on the scene.

He could leave now, report the incident to his superiors, and come back later for the interview he'd planned with Bishop Berhanu Astatke. That was, if the clergyman was still alive after the melee in the temple moments earlier. And if he wasn't—then, what?

Halloran would have to forge ahead without the information he had hoped to gain in Addis Ababa. Not unprepared, exactly, but with greater odds against him than he would have faced with full intelligence at hand. A greater risk of martyrdom, albeit in a worthy cause.

Or could the new arrival help him? Was he operating on his own, or—as seemed likely—on behalf of some official agency? The CIA, perhaps? Or MI-6? The French DCRI seemed an unlikely candidate, but Mossad might have a passing interest in the matter. Likewise, if they were fully briefed, Italy's own External Information and Security Agency, the AISE.

Any of which might prove useful to Halloran, if they owed him a debt of gratitude.

While he stood weighing risks against the possible rewards of stepping in, the Keepers gathered at the alley's mouth were stoking up their nerve to make a move. He saw it in their posture, read it in the urgent way they whispered back and forth, clutching their weapons. Any second now they'd rush the cornered gunman, firing as they went, and Halloran would lose whatever chance he had of learning something from the stranger.

Damn it!

They were up and moving now. Resigned to whatever might happen next, Halloran left his hiding place and jogged across the street.

BOLAN HEARD SCUFFLING footsteps to his right, still nothing from the left as yet, but if they flushed him from his alcove it could all be over in a moment. Best case, if he beat the cautiously advancing shooters to the punch, he might surprise them, either take them down or make them cut and run, clearing a path to Congo Street, his car and freedom.

Worst case, he would take some of them with him as

they cut him down, maybe some others in the cross fire if the gunners lurking to his left were careless joining in the turkey shoot.

He braced himself, trying to judge the distance as his enemies advanced, planning the dive from cover that would leave him lying prone, beneath their line of fire if he was lucky. Hopefully, he'd stitch a couple of them before the feces hit the fan.

And after that? The only thing he could predict was bloody chaos.

Sirens closer now, a few blocks out. Their singsong rhythm emphasized the numbers falling in his head. The doom clock counting down to zero.

Bolan took his dive and heard the reports of large-bore pistol fire before he hit the gravel belly-down. He found his targets as they crumpled, three men dropping to the pavement, stunned expressions frozen on their dying faces. Farther back, a fourth man dressed in black, ebony-skinned, was aiming *over* Bolan with a pistol, braced in a solid isosceles stance.

He caught the other gunmen rising out of cover to support their comrades, muzzle-flashes from his weapon lighting up the alley as the gunshots slapped at Bolan's ears. Aware that he was being helped, without a notion as to why, Bolan rolled over and reversed direction, leveling his Uzi at the shooters who'd been caught flat-footed by the new arrival on the scene. He joined the fight with short, near-silent bursts that made a couple of the shadow figures dance before they dropped in flaccid attitudes of death.

And it was over, just like that.

Or was it?

Turning back to face the last man standing, Bolan rose, holding his submachine gun ready, muzzle hovering around knee level. At the alley's mouth, the stranger let his pistol dip a bit and said, "We ought to get away from here."

"Sounds like it," Bolan said, acknowledging the sirens. "One thing, though…"

"The introduction, eh? All right," his savior said. "I'm Brother Joseph Halloran."

"Brother?"

"It's a title, not my name. I'm with the Congregation for the Doctrine of the Faith."

"That rings a bell."

"Why don't we talk about it on the road," Halloran said. "Your car, for now?"

"Suits me," the Executioner replied, already moving out toward Congo Street.

CHAPTER FOUR

Driving aimlessly in the Tekeze hatchback, Bolan said, "I'm trying to remember where I've heard about the Congregation of the Faith."

"Congregation for the *Doctrine* of the Faith," Halloran corrected him. "It's in the news from time to time, but rarely mainstream media."

"It's Catholic?"

"Most definitely," he confirmed.

"And someone famous was associated with it, if I'm not mistaken."

"You're probably thinking of Pope Benedict XVI," Halloran said. "Before his election to the papacy, as Joseph Ratzinger, he served as prefect of the Congregation from 1982 to 2005."

"That's him," Bolan agreed. "What *is* the Congregation, anyway?"

"It's gone through several names since its creation in the sixteenth century," Halloran replied. "The present title dates from 1988. Before that, in December 1965, it was named the Sacred Congregation for the Doctrine of the Faith."

"Not sacred anymore?" Bolan asked.

Halloran shrugged. "Depends on who you ask. From 1904 to 1965 it was called the Supreme Sacred Congregation of the Holy Office."

"Still pretty vague."

"All right. At its creation by Pope Paul III, in 1542, it was the Supreme Sacred Congregation of the Roman and Universal Inquisition."

Bolan blinked at that. "Witch hunters?"

"Not to begin with," Halloran said, "although it did get sidetracked for a while. The Congregation's mission was to maintain and defend the integrity of the faith and to examine and proscribe errors and false doctrines."

"Sounds like you're quoting," Bolan said.

"I am," Halloran acknowledged. "No one serves the Congregation without studying its history. And its mistakes."

"I don't hear much about witches these days," Bolan said. "What's the current job description?"

"We still deal with cases of heresy," Halloran said. "Six nuns in Arkansas were excommunicated for their association with the so-called Army of Mary in 2007, but that's an unusual case. Overall, the Congregation is a promoter of justice within the church. It deals with *delicta graviora,* grave offenses that the Vatican takes most seriously."

"Examples?" Bolan prodded.

"Crimes against the Eucharist or against the Sanctity of Penance," Halloran said. "And since 2001, of course, we've been dealing with cases of pedophile priests."

Bolan couldn't resist saying, "You got a late start there."

"Admittedly. Pope John Paul II issued an order giving the Congregation jurisdiction in such cases. Before that, cases often languished at the local diocesan level."

"So," Bolan said, "I obviously have to ask what brings you here."

"To Addis Ababa?"

"To Congo Street, tonight, taking those shooters off my back."

"Unless I miss my guess, the same thing that caused

you to drop in on the Temple of the Holy Covenant with your grenades and Uzi."

So the padre knew his hardware. "And that would be…?" Bolan said.

"You're after the Ark of the Covenant," Halloran replied.

"You take that seriously?" Bolan asked.

"I don't know what to think about it, honestly. I hate to think the Ethiopian Orthodox Tewahedo Church would perpetrate a fraud, mounting armed guards over nothing, but stranger things have happened."

"And you were sent to check it out," Bolan said.

"More or less. Between my race and my affinity for languages, I draw assignments throughout Africa from time to time. The Vatican believes I can relate to Africans more easily than might a brother from Calabria, let's say."

"Sounds right to me, if you don't mind type-casting."

"I submit to discipline and go where I am ordered. Where I can be useful."

"Well, you earned your pay tonight," Bolan told him. "But I have to say, I didn't know the Vatican had soldiers."

"Sometimes," Halloran said, "the issues we confront may be…extreme."

"Like Custodes Foederis planning a hocus-pocus attack on the Vatican?"

"If it *is* what you call hocus-pocus," the man replied.

"You think they've really nabbed some superweapon from the days of Moses?"

Halloran responded with a shrug. "Reality as you or I perceive it may be less important than belief. Custodes Foederis has called for attacks against the church and all its works, the so-called Scarlet—"

"Whore of Babylon." Bolan finished the sentence for him. "Yeah, I heard that line."

"Even without a supernatural weapon, dedicated zealots pose a threat to Catholics everywhere. Ending their madness is a prime concern of the Congregation."

"You can't kill madness with a SIG P-226," Bolan advised. "Only its carriers."

"I use the tools at hand for a specific task," Halloran replied.

"Been there myself. But I may have missed my chance this time."

"Bishop Astatke?"

Bolan nodded. "I was hoping we might have a word. For all I know, he's dead by now."

"You injured him?" Halloran asked.

"Try 'shot.' He pulled a piece and jumped into the mix."

"A true believer," Halloran said. "Willing to kill or die for his faith."

"Like you."

"And yourself?" Halloran asked.

"I'm not that big on faith these days, but I've got the killing down."

"You may surprise yourself. May I suggest that we collaborate?"

Tikur Anbesa Hospital, Addis Ababa

BISHOP BERHANU ASTATKE swam back to fitful consciousness through a haze of medication, and found faces hovering over him. He recognized Tamrat Gessesse, focused on his parishioner's anguished eyes, and rasped out the question, "Where am I?"

"Tikur Anbesa, Your Eminence," Gessesse said. "You're safe."

Tikur Anbesa meant "black lion" in Amharic, and

Astatke understood the reference even in his hazy, drugged condition. Black Lion Specialized Hospital was Ethiopia's largest, attached to Addis Ababa University. In a nation where forty-four percent of all residents died before reaching age forty, Black Lion trained hundreds of doctors and nurses, generally working with outdated equipment and facing a shortage of critical medicines, and laboring under a defective ventilation system, with patients crowding the wards and hallways. Still, it was the best Ethiopia had to offer, and the country's only cancer treatment center.

Not that Bishop Astatke had to concern himself with death from a wasting disease. His wounded legs ached bitterly, despite the drugs that he'd been given. Even reaching out to clutch Gessesse's slender arm caused him to moan and grimace, hissing through clenched teeth to speak.

"Did you contact...Dextera Dei?" he demanded.

Gessesse's eyes darted away from the bishop, sweeping the space near his bed for eavesdroppers. There were few private rooms at Black Lion, and those they had were reserved for rare patients of wealth and influence. Bishop Astatke's bed of suffering was situated at the far end of a ward containing twenty more, each occupied with trauma victims.

"Answer me!" he grated, through another wave of pain.

"I tried," Gessesse whispered. "No one answered at the number I was given, but I left a message. No, don't worry. I was not foolish enough to be specific. If the wrong ears listen, they will just be...curious."

"You mean no help is coming?"

"I don't know. If they had answered when I called—"

"God help us!" Eyes half-closed, Astatke rode another wave of wrenching agony. When he was able to control his voice, he rasped, "I cannot stay here."

"You must heal," Gessesse said. "The doctor says that if you're moved, you may not live."

"We all die," the bishop replied. "Better that than to betray the faith."

"You have betrayed nothing. Your courage shines as an example to us all."

"When the police come…"

"They are here," Gessesse told him. "Questioning the others as we speak. No one will tell them anything."

"I may," Astatke said.

"No, no. You're far too brave for that."

"The pain…the drugs…I cannot trust myself," Astatke groaned.

"Have courage."

"You must help me, Tamrat."

"If I can. You have only to ask."

Astatke swallowed, clenched his teeth against the rising swell of pain, and said, "You must release me from this broken shell."

Gessesse frowned at that, looking confused, then gaped as understanding pierced the veil. "You must not ask me that!" he said. "I cannot—"

"Yes, you can! You will! It is your duty."

"I don't know…."

"You speak to me of courage? Prove your own."

Gessesse looked around the ward, Astatle following his gaze as best he could. Black Lion was perpetually understaffed, with those on duty vastly overworked. Just now, there were no nurses or physicians in the ward.

"Get on with it!" Astatke ordered, his dry voice harsh, commanding.

Weeping silently, Gessesse drew the pillow from beneath Astatke's head and held it poised above the bishop's sweaty face. He said, "Forgive me please."

"The Lord forgives you," Astatke said. "And I thank you."

Silently, the pillow pressed against his face, obliterating light and breath.

Custodes Foederis Headquarters, Rome

UGO TROISI LISTENED to the short recorded message for a third time, frowning as a man's excited voice tried to convey his meaning without leaving any evidence on tape that might be useful to an enemy.

"Emergency!" his unnamed caller said. "The Temple of the Holy Covenant is compromised. Bishop Astatke is in hospital. Others are dead. Security is jeopardized. Beware!"

And nothing more.

The tracking software on his phone informed Troisi that the call had come from Addis Ababa, a fact already known to him, since each Custodes Foederis congregation worldwide had a unique title. Likewise, Bishop Astatke was well-known to ranking members of the sect at the Sedem Illustratio, a key supporter of their latest move against the Scarlet Whore. In fact, he'd been so involved in the coup that Troisi cringed to think of him confined to a hospital bed, subject to questions and coercion from authorities.

Steps should be taken to relieve the bishop—or to silence him—without delay.

As for the rest, Troisi had to follow up at once, determine what had happened at the Temple of the Holy Covenant, how many of the Keepers had been lost, how many others were in custody. Without providing details, his unknown caller had conveyed the essence of a strike against the sect.

By whom? Troisi couldn't say. But there was no need to ask why.

Someone was clearly bent on frustrating their plans to purify the faith. That narrowed down the field of suspects, but more research was required before Troisi could prepare to strike specific targets. In the meantime, he must share the grim news out of Ethiopia with Janus Marcellus and Mania Justina, his exalted Pontifex and Reginae.

That promised to be one unpleasant interview, but he couldn't postpone it. Every moment wasted now was a forsaken opportunity. And seeing Mania in a state of agitation, with her skin flushed, was a bonus for Troisi, even in the midst of a potential crisis.

There was nothing he could do immediately for the faithful in Addis Ababa. Someone had to be sent to find and help Bishop Astatke—Troisi could do that on his own authority, before sharing the news—but any other action called for consultation with his masters.

Or, rather, his master and his mistress.

The sharp twinge of anxiety Troisi felt—not guilt, but more akin to fear of being caught and punished—passed almost immediately. They were on the verge of great things, changing history in fact, and opposition from the dark forces confronting them was only natural. What tyrant ever willingly surrendered power? From the days of Caesar to the machinations of vast multinational corporations, avarice and lust had always ranked among the greatest motivators of corrupt humankind.

What could defeat them? Only faith, supported by a righteous army.

Prayer alone, Troisi had discovered, rarely made a difference in life—and never on a global scale. God was all-powerful, of course, but helped those who stood up for themselves. More to the point, He aided those who stood for Him. The weapon He had placed into their hands would cleanse the planet of a cancer that had claimed millions of lives since the Middle Ages, blighting countless others and leading their immortal souls into damnation. Having granted them that power, though, it was expected that the Lord would stand back and observe what use they made of it themselves.

And if they failed? Then what?

According to the gospel as Troisi understood it, God would be content to watch and wait until a stronger union of believers came along to carry out his will. A year, a century or a millennium, it made no difference to Him. If God ran out of patience, sometime in the future, He could always send another flood or rain of fire to rid the world of infidels. But He preferred to see His faithful do as they'd been ordered and achieve the victory themselves, through faith and perseverance.

Triumph, thought Troisi, would absolve the victors of whatever petty sins they had committed during their campaign on God's behalf. Salvation was its own reward. But if his earthly lord and master recognized Troisi's passion for the sect's queen mother, there would certainly be hell to pay.

Amen.

Addis Ababa

BROTHER JOSEPH HALLORAN was curious about his new comrade, this Matthew Cooper. He knew the soldier's name translated from Hebrew as "gift of God," but what did that prove? Modern Americans more often named their children after decadent celebrities than for disciples of Christ. A useless factoid—one of thousands stored in Halloran's brain by his eidetic memory—reminded him that Matthew ranked as one of the English-speaking world's thousand most popular names since the 1970s, one of Britain's top one hundred, fifteenth in Ireland, and—

He caught himself and broke the rambling chain of thought, returning to the here and now with Cooper's voice in his ears.

"I thought this anti-Catholic business went out with the old Ku Klux Klan," Bolan stated. "Or at least with JFK's election to the White House."

"Hardly," Halloran replied. "Some Protestant sects devote as much time to reviling the papacy as others spend condemning gays or abortion. Or consider Northern Ireland, where sectarian violence between Protestants and Catholics is historically indistinguishable from political strife. Thousands of Catholics were slaughtered by Muslims in Sudan's civil war, between 1983 and 2005. Even in predominantly Catholic countries—say, Latin America—leftist guerrillas often target priests and nuns for violence."

"But this Custodes Foederis stands out, somehow?"

"Indeed it does," Halloran said. "From small beginnings and employment of the age-old propaganda, it has grown into a movement geared toward action. Individual adherents have been linked to desecrations of Catholic churches, schools and graveyards, even to the murder of a priest in San Antonio—your Texas—late last summer."

Frowning in the dashboard's light, Bolan told him, "I've missed all that."

"Most of the cases received only local attention, and some of them were in Europe. The Texas murderer was killed by police while resisting arrest. His connection to the Keepers wasn't widely known."

"But you're aware of it."

"The Congregation for the Doctrine of the Faith keeps track of enemies who pose a threat."

"You work with the police?" Bolan asked.

"Whenever possible. The present instance is, of course, rather unusual."

"So, you're...what? Like a one-man crusade?"

Halloran smiled at that. "The Crusades were mounted to regain the Holy Land from Islam. Warriors who enlisted were absolved of any sins they might commit on God's behalf, by means of plenary indulgence. The Crusades continued, with brief interruptions, from AD 1095 to 1272, ending rather inconclusively."

"Is that a yes or no?" Bolan asked.

"You may consider my assignment a crusade of sorts," said Halloran, "against an enemy devoted to destruction of the world's largest Christian denomination. I trust that it won't drag on for 177 years."

"And what about the plenary indulgence?"

"No," Halloran said. "I act as I see fit, in self-defense or to defend the faith, but I'm still expected to confess and purge myself of sin whenever it is feasible."

"Back there, you killed three men," Bolan said. "I'm not complaining, understand, but that's not something I imagine would be sanctioned by the church."

"The fifth commandment says 'Thou shalt not kill,' but most authorities agree that the original translation is a reference to *murder*. Killing in defense of innocents, to halt atrocities, or in a righteous war isn't defined as murder. Neither is the execution of a legally convicted and condemned offender. Still, when I have time and opportunity, I will confess those actions and make a good act of contrition."

"And all's forgiven."

"According to the Gospels and Ephesians, chapter one, that is correct," said Halloran. "What are your own beliefs, if I may ask?"

"They wouldn't mesh with any given system of theology," Bolan said. "My family was Catholic."

"Yet you perceive morality and risk your life on its behalf."

"You'd get an argument on that, from some."

"I don't concern myself with the opinions of the world," Halloran replied.

"But your ecclesiastical superiors," Bolan said, "might not appreciate our joining forces."

"Why should they be burdened with the fact, as long as I pursue my mission?"

"Easier to get forgiveness than permission, I suppose."

"Where were you planning to go next?" Halloran asked. "After you'd spoken to Astatke?"

"I was hoping for a pointer there."

"In which case," Halloran replied, "I think that I can help."

Custodes Foederis Headquarters

ACCESS TO THE royal apartments of the Sedem Illustratio was by invitation only. Even Ugo Troisi couldn't enter uninvited by Janus Marcellus or Mania Justina. Burly guards with automatic weapons stood watch at the entrance to their quarters day and night, with orders to use deadly force against would-be intruders. As it was, Troisi had already phoned ahead and spoken to the servant supervising household staff, citing an emergency, and waiting on the line until his visit was approved.

Two hours difference between the time in Rome and Addis Ababa. All things considered, he had been alerted quickly of the raid against the Temple of the Holy Covenant, but the attackers still remained at large, as far as he could tell. Whether police eventually apprehended them or not, Troisi had a duty to inform his masters of the incident, enabling them to be prepared for any repercussions.

There was no need to announce himself as he approached the royal living quarters. Brother Guido Turriano, the royal butler, waited in the outer corridor to lead Troisi past the guards, advising in a whisper about the situation he would face.

"There is uneasiness tonight," Turriano said. "Your emergency has further agitated troubled waters."

Trying to make sense of that, Troisi wondered whether he had walked into a trap. If Marcellus knew about his private meetings with the Queen Mother...

"What else disturbs them?" he inquired.

A shrug from Turriano was the only answer he received, before they reached a tall door and the butler knocked, waiting until a male voice called, "Enter!"

Turriano held the door open, then closed it firmly when Troisi had passed through. Before Troisi, Marcellus stood resplendent in a purple satin robe, with gold around the collar, cuffs and hem. Its back, Troisi knew, was decorated with the golden symbol of an ever-watchful eye.

Mania Justina was nowhere in sight. A bad sign, or nothing at all?

"You spoke of an emergency, Ugo," Marcellus said. "Be so good as to explain."

Troisi shared the sparse details at his disposal: the preliminary call, his own brief conversation with an officer the sect employed to gather information for its benefit in Addis Ababa. A shooting at the temple, seven dead, that count including Bishop Berhanu Astatke. "He was wounded in the legs, from what I understand," Troisi finished, "but has since died at a local hospital."

"And those responsible?"

"Still free and unidentified, Your Grace."

"So, we have no idea?"

"Only a sparse description at the present time. Two men. One black, one white."

"A white man in Addis Ababa? What does that suggest to you?"

"A foreign agent, obviously. As to who he serves, Your Grace—"

"The options must be limited," Marcellus said, interrupting.

"If not the Vatican directly, possibly the GIS," Troisi said, referring to the Gruppo di Intervento Speciale attached to Italy's Carabinieri.

"No one heard him speak, I take it?"

"No one who survived, Your Grace."

"Unfortunate. The black man could be local, from their national police perhaps, but why would he be working with a white man?"

"If another country was involved, Your Grace, it is conceivable. We can't rule out the CIA, who have pursued the Ark for thirty years or more, albeit unofficially."

"They're all preoccupied with Arabs since the towers fell," Janus replied. "Who else?"

"The British are an outside possibility, Your Grace. Their SIS, or MI-6."

"If only he was heard to speak! An accent could betray him."

"I suspect all white men sound alike to Ethiopians, Your Grace," Troisi said.

"Surely they know a Brit from an American."

"He might represent the Congregation for the Doctrine of the Faith," Troisi offered.

"Ah! In which case, a response is all the more important, eh?"

"Indeed, Your Grace."

"You have something in mind, Ugo?" Marcellus inquired.

"With your permission, I suggest a broad response on several fronts. Our enemies must learn that they cannot attack us with impunity."

"Agreed. But at the same time, we must exercise a certain...circumspection," Janus answered.

"Absolutely. As you say, Your Grace."

"I leave the details in your able hands, Ugo."

Meaning that if he failed, the blame was his and his alone. He smiled, projecting confidence, fighting the urge to ask about Mania's absence.

"You may trust me absolutely," Troisi replied.

CHAPTER FIVE

Boston, Massachusetts

Streets were narrow and perpetually crowded in the Old North End of Boston. Tourists often cursed the traffic, likely wondering if any new construction had been undertaken since the days of Paul Revere. A horseman would make better time on Salem Street than any out-of-towner in an SUV, particularly since the locals had a tendency to double park and leave their engines running while they wandered into nearby stores.

Brent Houston didn't mind the traffic. He was walking on this final morning of his life, taking his time, absorbing all the sights and smells as he proceeded south on Endicott, already getting scowls and stares but ready to accept them. Nothing mattered anymore, except the mission that he'd volunteered for. Setting free his soul.

The neighborhood was old Italian, known for restaurants like Massimo's and Filippo's, for street processions on the Feast of San Gennaro, and occasional *Globe* articles about the Mafia. Houston liked his pizza and lasagna as much as the next guy, and he figured most of the people giving him stink-eye that morning were probably nice enough once you got to know them, but who had the time?

An apocalypse was coming and he had his tiny part to do, lighting the fuse.

It's nothing personal, he thought, and smiled back at a

stumpy gray-haired man who muttered something at him in Italian, shaking his head in disgust.

Whatever.

Houston had made the sandwich sign himself, from sheets of poster board, with shoulder straps cut from his dachshund's leash. The dog was kenneled with her vet this morning, and he'd left a wad of cash—the last he had—to cover boarding for a while. Once people at the office heard the news that evening, they'd make arrangements to find Noodle a new home.

The front of Houston's homemade sign read Damn the Scarlet Whore of Babylon. For anyone who missed the point, the back read Vatacan Must Go! He'd caught the spelling glitch too late and didn't want to start from scratch. Some TV talking head would likely have a laugh at his expense, but Houston had the last laugh coming. Any minute now.

Beneath the sandwich sign, affixed with duct tape to the poster board, were six dozen large freezer bags filled with homemade plastic explosive. Houston was no chemist, but the poor man's C-4 wasn't hard to make if you had petroleum jelly, bleach, potassium chloride, wax and a fair amount of patience. He'd experimented with a recipe he found online, fiddled around with the proportions and tested a small batch, just cherry bomb size, at the Belle Isle Marsh Reservation.

Rigging the detonators was the hardest part, but Houston had gone back online and found a handy booklet that walked him through the steps of fabricating blasting caps at home. Once he'd produced enough, handled with loving care, and wired them up to the handset from a slot car kit, Houston was good to go. The fully loaded sign weighed close to fifty pounds, but what the hell. He had to wear it only once.

One block ahead, he could see people entering the Church of Saint Francis Caracciolo. Houston had done his homework, looked it up, and learned that this particular Saint Francis was Italian, that he'd died in 1608 and been canonized two hundred years later. He was the patron saint of Naples and Italian cooks, which made him perfect for the neighborhood.

And marked the church named in his honor as a perfect target.

Houston climbed a flight of concrete steps to reach the double front doors, which were standing open. Stopping there, he began to sing "A Mighty Fortress Is Our God." His voice was nothing special, but that was fine. Brent Houston had a reservation booked in Paradise.

The song he chose had been penned by Martin Luther, first to stand and shout against the Scarlet Whore, although Houston understood that it was sometimes sung at masses now. So what? He was only killing time until the priest arrived—and here he came, a fairly tall man, middle fifties, almost certainly Italian from the look of him.

Perfect.

"Excuse me," the padre said. "I must ask you to remove yourself. These steps are private property."

Instead of moving, Houston started belting out the next verse, louder than before. He raised his right arm, the one trailing insulated wires connected to the handset in his fist. The priest saw that and gasped, lunging for Houston's hand.

Too late.

His thumb depressed the handset's plunger. Suddenly, the world went white and very loud.

Fulham, London, England

DRIVING NORTH ON Harwood Road past Fulham town hall, Percy Collins kept a sharp eye on the rearview mirror of his aged Mini Cooper sedan, watching out for the blue-and-orange cars used for routine patrol by officers of London's Metropolitan Police Service. None was in sight, and while he stayed within the speed limit, giving law officers no reason to detain him, paranoia gnawed around the raw edge of his nerves and had him fairly bouncing in the driver's seat.

Why not, considering the cargo he carried? In a black gym bag immediately to his left, filling the rider's seat, there lay a Sterling L2A3 submachine gun, its metal stock folded beneath its ventilated barrel shroud, together with a dozen magazines of 9 mm Parabellum hollow point rounds. The gun had been his father's, smuggled home from service in the Northern Irish troubles of the early seventies, together with the Webley Mk VI revolver Collins carried in a holster underneath his knee-length raincoat. The coat's pockets were heavy with .455 Webley cartridges, some of them loose, a couple dozen slotted into half-moon clips for rapid loading.

Percy Collins was prepared to leave his mark on history.

The call had come the previous night, from Pastor Leo Berkus at the Temple of the Crucifixion. Collins had been chosen from a list of volunteers to carry out the first strike executed by Custodes Foederis on British soil—an honor that thrilled him, even as it set imaginary insects to scrabbling inside his stomach. This day his name would be inscribed on Christ's own honor roll.

Written in blood.

His designated target was the Saint Ignatius Academy on Vanston Place, near Walham Grove. The school had thirteen hundred students, mostly boys, though females were admitted in the sixth form, preparing for their A-level examinations. Collins knew he couldn't kill them all, with some five hundred rounds of ammunition, but he'd make a start.

And more importantly, he'd leave a message.

Tucked into an inside pocket of his best tweed jacket, underneath his raincoat, an eight-page manifesto nestled in the plastic bag he'd picked to keep the papers free of bloodstains when armed response units arrived to gun him down. Collins had already resigned himself to death, wouldn't subject himself to public scrutiny like something from a freak show. But his words would live on, echoing across the ages to a time when humankind was liberated from the Scarlet Whore of Babylon.

Sooner, perhaps, than anyone had dared to hope.

There were no open spaces at the curb within three blocks of Saint Ignatius, but Collins didn't care. A citation for a parking violation was the least of his concerns this day. He stopped beside a hydrant, switched off the Mini Cooper's engine and reached into his gym bag, slotting a curved double-column magazine into the Sterling's receiver. A sharp yank on the cocking handle put a live round in the chamber, and Collins left the safety off, ready to fire, as he replaced the weapon in its bag.

He stepped out of the car, taking the heavy bag, leaving his key in the ignition with the door unlocked. Perhaps some wayward lad—or lass, these days, who knew?—would come along and lift it for a joyride. Collins had no further use for it. His next ride would be in a hearse.

Classes were under way at Saint Ignatius, midmorning, all the hapless children having blasphemy drilled into them by servants of the Great Deceiver. Some of them were listening to their last lectures even now, unconscious of the fact that Death was moving toward them with determined strides, a broad smile on his face.

Some sort of monitor was standing watch outside the building, a portly man of early middle age dressed in the school's colors, maroon and black. He frowned as Collins turned in from the public sidewalk, and, moving toward the front door, raised his hand to halt this stranger with the odd smile on his face.

"A moment if you please, sir."

Collins drew the Webley, cocked and fired it in a single fluid motion, opening a keyhole in the watchman's forehead, blowing out a mist of gray and crimson at the back. Without missing a stride, he passed the fallen corpse and pushed into the school's foyer, as brakes squealed in the road behind him, someone grabbing for a cell phone to summon the police.

So it began.

Axum, Ethiopia

THE DRIVE FROM Addis Ababa to Axum took six hours, covering 350 miles and change on roads that ranged in quality from adequate to poor. Ethiopia's only expressway was the four-lane Addis Ababa Ring Road, a limited-access thoroughfare encircling the capital. Bolan and Halloran traveled over Highway 1, northbound from Addis Ababa through Dessie to Adigrat, where a winding side road branched off to Axum. On the final stretch, a dust plume trailed behind them, as if the Holland Tekeze was laying down a smoke screen.

They parked a half mile from the Chapel of the Tablet and walked back, Halloran sketching the history for Bolan's benefit while locals wondered at the sight of white and black together on the street, the black man wearing clerical garb.

"Saint Frumentius brought Christianity to the Aksumite Kingdom during the fourth century," Halloran said. "Today, he's known as Abune Selama Kesatay Birhan, translating into English as Our Father of Peace, the Revealer of Light."

"That's some reputation," Bolan remarked.

"He earned it as a prisoner who won his freedom with the gospel and converted his captors, going on to serve as bishop, confessor and apostle to Ethiopia."

"So, what went wrong?" Bolan asked.

"Wrong?"

"I understand they're not exactly Catholics today."

"Ah. Long story short, Eastern Orthodox churches broke with Rome over doctrinal issues in 1054. Both factions worship Christ, of course, but fell out over other theological disputes. One branch, the Coptic Orthodox Church of Alexandria, claimed primacy over Ethiopia until 1959, when the Ethiopian Orthodox Tewahedo Church asserted independence."

"What's Tewahedo?" Bolan asked.

"A word from the Geez language common to the Horn of Africa, established as the official tongue of the Aksumite Kingdom and Ethiopia's imperial court. It translates as 'being made one,' a reference to divine and human natures merged in the person of Jesus."

"And they claim they got the Ark of the Covenant... how, again?"

"According to the *Kebra Nagast*—that's a book, *The Glory of Kings,* dating roughly from the fourteenth century—Emperor Menelik I brought the Ark with him to Ethiopia when he married Makeda, the Queen of Sheba, around 950 BC. Menelik presumably got it from his father, King Solomon of the Old Testament."

"Guy with the mines that nobody can find."

"That's the one."

"Cutting babies in two."

"He didn't follow through on that," Halloran said. "It was an object lesson."

"And the Ark's been sitting here for better than a thousand years."

"Supposedly."

"No point in asking anybody here, I guess."

"I shouldn't think so," Halloran agreed. "Believers are invested in the legend, true or false, and nonbelievers won't have any useful information."

"So, plan B," Bolan replied.

"I think so. Yes."

"You think they staged the hit out of Eritrea."

"I can't be positive, of course," Halloran said. "But Custodes Foederis has a congregation at Massawa, some ninety miles due north. They call themselves the Temple of the Guiding Light. If they weren't involved…"

"Somebody there may know who was," Bolan suggested.

"That's what I surmise."

"Makes sense."

"We may experience some difficulties at the border," Halloran observed. "You may know that Eritrea and Ethiopia were at war from 1998 through 2000. Despite the eventual peace treaty, tensions remain. United Nations peacekeepers were stationed on the border until 2008, then withdrew, citing Eritrea's failure to cooperate. Both sides patrol the border heavily, one might say seeking an excuse for the renewal of hostilities. As for tourist visas, well…"

"In other words, we'll have to sneak across," Bolan said.

"It saves a world of time and explanation, not to mention lying."

"Which would be a sin."

"Albeit venial," Halloran added, half smiling.

"You've been here awhile," Bolan remarked. "What did you have in mind?"

"There is a man who may be useful," Halloran replied, already reaching for his phone.

North Montreal, Quebec, Canada

BRIGITTE LECLAIR NOSED her Opel Astra G into the parking garage of Hôpital Saint-Rémi on Boulevard Lacordaire. She took a ticket from the meter, let it drop beside her car as she drove underneath the rising barrier, and circled upward through the floors reserved for doctors, staff and patients visiting the hospital for tests or therapy. On level five she found a space, pulled in and killed the Astra's engine.

On the seat beside her, in a cloth Loblaws shopping bag, were twenty hand grenades, the green C13 model which, she understood, was simply a relabeled version of the American M67. Each grenade weighed fourteen ounces, roughly half of which was Composition B, an explosive mixture of RDX and TNT.

Leclair knew that because she had been forced to study for her mission, and to toss one of the blue training grenades in practice sessions, in a secluded corner of Cap-Saint-Jacques Nature Park on the West Island. Her aim wasn't precise, but she supposed that with a killing radius of five meters, and a wounding radius of triple that, it didn't have to be.

She left the car and slung the cloth bag over her left shoulder. At close to eighteen pounds, it was uncomfortable, chafing through her blouse and lightweight sweater, but the weight was unimportant. And it would get lighter as she went along.

She'd been initially put off by the idea of terrorizing patients in a hospital, but the situation had been explained to her. The individuals she would be facing had elected to have treatment in a warren of corruption run for profit by the Scarlet Whore of Babylon. Most were diseased because of their licentious lifestyles, having brought it on themselves. The innocents—if there were any to be found inside the walls of Hôpital Saint-Rémi—would look down from heaven afterward and bless her for releasing them from hell on earth. The more Leclair considered it, the more it all made sense.

She passed a constable on entering the hospital, but he hardly glanced at her. Another visitor with gifts for some unfortunate, no doubt. She passed the information kiosk and headed for the elevators, silently repeating the instructions she'd been given: Ride it to the top, Intensive Care, then work your way back down.

Where the authorities, by then, would certainly be waiting for her. And she planned to save one last grenade for them. Or for herself.

The topmost floor of the hospital was a nearly silent place. Although Leclair had never visited Intensive Care before, she recognized it more or less from television programs. All the rooms were private, glass-walled, with signs warning of oxygen in use, forbidding all unnecessary noise. A small space set aside for visitors was nearly empty at the moment, except for one man lying on a sofa, seemingly asleep.

But not for long.

Two nurses at their station watched Brigitte Leclair approach the nearest room, where a young woman lay unconscious in a bed festooned with tubes and wires. One of them called to her as she approached the door, her right hand dipping into the cloth bag.

"Vous ne pouvez pas aller là-bas, madame." She was forbidden to enter there.

"Don't worry," she replied. "It's fine." With a grenade already primed, she rolled it toward a tall oxygen tank near the bed, then retreated as its four-second fuse burned down.

She was halfway to the service stairs—the elevator was far too slow to help her now—when the explosion came, a double wham from the grenade and the tank of oxygen. The nurses started to scream, but Brigitte heard them for only a second. Then the heavy door swung shut behind her, cutting off the sound.

Rio de Janeiro, Brazil

CHRIST THE REDEEMER stood overlooking the city, arms spread as if still crucified—or perhaps in a gesture of welcome to all who approached him. He was hard to ignore, at 125 feet tall with a thirty-one-foot arm span, perched atop Corcovado mountain 2,300 feet above sea level, with a panoramic view of Rio de Janeiro below and the blue Atlantic beyond.

Each year, more than three hundred thousand pilgrims and tourists boarded the Corcovado Rack Railway for a twenty-minute ride to meet Christ on the mountaintop. How many lives were altered by that trip would be impossible to say.

Duarte carried a camera bag, but planned to take no photographs. Inside the bag he'd packed a short Patria Mod 2 machine pistol, made in Argentina during the mid-1980s, chambered in 9 mm Parabellum. The remaining space was filled with 30-round box magazines—enough to kill a hundred people, maybe more, if he was able to control the little stuttergun he'd barely practiced with. Its folding foregrip, similar to that on the Beretta 93-R, ought to help.

Arriving at the mountaintop, Duarte was among the first riders to disembark. Above the railroad platform at least a hundred gawkers were already clustered at the statue's feet, some of them slowly descending to meet the train, ready to leave, while others showed no inclination to depart. Of course, it didn't matter what they wanted now, or what they'd planned to do for the remainder of their day in Rio.

Time stopped here, as Duarte drew the Patria Mod 2, cocked it and shouted in a high-pitched voice that made his cheeks flame with embarrassment, "Death to the Scarlet Whore of Babylon!"

Before his words had time to register, Duarte opened fire. His weapon's cyclic rate of fire matched that of an Uzi at six hundred rounds per minute. He fought to control it, blasting short bursts toward his running, screaming targets, all the while imagining the havoc his brothers and sisters of Custodes Foederis were wreaking worldwide, a tide of blood, rising before the final stroke of Armageddon fell and purged an ancient cancer from the world. Duarte knew he wouldn't live to see the day of glory in his present form, but planned to watch it all unfolding from his place in Paradise.

Loading his second magazine, the first one gone in seconds, Duarte heard the tourist train reversing gears, its engineer bent on escape, saving himself and anyone on board. Running as if to catch the train himself, Duarte fired in through the windscreen of the driver's cab, rewarded with glass imploding and a splash of blood. The train began accelerating in reverse, the few tourists aboard it clinging to their seats and crying out in panic. Duarte pictured carnage at the station two and a half miles below, when the train arrived with no hand on the brake.

An unexpected bonus, and its crash would stall police heading for the peak of Corcovado with their guns, to take him down. By the time they cleared the track and launched another of the four tourist trains up the mountain, Duarte's work would be completed. They could kill him then, with nothing lost. His name would be enshrined forever in the pantheon of martyrs blessed by God.

But still, he had no time to waste. Terrified pilgrims were still on the run, some scrambling for safety above the railroad platform, slogging up the 220-step staircase or clinging to the escalators installed for weaker tourists. Duarte followed them, chased them with automatic fire, and laughed to see them tumbling down again, splashing the steps with blood. The survivors scurried like rats, squealing in panic, while their killer reloaded on the move.

Perfect.

They had nowhere to go, no one to save them now. Would those who stammered hasty prayers before the statue find forgiveness for their sins? Duarte didn't know and didn't care. He had a job to do, and it was far from done.

CHAPTER SIX

Massawa, Eritrea

Halloran's useful man turned out to be a smuggler who supported himself and a large family by running contraband across the border between Ethiopia and Eritrea. The latter country, prized for its coastline along the Red Sea, had been invaded and conquered in turn by Arabs, Ottoman Turks, Portuguese, Egyptians, Sudanese, Brits and Italians, until it was federated with Ethiopia by United Nations mandate in 1951. Ethiopian disregard for Eritrea's culture and language sparked a thirty-year war for independence in 1961. International recognition of Eritrean sovereignty failed to end the bitter fighting, however, and hostility continued to the present day, albeit it formally defused by treaty in 2008.

Passage of goods and travelers across the still-disputed border was, therefore, a matter of contention—and a bounty for smugglers who greased the wheels of commerce with bribes. Halloran's contact, a thirty-something Ethiopian named Alemayehu Teka, had agreed to transport Halloran and Bolan with a truckload of coffee that concealed a stash of khat, and Bolan paid the tab out of the war chest he'd collected in D.C. Teka concealed their weapons with his cache of drugs, while Bolan donned priest's garb that Halloran produced out of his meager luggage.

Bolan was an expert in "role camouflage," assuming

guises that allowed observers to see what they expected in a given situation, but it was the first time he had dressed up as a member of the clergy. Father Executioner. When lightning didn't strike him on the spot, he took it as a sign of sorts and climbed aboard the aged SNVI truck, a model manufactured in Algeria on some date long forgotten.

The border crossing was easier than Bolan expected, once money changed hands with guards on both sides of the line. They might hate each other's guts, but the Eritreans and Ethiopians alike were willing to be greased with cash. From there, Bolan's party drove fifty miles to the capital city, Asmar. Halloran rented a car there—a two-year-old Toyota Corolla—then picked up one of Eritrea's principal highways, P-1, to Massawa by way of Ghinda. It was asphalt all the way, the smoothest ride Bolan had enjoyed since leaving Addis Ababa.

But leading him to what?

More bloodshed, absolutely. As to *whose* blood would be spilled...well, only time would tell.

As they pulled into town, Halloran said, "The Temple of the Guiding Light is run by a member of Custodes Foederis who calls himself Bishop Yegizaw Sultan. That may or may not be his name, in fact. It hardly matters for our purposes."

"You think he'll spill?" Bolan asked. "Those were tough nuts back in Addis Ababa."

"Even the toughest nut will crack, with pressure properly applied."

Here comes the Inquisition, Bolan thought, but kept it to himself. Inflicting pain on others never pleased him, though there had been several occasions when he'd felt a rush of satisfaction, when sadists fell into his hands and got a dose of their own medicine. More often, when he had to squeeze someone for information in the middle of a life-or-death campaign, Bolan accomplished what he could with threats and promises, reserving brute force as a last-ditch option.

Presently, he reckoned that no matter what this Bishop Sultan said or didn't say, allowing him to live and blow the whistle to his masters was a bad idea. But Bolan would play the cards as they were dealt, see how they fell.

And leave the moment to decide who lost it all.

Temple of the Guiding Light, Massawa

BISHOP YEGIZAW SULTAN was troubled by reports from Addis Ababa. The death of Bishop Berhanu Astatke was a bitter loss, since they'd been friends as well as brethren in the faith. Astatke had facilitated the capture of the Ark, as Bishop Sultan had secured safe passage for its liberators and their cargo through his own parish. In truth, he'd hoped to catch a glimpse of it in passing, but his plea had been denied by Janus Marcellus.

Bishop Sultan knew his scripture, specifically the books of Samuel, wherein God killed seventy men of Beth Shemesh for peering inside the Ark, and later struck down faithful Uzzah when he touched the Ark, to steady it from falling when the oxen drawing it had stumbled. Compromise was sin, and Sultan had chastised himself for his passing weakness in seeking a special privilege.

The Ark had power. It had changed the ancient world and it could do the same in modern times, but on a broader scale. God's sacred gift to humankind had been forgotten and ignored for centuries, while false prophets led millions from the path of righteousness to sure damnation and the fires of hell.

All changing soon, unless…

It seemed unthinkable, but still the notion nagged at Bishop Sultan's mind. Would God permit the infidels to win, after his loyal believers had done everything within their mortal power to secure the victory for His sake? And if so, what did that say about their faith? Was it misplaced?

Sultan stopped short, muttered a prayer of supplication as he realized how close he'd come to blasphemy. Mere doubt alone could weaken people. It could erode their very souls.

He felt a sermon coming on, was sitting down to sketch an outline of it, reaching for his fountain pen, when voices from the courtyard startled him. Rising, Sultan started toward his office window, but a blast of gunfire stopped him in his tracks. Quickly retreating to his desk, he reached inside the upper left-hand drawer to find a Walther PPQ pistol, one of its fifteen .40-caliber rounds already in the chamber. Its double-action trigger with the integrated safety meant that all the bishop had to do was aim and fire, if enemies confronted him.

But first, before he joined the fight, he had to make a call.

His hands were trembling, and he nearly dropped the satellite phone as he tapped in the digits one-handed, darting anxious glances at the window all the while. More shooting from the courtyard was punctuated by a bullet drilling through the window glass, ripping a furrow in the ceiling of his office. Bishop Sultan dropped behind his desk, kneeling as if in prayer, but wholly focused on the LED screen of the phone clutched in his hand.

Ringing.

"Answer!" he rasped. "For God's sake, pick up!"

Finally, on the eleventh ring, his plea was answered.

Small and distant came a voice he barely recognized. Instead of salutations, it said, "This line is not secure."

"No matter," Sultan blurted out. "You know who this is?"

"Yes."

"We're under fire! And yesterday there was a raid in Ad—"

"I know that. We cannot help you."

Startled by his sudden anger, Sultan replied, "*I know that!* I didn't call to ask for help. I'm warning you!"

"Message received," the distant voice acknowledged.

And the line went dead.

Furious, Sultan fought an urge to hurl his sat phone at the nearest wall. It would have been a pointless, childish act, counterproductive at the very least. Instead, he ought to call the Sedem Illustratio, alert the Pontifex and Reginae.

Sultan was fumbling with the sat phone's buttons, punching in a second number, when the office door burst open, slamming back against the wall.

THE TEMPLE OF the Guiding Light reminded Bolan of the Spanish missions he had seen in the American Southwest. It was a hollow rectangle, the spacious courtyard in the middle paved with slate, except where spiky aloe plants rose waist-high out of arid flower beds. The walls were plaster, painted beige and faded by the sun, beneath a brown tile roof. Bolan and Halloran had scouted the location with a drive-by, noted two guards at the red front door, and drove on past.

"I didn't see their guns," Bolan remarked.

"You wouldn't, on the street," Halloran said. "Civilian ownership of guns is banned by law throughout Eritrea, which doesn't mean they don't exist, of course. Official estimates claim there are twenty thousand guns floating around illegally—that's one for every two hundred people. *Unofficially,* who knows? The street price for an AK-47, as of last week, was 250 U.S. dollars."

"Pretty cheap," Bolan observed.

"Ah, but that's roughly one-third the average citizen's yearly income."

"No sniping from the neighbors, then."

"As for the Keepers," Halloran replied, "you've seen how they greet uninvited visitors."

Passing by the south side of the temple square, the two men saw a wooden gate that led directly to the courtyard. No guards on the street there, though for all they knew an army could be waiting on the other side. Still, it was better than approaching from the front, with sentries raising the alarm and maybe hauling automatic weapons out from underneath their muslin robes.

Predictably, the gate was latched from the inside. A muffled 3-round burst from Bolan's Uzi dealt with that and sent the shattered latch flying across the courtyard. As Bolan led the way inside, two Covenant Keepers in casual denim leaped up from a bench, reaching for weapons hidden underneath their loose shirttails. Bolan stitched one across the chest and put him down, but number two got off a hasty shot before the Uzi caught him with a second burst.

And that was all it took.

Three doorways opened on the courtyard from surrounding temple wings, all of them spilling gunmen within seconds flat. Bolan met them with autofire, Halloran joining in with a Beretta M12S submachine gun he had packed before they left Addis Ababa. Ducking, rolling, with bullets whining off the dark slate paving stones around them, Bolan and the brother fought back with everything they had. Their human targets dropped, sprawled, slithered in a spreading lake of blood, while cartridge casings rattled on the pavement.

Amid the firing, Halloran called out to Bolan, "Can you hold here, while I check the bishop's office?"

"Go for it," he replied.

Halloran was up and running, Bolan not at all surprised that he'd found some way to research the temple's floor plan in advance. Bishop Yegizaw Sultan was the man they wanted, and Bolan only hoped that Halloran could bag him alive. If not, it came down to another wasted gamble, and they still might not be able to get out.

More shooters kept on coming through the courtyard doors, like clowns emerging from a circus funny car, except that all of these were armed and bent on killing any trespassers they found on temple property. Right now, with Halloran already out of sight, the list came down to one: Mack Bolan, feeding a new magazine into his SMG and reaching for a frag grenade in hopes that he could shave the odds.

IT PAID TO do your homework in advance. Halloran knew where Bishop Sultan ought to be, unless the cleric had already found an exit from the temple, fleeing for his life. He might not be a fighter like Bishop Astatke, back in Addis Ababa, but there was only one way to find out.

Halloran crashed the office door and saw a figure crouched behind the bishop's desk. He'd memorized Yegizaw Sultan's face from various surveillance photos, would have known him anywhere, along with every other ranking member of Custodes Foederis. This was Sultan, absolutely, and he'd caught the man alone.

But not unarmed.

An instant after Halloran bulled through the door, his quarry raised a pistol, squeezing off a rapid double-tap from twenty feet. His aim was off, a product of his shaky hand, but even so the bullets passed within an inch or two of Halloran's left ear. He answered with the short Beretta SMG, firing one-handed as he dived behind a sofa to his right.

Poor cover there, Halloran discovered, when the slugs from his opponent's pistol started punching through it, raining plaster from the wall behind. Halloran wished that he had one of Cooper's grenades, but hadn't thought to ask for any when they left the hired car on the street a half block from the temple. As it was, the only tools at his disposal were the power of persuasion and a dose of deadly force—always assuming Sultan let him raise his head to try a shot.

Halloran didn't speak Tigrinya, and his Arabic was spotty, but he knew that English was the third official language of Eritrea. He tried it, calling out to Sultan from his hiding place, "You can't get out of here. We've got the place surrounded."

Bluffing, but it couldn't hurt to try.

"I don't expect to live," Sultan replied. "My sacrifice is nothing if I take you with me."

"All we want is information," Halloran replied. "It needn't cost you anything."

"Except my soul! Damn you for tempting me, you spawn of Satan!"

So much for negotiating, then. Halloran heard a sound of scuffling footsteps and propelled himself across the floor with knees and elbows, scuttling toward the far end of the sofa, where he'd have a line of fire across the bishop's office. If he hadn't timed the move too late...

He cleared the couch as Sultan charged around the near end of his desk, blazing away with his black semiautomatic pistol. It seemed loud as thunder in the confines of the room, a heavy caliber in rapid-fire, but wasting rounds before the bishop realized his target had already shifted places. With a shout, he brought the gun around to bear on Halloran, and met the small Beretta's rising muzzle spitting fire.

Halloran's stream of Parabellum manglers ripped across his target in a rising arc from groin to throat. Fighting for his life, he had no time or opportunity to angle for debilitating flesh wounds, much less blast the gun out of his opponent's hand as if it were a Hollywood production with the mayhem all precisely staged. Halloran saw the bishop spin, his legs folding under him, and hit the floor with force enough that blood sprayed upward from his wounds.

Crouching beside him in another second, Halloran was poised to shake the dying man and question him while any trace of life remained, but he was already too late. The cleric's glassy eyes stared off a thousand miles beyond the ceiling overhead, perhaps in search of Paradise.

A hand grenade exploded in the courtyard, trailing screams behind its thunderclap. Halloran rose, was turning to rejoin the fight and Cooper, when he glimpsed something on the bishop's desk. A satellite phone, he surmised, from its chunky antenna and larger-than-usual size. With a grim smile on his face and cautious hope in mind, Halloran snatched the phone and then retraced his path to the battleground.

BOLAN WAS STANDING in the midst of an open-air slaughterhouse when Halloran reappeared on the scene. The human tide had broken moments earlier, his Uzi fire and shrapnel slicing through the ranks till there was no one left standing before him. Two of those who'd come in late and died immediately were the robed men who'd been standing watch out front.

All gone.

Now Halloran was back without the bishop, a grim expression on his face, a sat phone in his hand.

"What happened?" Bolan asked.

"I couldn't talk him out of dying," Halloran replied. "But I have this."

"His phone?"

"I'll get the numbers from its memory. Perhaps if we can trace them—"

"I can help with that," Bolan replied, thinking at once of Stony Man Farm. "We'd better get on the road, though."

Sirens emphasized his point, still several blocks away but closing fast. At the Toyota, Halloran told Bolan, "If we pass them, you shouldn't be seen."

"Backseat," Bolan agreed, and piled in through the left rear door. Halloran slammed it shut behind him, slid into the driver's seat and powered out of there while Bolan lay below the line of sight from any passing vehicles.

He used the time to look over the sat phone Halloran had lifted from their quarry, now deceased without spilling the beans. The phone was fairly new but relatively simple, as befitted an instrument that might be passed around through more or less uneducated hands. Its memory gave up a list of numbers on command, outgoing calls from Bishop Sultan to whomever, with nary a country or area code to be seen.

"He's calling other sat phones, maybe cellulars," Bolan advised, seconds before a cop car passed them going in the opposite direction, siren peaking, then diminishing in Doppler drama.

Halloran, when they were clear, asked Bolan, "Are they traceable?"

"It's worth a shot. I'll have to reach out to a buddy in the States."

"We all have masters, eh?" Halloran said. There was the faintest echo of a smile behind his words.

"Associates," Bolan corrected him. "Do you see any more police?"

"Not yet. Another mile or so, and I will find a place to stop."

"Suits me."

Ten minutes from the temple battleground, Halloran turned once more, then stopped the car. Bolan sat up to find them in a spacious parking lot adjacent to a some kind of marketplace. He came around to the Corolla's shotgun seat—the Uzi seat, in his case—and produced his own sat phone from hiding. Turned it on and angled the antenna, checked reception on the screen, then started tapping numbers on the keypad.

On the far side of the world, a bland voice answered, "Good day. How can I help you?"

"Striker calling," Bolan said. "And scrambling...now."

He thumbed a switch to scramble his transmission, heard the hiss of static for a moment, then the voice returned to say, "We're scrambled. How may I direct your call, sir?"

"I've got something for the Bear."

"Affirmative."

More clicks, and then a voice he recognized. "Long time, no speak," Aaron Kurtzman said. "What's the flap?"

"I need locations for a list of cell or sat phone numbers, if it's possible."

"Should be," Kurtzman replied, "if they're in use. If not, we'll monitor until they activate, and call you back."

"Sounds good." Bolan began to read the list of numbers, eight in all. Long seconds passed before his friend and contact spoke again.

"We have two active at the moment. One's in Rome

and stationary. Number two is on the move through…let me double-check this…yep, it's Konya Province, Turkey."

"Right. I'll see what I can do with that," Bolan said. "Keep me posted on the others, will you?"

"Sure thing. And before you go…have you been following the news?"

"ATTACKS?" HALLORAN ECHOED Bolan's word as if the term was unfamiliar to him.

"Half a dozen, as of now, and they're anticipating more," Bolan confirmed.

"By members of Custodes Foederis?"

"Two confirmed so far. They're guessing on two others, but the timing and coordination make it pretty clear. I guess they'll have to work from DNA in Boston and Montreal, getting IDs on the others."

"It's begun, then. I had hoped that they would only try to use the Ark, without employing any other tactics."

"And it's still our focus," Bolan said. "We can't be everywhere at once."

"But all those lives—"

"Word's out, okay? The FBI and MI-5, RCMP in Canada, Brazil's DPF, they've got the Keepers covered. Rounding up the leaders for interrogation, shadowing the flock."

"It isn't good enough," Halloran stated. "You must know that."

"They're doing all they can, under the law," Bolan replied. "The rest comes down to us."

Halloran heaved a weary sigh, then said, "You're right. What of the phone numbers?"

"Two were active. One in Rome, the other one someplace in Turkey. Konya Province."

"But in transit?"

"Right. You're psychic now?"

"Hardly," Halloran said. "It only stands to reason that they must be moving westward, toward Çorlu."

"Because…?"

"It's the location of the sect's Turkish church. More specifically, the Temple of the Resurrection, under Bishop Mehmet Akdemir. The raiders would consult with him, of course, en route to Rome."

Bolan considered tipping off Brognola, having him get in touch with someone from the Turkish National Police to drop a net on Akdemir and company, but what would happen to the Ark in that case? Did they want an international incident blown up in headlines and streaming on CNN hourly, if there was any other option?

As if reading his mind, Halloran said, "There could be panic in the streets, you know. And certain churches, if they thought the Ark existed and was being used for evil."

Bolan tried to picture it and came up with only a vague image of people milling in the streets. The closest thing to a religious panic that he knew of was the Indian phenomenon of temple stampedes that killed dozens, sometimes hundreds, at regular intervals. Those, he understood, normally started out as shoving matches or a crush for handouts, then turned deadly. If large numbers of religious folk believed the Day of Judgment was at hand—or that their sect was threatened by a band of heretics—how might the scene play out?

In carnage, sure. What else?

"We'll need a charter flight," Bolan said.

Halloran nodded. "We should find something at Massawa International. The name exaggerates its greatness, as you may imagine, but they do have private charter services."

"To Turkey?" Bolan asked.

"I hope for El Nouzha Airport, in Alexandria. From

there, it is approximately seven hundred miles to Istanbul. Çorlu lies westward of the capital, en route to Turkey's border with Greece and Bulgaria."

"Right, then," Bolan said. "It looks like we fly."

CHAPTER SEVEN

Bilecik Province, Turkey

Claudio Branca grimaced when his sat phone uttered its demanding thrum of sound, certain that it could be only bad news. He was on schedule, moving toward his target on the course agreed in countless planning sessions; there was no reason for anyone to call him for a simple update or to tell him he'd done well.

Therefore, a hitch.

He answered brusquely, gave nothing away. *"Ciao."*

And recognized the voice that greeted him by title, rather than by name. "Dei Legatus."

God's Lieutenant.

Branca answered Ugo Troisi in kind: "Dextera Dei, how may I help you?"

"Today it is I who helps *you.* Is your scrambler engaged?"

"It is."

Troisi hesitated for a beat, then said, "There have been… complications."

"Please explain," Branca urged his superior.

"Our temples in Massawa and in Addis Ababa have been raided. Bishops Sultan and Astatke are among the casualties. It can hardly be coincidence. Someone is seeking you and what you carry."

"How can they find us," Branca asked, "unless we are betrayed by someone in the fold?"

"In times like these," Troisi said, "we must be doubly vigilant. Be prepared to fight at any moment, without warning."

"We are ready," Branca said, and meant it.

"If you find yourselves cut off and in a hopeless situation," Troisi said, "use your own initiative in dealing with the object."

Even on a scrambled line, he didn't want to speak the word. In other circumstances Branca might have found that humorous, but not today.

"I understand, sir."

"It must not be captured by the infidels."

"I guarantee it," Branca answered.

"With your life?"

"Yes, with my life."

"May God protect you, Dei Legatus."

"And you, Dextera Dei."

Switching off the hiss of dead air in his ear, Branca considered the warning and orders. Of course his soldiers were ready to fight. Why else had he handpicked them for this mission? Only proved killers of the highest quality had been recruited for the team.

The problem, as he'd told Troisi, was betrayal from within. It seemed impossible to Branca that an enemy could track him overland through Europe without guidance from a traitor. Even guessing—knowing?—that his target was the Holy See, there were too many routes across the continent for any normal force to set a trap with confidence. They could defend the Vatican itself, or try to, with a wall of armored vehicles and guns, but what would that avail them in the face of God's own wrath?

Only betrayal could undo him. And betrayal, God's

Lieutenant understood, could only come from certain individuals. One possibility, the topmost leadership of Custodes Foederis, seemed so unlikely as to be essentially impossible. That left the bishops who had helped him on his way, or who were scheduled to assist him in the future.

Two of those were dead, according to Troisi. Had they been compelled to speak before they died? Or was a traitor waiting to receive him somewhere on the winding road ahead?

His orders had been simple and explicit: "Be prepared to fight at any moment, without warning."

And to execute a traitor, if it came to that. No mercy would be shown to anyone who broke faith with Almighty God. On earth, as in the fires of hell, their punishment would be severe.

His mission had to proceed to final victory.

The mission *would* proceed, no matter if he had to wade in blood from Istanbul to Rome.

Massawa International Airport

HALLORAN'S ASSESSMENT OF Eritrea's second-largest airport had been accurate. The layout featured a small terminal and a single concrete runway, serving one commercial airline. Nasair could take you anywhere on earth—as long as you wanted to visit Asmara, Doha, Dubai, Jeddah, Khartoum or Nairobi. Beyond those destinations, forget it.

Fortunately, Halloran had also been correct in thinking that the airport harbored private pilots who would take on charter flights, no questions asked beyond the client's destination and negotiation of a price. Their chosen pilot—one Ibrahim Abdella, owner-operator of a no-name, one-plane airline—quoted an outrageous price for flying two men and their bags to Alexandria and on from there to Istanbul, then bargained down to the equivalent of two years' salary plus standard rates for fuel and "overhead."

Before takeoff, a customs officer appeared, nosing around, and spoke with Abdella in a language Bolan took to be Tigrinya, since it clearly wasn't Arabic or English. Smiling at his customers, Abdella named the cost of doing business at Massawa International and palmed another wad of Bolan's cash. The customs officer departed with a smile, after he wished them bon voyage.

When it was just the three of them again, Abdella said, "We should be on our way, before his friends demand their own inspection fees."

Airborne ten minutes later, they were winging over the Red Sea, skirting Sudanese air space and any potential contact with that troubled nation's motley air force. Egypt was safer, Abdella explained, although officials at Alexandria's Borg El Arab Airport would certainly demand the standard fees and taxes for arrival and departure on their way to Istanbul.

No problem, Bolan thought. His bankroll from D.C. was holding up so far, and he could always find more cash if it was necessary. Money was the least of their concerns, in fact.

What worried him was time.

The raiders who had taken whatever it was from Axum were ahead of Bolan, call it halfway to their target now. It seemed that they were traveling by land, presumably to keep from trundling their cargo through airport security time and again with the risks that entailed. Bolan was gaining on them, thanks at least in part to Halloran, but whether he could catch the team before they found their way to Rome was still an open question.

And if he got lucky…then what?

There'd been no survivors at the Chapel of the Tablet, leaving Bolan no idea as to the number of opponents he'd be dealing with, how they were armed, or any other vital matter. Then there was the question of the Ark itself. Assuming that it wasn't just another tricked-up relic like the "yeti scalp" from Kathmandu he'd read about, which proved to be a phony stitched from goat's hide, what *was* it? And what power might be caged inside it, other than the grip it held on some people's minds?

Even Halloran, seemingly a true believer in the supernatural, stopped short of granting any special powers to the Ark. His fear involved the purely human actions of fanatics drawing inspiration from a symbol of divinity, the very terrorist attacks now being carried out worldwide by members of Custodes Foederis. Would recapturing the Ark—or, as a last resort, destroying it—stem the tide of violence the cult had unleashed?

Or was it all in vain?

Just focus on the job, Bolan thought. Don't get distracted.

Words to live by, on a mission where just living had become a challenge in itself.

And at the end of days, it was the best that he or any other warrior could do.

Robert F. Kennedy Department of Justice Building, Washington, D.C.

HAL BROGNOLA WAS on Google News, tracking the carnage as it spread, and feeling helpless in the face of so much violence. It wasn't like a war with static battlefronts, or even a guerrilla conflict where the action was at least confined within a province or a given nation. Terrorism on this scale, propelled by pure religious hatred, was unprecedented in his personal experience.

Okay, the body count so far still hadn't rivaled Oklahoma City, much less 9/11, but the dead and maimed were piling up. If things kept going as they were, Janus Marcellus and his acolytes might yet eclipse the older, more established groups that fought for a political objective, rather than a tenet of religious faith.

So far, as suited to the cult's vitriolic propaganda, all the targets had been Roman Catholic, which didn't mean that all the *victims* had been members of that faith. Machinegun fire and shrapnel from explosives didn't recognize or care whose flesh they shredded. Anyone within the line of fire was going down, with no exemptions based on age, sex, race or creed.

Unless somebody stopped the bastards cold.

So far, it wasn't working. Law-enforcement agencies from New York City to Los Angeles, Montreal, Johannesburg and Adelaide had rounded up known leaders of the cult—its "bishops"—but the prisoners weren't cracking, weren't revealing anything. What violence? they asked, all injured innocence. What ark?

And still, the lone-wolf strikes went on. A man here or a woman there, with guns, grenades, Molotov cocktails—name your poison. Schools, churches and hospitals appeared to be the favored targets, but one Keeper in Illinois had shot up an Irish-themed bar, then doused himself in turpentine and struck a match as cops arrived. Eyewitnesses reported that his dying words were, "Fires of hell!"

Brognola wondered whether he was down there now, or if "down there" even existed in some parallel reality beyond the reach of scientists and all their instruments. It had been years since he'd given any thought to questions of an afterlife, but as his own time slowly dwindled, he was prone to think about it more and more.

Bolan had told him once, in passing, that if there was

such a thing as Judgment Day, warriors would be examined for their scars, not for awards and commendations. Brognola himself had no idea what happened after death, beyond the obvious collapse, decomposition and the rest of it. He'd done some things he wasn't proud of, granted, just like everybody else on earth, but if there *was* a judgment waiting, he believed he could defend most of his actions based on an objective code of right and wrong.

You helped defenseless people when they were beset by predators. If that meant killing, then you killed, without considering the legal niceties. The big Fed was prepared to stack his love of law and order against anybody else's, but the system didn't always work. Some evil shits had made themselves untouchable within the law, he knew, for all intents and purposes. To stop them and relieve the suffering of those they preyed upon, a person had to get down in the gutter with the scum and fight on their terms.

To the death.

His system wasn't perfect, either, but it had an excellent success rate. And you couldn't judge it by the fact that predators always waited to replace the ones you'd taken out. That was the nature of the human race, and barring some apocalypse or revelation that Brognola had no power to predict, it wouldn't change.

Evil, from what he'd seen so far in life, appeared to be immortal. But the men and women who advanced its cause were not. They bled and died the same as saints. And that was where the Executioner came in.

This time, Brognola hoped he hadn't come too late.

Custodes Foederis Headquarters, Rome

SOFT MUSIC WITH a vaguely Far Eastern air played from concealed speakers in the private apartment of Queen Mother

Mania Justina. She lay nude atop sheets of Egyptian cotton, sprawled across a bed that was, appropriately, queen-size. Stretched out at her side, Ugo Troisi used his hand to trace aimless teasing patterns on her flat, tan stomach.

"If he saw us now," Mania said, "what do you think he'd do?"

"Who knows?" Troisi answered, though a number of unpleasant possibilities came instantly to mind. "If we were...well...I'd never shunt you off to sleep alone this way."

She stretched beneath the ministration of his hand. "He needs his privacy to meditate. And frankly, as you may have noticed, so do I."

Troisi wondered whether that would qualify as blasphemy, not as a reference to her husband, but the Lord and Master of them all. The lines between permissible behavior and a violation of the Keepers' code were prone to blurring. Any way he thought about it, though, bedding the sect's Reginae Matris was a mortal sin and capital offense.

Then I am damned, Troisi thought. So be it.

"We could leave together," he suggested, and was startled that he'd dared to speak the thought aloud.

"Leave?" she repeated, as if he had used a word she didn't recognize. "All this? You don't know where I've come from, Ugo. How it was for all those years before he saved me from myself."

Troisi blinked at that. "Saved you?"

"Of course! He's saved us all, don't you agree? You must, Ugo. You are his right hand, after all."

"That's just a title, Mania. And it's Right Hand of *God,* not any certain man."

"But you'll admit he has a godlike quality about him, eh? How else could he influence thousands as he does?

And now, with victory before us… Ugo, I couldn't consider leaving under any circumstances. It would cast me into outer darkness. I'd lose everything!"

"Not everything," he said. "I'm hardly destitute. And you'd have love."

"I have that now," she said, and gripped his hand to guide it. "Yes. Right there."

Hardly conscious of his fingers moving, Troisi said, "You still believe he loves you?"

"Absolutely. Why else would he name me as his queen?" She gave a little gasp before adding, "Slower, please."

Troisi dared not tell her that he had misgivings, secret fears that something would go wrong. The Ark would fail them, or, worse yet, backfire and kill them all for daring to disturb it. He couldn't confess a lapse in faith. If she tired of him or turned against him for whatever reason, he'd have placed a lethal weapon in her hands.

Mania purred and arched her back, brought both hands down to trap his own and guide it. "Here," she said. "Like this. Ooh, yes!" One hand released his wrist, rummaged between his thighs, cupping him. "Ugo? Is something wrong?"

"No, no," he said. Perhaps too quickly? "But the first two times…"

She laughed. "Perhaps I need a younger consort, eh?" Her hand released his flaccid manhood, came to rest atop his head and pushed him toward the juncture of her open legs. "No matter. You will think of something else, I'm sure."

Troisi did. And as he worked, Mania's moans rising to breathless cries of pleasure, he was thinking all the time about his future and the possibility that he had made a very dangerous mistake.

Borg El Arab Airport, Egypt

MACK BOLAN'S FIRST impression of the airport, situated twenty-five miles southwest of Alexandria, was that it needed work. In fact, construction was ongoing and expected to be finished by year's end, expanding from the airport's roughly boat-shaped, three-story passenger terminal and administration building. With Alexandria International Airport's having closed for remodeling in December 2011, Borg El Arab was—however briefly—the region's principal airport, with a capacity for handling one million passengers per year.

If he'd been hungry, Bolan could have ducked inside the terminal and patronized the food court, but he didn't plan to hang around that long. Ibrahim Abdella had already greased the necessary palms, and now was supervising the refueling of his aircraft. No inspection had been necessary once the bribes were paid, and they should soon be on their way to Istanbul.

Beyond that, Bolan couldn't say.

The soldier had made several visits to Turkey, a land where East literally met West at the Turkish Straits, a geographical dividing line between Europe and Asia. The country itself was divided along that same line, with East Thrace—also known as European Turkey—to the west, and Anatolia, or Asia Minor, to the east, home to the fabled city of Troy.

Unlike the Spartans, who had come before him, Bolan didn't plan on laying siege to anything. His style was very different, the classic hit-and-git, employing tactics that the media had lately labeled "shock and awe." Bolan hadn't required a name for it when he began his lonely war against the Mafia, since he was issuing no press releases, and he didn't care what television pundits called it now. It worked, and that was all that mattered to a warrior on the firing line.

His prior experience with Turks had taught him that they were a proud and stubborn people, fierce in battle, quick to take offense and slow to make amends. Once he and Halloran began their Turkish blitz, there'd be no room for hesitation, second-guessing or retreat. If Halloran could lead him to the Temple of the Resurrection, he would treat it just like any other target. A facade of faith disguising malice and aggression rated no consideration from the Executioner.

"Ready!" their pilot called, and Bolan walked back to the plane, perfectly at ease within his priestly garb, black jacket large enough to hide the shoulder rig he wore underneath his arm. Bolan had never preached a sermon in his life, but he could dish out hellfire with the best of them.

This was the edgy time, when they were seated, buckled in and had begun to taxi toward the airport's single asphalt runway. Anything could happen at the final instant prior to takeoff: a denial of permission from the tower, soldiers or police racing to meet them in official vehicles, even a blowout that would send them cartwheeling to fiery death.

But nothing happened, and a moment later they were airborne once again, with less than seven hundred miles remaining on the last leg of their journey out of Africa and into Europe. While remaining in the same time zone—no jet lag to concern them—they were leaving one culture behind and soon would be immersed in yet another.

Not that it made any difference.

Bolan's assignment and his enemy remained the same. As always, right. When it came down to hunting human predators, he had found that there was nothing new under the sun.

Temple of the Resurrection, Çorlu, Turkey

BISHOP MEHMET AKDEMIR surveyed the stock of groceries that had been purchased for his expected visitors, satisfied that there would be enough to feed fifteen with no one going hungry. As for wine, he had enough to keep a village tipsy for a week, but he supposed the travelers would limit their intake of alcohol. They still had far to go, with deadly peril waiting at the end of their heroic quest.

And following them, too, as Akdemir had learned through warnings from the Sedem Illustratio. Already, infidels had struck at temples in Addis Ababa and Massawa, indicating knowledge of the path Dei Legatus and his soldiers were pursuing with the mighty weapon in their custody. Would enemies target Mehmet's Temple of the Resurrection next?

If so, they would be in for a surprise.

Despite Turkey's restrictive firearms legislation—banning civilian possession of automatic or semiautomatic weapons, permitting ownership of other guns to persons who had reached the age of twenty-one, with licensing dependent on a demonstrated need—the temple had acquired a decent arsenal of small arms used by Turkish military forces: Heckler & Koch G3A7 battle rifles, M4A1 carbines, MP-5 submachine guns, and Yavuz 16 semiautomatic pistols—the classic Beretta 92, produced under license by Turkey's Mechanical and Chemical Industry Corporation. When trouble came, as it was bound to do during the Final Days, Bishop Akdemir's parishioners were well prepared.

The Final Days.

How long Akdemir had dreamed and prayed for this moment, when battle would be joined against the infidels and the corruption of the Scarlet Whore would be obliterated. There would be sacrifices, certainly—his own life possibly among them—but that was a price all members of Custodes Foederis accepted on initiation to the church. They understood what God required of them, how they had to fight and suffer for their faith before the final victory was theirs. No prize of any worth came cheaply; what, then, was the price of an eternity in paradise?

In truth, when Akdemir had learned he would play host to liberators of the Ark, he had been both excited and intimidated. So much power resting, even for a moment, at the temple he was privileged to supervise, caused Akdemir to wonder whether he was worthy of the honor. Then, casting false modesty aside, he knew that he was equal to the task.

A brief stop only, since Dei Legatus and his men had an exacting schedule to keep. A literal appointment with destiny. The fate of all humankind hinged on their mission, its success or failure in the coming days.

And they *could* fail. Akdemir realized that, felt the truth of it like a lead weight in his stomach. Scripture overflowed with tales of heroes who had done their best but fallen short in some respect of God's exalted expectations. Adam, Abel, Noah, Moses, David, even Christ Himself had weakened for a fleeting moment at Gethsemane. The smallest doubt, the slightest second thought, could ruin everything and snatch defeat from the jaws of victory.

The best that Bishop Akdemir could do was feed the warriors, offer them a place to rest, and pray with them for strength to see their holy mission through to its conclusion. And if need be, he could spend the last drop of his blood crushing the enemies who stalked them, seeking to derail their quest before it could succeed.

In which case, he'd have spent his final moments on

earth in righteous struggle and would be rewarded in due time. Of that, Akdemir had no doubt at all.

In death was life. In sacrifice, salvation.

Let the devils come.

CHAPTER EIGHT

Atatürk International Airport, Istanbul, Turkey

Flying into Istanbul cost Bolan nearly twice as much as he had spent at Alexandria. It was to be expected, he supposed: eighth busiest airport in Europe, twelfth busiest on earth, and the customs officers were underpaid for long days hunting terrorists and smugglers. Or it may have just been bribery in the grand old Turkish tradition, stretching from the days of camel caravans to massive Afghani heroin shipments.

Bolan was prepared to fly with empty pockets if he had to, but he also thought a certain measure of negotiation would prevent the men in uniform from thinking twice and coming back for more. He ultimately talked them down by ten percent from what they'd asked up front, and paid out twenty-seven hundred Turkish lira, the equivalent of fifteen hundred U.S. dollars. Halloran had helped interpret—yet another language that he managed well enough to get them by—while their pilot stood waiting for his cut, bemused at the actions of his passengers.

They were leaving Ibrahim Abdella there, or he was leaving them, returning to Massawa with enough cash in his pockets for a long vacation, plus a story he would no doubt tell to everyone he knew. That didn't worry Bolan, since nobody in Eritrea could reach them now, and any warnings likely to be sent ahead had probably already been received.

Next stop, the acquisition of a rental car. They went with Hertz, Bolan a little edgy as he walked along the concourse with a pistol strapped beneath his arm, a bag of weapons in his hand and uniformed police passing in both directions. No one seemed to notice them, however, even with the garb that marked them as spokesmen for a tiny religious minority. In flight, Halloran had informed him that the country harbored some thirty-five thousand Catholics, nearly invisible among seventy-five million Turks.

They wound up with a Fiat Stilo, rated as a "five-door" with its hatchback. It was beige, the next best thing to gray for passing unobserved in traffic, and was powered by a 2.4-liter straight-five engine with a six-speed manual transmission. Bolan saw that it was right-hand drive, as in Eritrea and Ethiopia, so nothing changed in that regard. He signed for full insurance, paying extra, in full knowledge that the car could be destroyed while they were using it.

Why stick a total stranger with the tab?

European route E80 lay before them, also known as the Trans-European Motorway or TEM. In fact, it ran thirty-five hundred miles from Gürbulak, Turkey, on the Iranian border, to Lisbon, Portugal, but Bolan and Halloran were traveling only a fraction of that distance, from Istanbul to Çorlu. Halloran's guidebook pegged the trip at seventy-five miles, passing through Kavakli at the midpoint of their journey.

Halloran wanted to drive and Bolan didn't argue. Riding shotgun gave him time to think and watch the scenery.

"There's a good chance we could miss them where we're going," he reminded Halloran.

"I know," the brother replied.

"You have a list of all the temples they might visit on their way to Rome?"

"Right up here." Halloran tapped his temple with an index finger.

"Fair enough," Bolan replied, hoping a bullet wouldn't blow that list out of his skull before they found their targets on the road.

Temple of the Resurrection, Çorlu

"WE ONLY HAVE a short time here, you understand." Claudio Branca spoke while watching as his soldiers ringed their van outside the temple, keeping weapons out of sight but close to hand.

"It's disappointing," Bishop Mehmet Akdemir replied. "We have a feast prepared, and beds if you need rest."

"We're sleeping on the road, in shifts," Branca stated. "Thank you for your preparations, but we'll need that food to go."

"I understand, of course," the bishop said. "Your mission takes priority."

"You've heard about the raids in Africa, I take it?" Branca asked.

"Indeed. And we're prepared to meet the infidels if they assail us here."

Branca lowered his voice. "It troubles me to say it, Bishop, but there may be traitors in the flock."

Frowning, the clergyman replied, "I vouch for every member of my congregation," but his voice was tinged with something that bespoke uncertainty.

"I don't accuse you or your followers," Branca said. Lowering his voice still further, almost to a whisper, he went on. "I thought, perhaps, someone in Rome."

The bishop stared at him, aghast. "You mean, within the Sedem Illustratio?"

Branca allowed himself a shrug. "Christ had his Judas, eh? I have no suspects, nothing to support it but my feeling that the enemy has followed us too quickly and too closely."

"It is known among the Scarlet Whore's disciples that we have the Ark," the bishop said. "No doubt they've charted the location of our congregations. If they reckon that the Ark must travel overland…"

"Perhaps you're right," Branca replied. "I pray you're right. If not, when we've fulfilled our destiny, we must determine who's attempted to subvert us."

"There'll be ample time for that when we have finished sifting through the ashes of the infidels," Akdemir said.

"Amen!"

"Amen!" the bishop echoed. "Now, as to your food…"

Branca directed half a dozen of his men to follow Akdemir inside the temple, help him box their meal and get it ready for the road. Two more were at work refueling the van and their cars, from cans of gas Akdemir had waiting for them at the church. No time spent at a local filling station, where they might be noticed and reported by suspicious witnesses.

Branca was briefly worried that he might have overstepped, by sharing his suspicion with the cleric. It was possible, he realized, that Akdemir could pass his words along to Rome, where they might fall on the wrong ears. It was a calculated risk, but if there *was* a traitor, and if he—or she—planned a move against Branca, it could be the maggot's undoing.

Judas had endured remorse after betraying Jesus, and had hanged himself. Branca determined that a traitor who betrayed their holy mission wouldn't have that opportunity.

Their modern Judas would die screaming at the hands of Dei Legatus—assuming Branca lived that long.

His men returned with plastic bags and cardboard cartons, one hauling an insulated cooler. Akdemir waited to see the food distributed among Branca's commandos, each man with an equal share to eat while traveling, with canned soft drinks to wash it down. Branca shook hands with Akdemir in parting and accepted his best wishes for the task ahead. Leaving the Temple of the Resurrection, he was moved to wonder if they'd ever meet again.

And realized it didn't matter, either way.

If he succeeded, they would have eternity. If not, at least his enemies would know a little taste of hell on earth.

Custodes Foederis Headquarters, Rome

Ugo Troisi switched off his sat phone, set it on his desk and prepared to face Janus Marcellus. There was good news from the Turkish front, with Branca's team on schedule and proceeding toward their target, thus far unencumbered by the raids on temples in the Horn of Africa. However enemies had gotten on their track, at least the infidels were still behind them, with no sign of catching up.

But could their good luck last?

Delivering the latest news to Marcellus was Troisi's job, but he couldn't help being nervous any time he faced his master. That was only natural, he thought, all things considered, but he feared that Marcellus might detect his guilt, smell his duplicity and call him out for violating one of their most sacred principles, the sanctity of home and family.

Marcellus had powers; that was understood. As Pontifex Rex, he had received successive revelations from the Lord instructing him to found the church and lead it toward a final cleansing of the world. Marcellus could read the hearts of men—and women, too, presumably—although he hadn't managed yet to see that Mania enjoyed the company of others when his back was turned.

Or *did* he know? Was it some kind of game they played, planned out between them? And if so, what was the benefit to Janus?

For a nauseating moment, Troisi wondered if Mania had been using him. Was Janus one of those who liked to watch, perhaps from hiding or on video, while his wife cavorted with other lovers? And if so, was the Pontifex privy to Troisi's greater betrayal, the offer to take her away from her husband? Away from the church?

It seemed unlikely, since Troisi still drew breath. He could name half a dozen Keepers who had sinned against the sect in lesser ways and paid the price in blood. It had been his task to deliver them for sacrifice, and to dispose of their remains after the executions were completed.

No. If Marcellus knew that he had shared Mania's bed, much less proposed elopement, Troisi would be dead and buried now. Their masquerade was still intact. So far.

Approaching the royal chamber where Marcellus met with his minions, Troisi forced himself to focus on Claudio Branca's brief message. The team had left Çorlu with fresh supplies from Bishop Akdemir and was proceeding toward their next stop on the road to Rome. Instead of following the TEM into Bulgaria, they would divert to Greece; a boat was already waiting to receive them for travel by water, defeating pursuers who sought them on land. Troisi gave full credit for that masterstroke to Branca, hoping that it would succeed.

Good news for Marcellus, and an opportunity for Troisi to read his mood, watching for any indications of suspicion.

Riflemen stood watch over the Pontifex, outside his study's ornate door. They recognized Troisi, snapping to attention and admitting him without the pat-down search that any lesser member of the sect would have endured. Not for the first time, it occurred to Troisi that he could kill Marcellus anytime he wanted to—but then what? Mania would likely shun him, while the wrath of God propelled his soul into the everlasting fires of hell.

Perhaps it was his destination anyway, considering his many sins.

Marcellus waited to receive him, seated on a throne plated with fourteen-karat gold. Some of the gems that decorated it were copies—garnets in the place of rubies, cubic zirconia instead of diamonds—but it still made an impressive show.

"What word?" the Pontifex inquired.

"My Lord," Troisi said, forcing a smile, "I have good news!"

European Route E80, Istanbul Province, Turkey

BROTHER HALLORAN FROWNED at the buzz of his sat phone, considering whether he should stop on the roadside to answer the call. It could be from only one source, and he could have left the car to have some privacy, but by the second tone decided that it didn't matter. He'd already been through hell with Cooper, and more of it still lay ahead of them.

He answered simply, "Halloran," and waited for the deep familiar voice to fill his ear.

"You're still alive, then."

"Yes, Prefect." Nearly fifteen hundred kilometers separated the men, and he still couldn't miss the undercurrent of displeasure in the voice of his superior. With nothing to lose, he added, "I suppose the tracker must have shown you that."

"Indeed," the answer came. "But we could not say whether you were traveling with purpose, if you'd been abducted or if someone had your corpse in transit."

Hardly plausible, Halloran thought, but kept it to himself. "You're right, Prefect. I should have called you sooner. I apologize."

"You haven't called me yet," the scolding voice replied. "I've just called you."

"Again, sir—"

"You're aware of what has happened at the sites in Africa?" The prefect was playing cagey, even though the phones they used for missions out of country scrambled all calls automatically.

"I am. Yes, sir."

There was a momentary pause before the next inquiry. "And were you in any way responsible?"

"I used my personal initiative," Halloran said. "If I am to succeed in my assignment, I must gather all available intelligence."

"And have you, Brother? Are you any closer to your goal?"

"Yes, Prefect. I believe so."

"Ah, belief. And what supports it, may I ask?"

"The cargo travels overland. It can't be flown, sir. Those transporting it will naturally seek to keep a low profile. Most of their needs, I think, will be supplied whenever possible by their associates along the way."

"I see. When you say overland…how would they reach the place where you are now?"

"A fast run through Sudan and Egypt, then through Jordan, circumventing the Israelis, and through Syria. You may recall, Prefect, they had the best part of a week's head start."

"Yes, yes. And they're advancing, Brother. How much longer will this take?"

No longer worried about body counts, apparently.

"Sir, I can hardly offer you a date or time. We're close, I think, and—"

"We?"

"Yes, sir. I meant to tell you."

"Then by all means do so, Brother."

"Back in Axum, I encountered someone with an assignment similar to mine."

"Assigned by whom? From where?"

Halloran glanced across at his companion and found him focused on the passing scenery. "America, I think."

"You think?"

"Most certainly."

"The CIA? NSA? DIA?" the prefect probed.

"Of that, I can't be sure."

"You haven't asked?"

"There seemed to be no point, Prefect."

"No point. And was there no point in consulting me before you entered into this unauthorized alliance?"

"Frankly, sir, I calculated that it would be easier to win forgiveness than approval."

Was that choking sound a growl of anger or a stifled laugh? Even in person, face-to-face, it could be difficult to tell.

"It seems that I've been too indulgent in the past. Now you confront me with a situation I cannot control, unless I call you back to Rome directly."

"And allow the cargo to proceed."

"Carry on, then. We shall certainly discuss this at a later time."

If I survive, Halloran thought. And said, "Yes, sir," before he broke the link. "My prefect, checking in," he said to Bolan.

"I got that part. You good to go?"

Halloran focused on the highway. "Yes, I am," he answered. "Good to go."

Feres, Greece

CLAUDIO BRANCA WASTED no time departing from Turkey. The coastal town of Feres, situated almost on the border in the Evros regional unit of East Macedonia and Thrace, boasted a population large enough that Branca's three-car caravan could pass unnoticed. Lying at the mouth of the Maritsa-évros River, the longest in the Balkans, it was also a convenient port on the Aegean Sea. From there, they would be traveling by water to the Cyclades, and on from there to Sicily, eluding any hunters who pursued them overland.

And on from there to Rome. The final act.

Their ferry captain, Nikolaos Anatolakis, was a member of Custodes Foederis who had volunteered to carry them across on this leg of their mission. His three crewmen hadn't been initiated to the sect, but they were silent, surly types who kept their mouths shut around strangers and policemen. By the time they went ashore next and were drunk enough to blab, it would not matter who they told of what they had or had not seen aboard the *Oceanus*.

It was an older, double-ended ferry, on the small side, capable of hauling two trucks or half a dozen compact cars, with forty passengers at maximum capacity. For this run, it would carry only Branca's team and their three vehicles, explained to other would-be passengers at dockside as a private party bound for Alonnisos in the Sporades. No one would question that in Feres—nor in Alonnisos, since the *Oceanus* was not stopping there. None of the island's twenty-seven hundred residents expected it, nor would they miss it when the ferry passed them by.

Branca was prone to seasickness, but he wore a scopolamine patch behind his left ear to hold the nausea at bay. Once they were well at sea, he let himself relax a little, still not backing off from full alert, but resting on a bench beside the starboard railing with the blue Aegean spread before him. He imagined those who stalked his party hastening to overtake them, unaware that they'd already lost the race. And by the time they worked it out...

Where would he be? In Sicily? On the Italian mainland, burning up the Autostrada A3 from Reggio Calabria to Naples? Perhaps already on the Grande Raccordo Anulare, circling Rome?

It was a grave mistake to be too confident, he realized. Pride ranked among the deadly sins and could betray the boldest, most experienced of warriors if it got the upper hand. It led to taking reckless chances, letting down one's guard, and thereby falling prey to enemies who watched and waited for an opportunity to strike.

Instead of celebrating his escape, he thought ahead to what awaited him in Rome, as they approached Vatican City. Officially, the sovereign city-state of 832 year-round inhabitants was defended by 135 members of the Pontifical Swiss Guard in their flamboyant medieval uniforms, plus 130 police officers of the Corps of Gendarmeria, attached to the Vatican's Security and Civil Defense Services Department. Sixteen guns against 265 would be a losing battle in itself, but the papacy also relied upon regular Italian troops for its military defense.

How many thousands, then? Branca couldn't begin to guess.

Nor did he care.

God's power, channeled through the Holy Ark, could vanquish any force on earth in seconds flat, provided that the soldiers wielding it had faith.

European Route E80, Approaching Çorlu

ÇORLU COULDN'T COMPETE with Istanbul for size, but it was growing rapidly. Its population had nearly tripled between 1990 and 2000, leaping from 75,000 to 206,000, mostly drawn to work in the city's three hundred textile factories and outlet centers.

It was a modern boomtown, with all that implied. Large blocks of public housing and fast-foot restaurants crowded downtown Çorlu, with little to show in the way of culture besides movie theaters and multiple large halls hired out for wedding receptions. Crime was an increasing problem, fueled in equal parts by the town's thriving red-light district and easy availability of drugs. A leading heroin producer in its own right, modern Turkey also served as a conduit for much of the Afghan smack moving westward, to feed addictions in Europe and North Africa.

None of which was Mack Bolan's concern, as he and Brother Halloran approached the city close to dusk. Halloran said, "The Temple of the Resurrection is on the east side of town. The area around it is…unsavory, I think you'd say."

"Expect police, then," Bolan said.

From prior visits he recalled their navy-blue uniforms, silver stars on the shoulders for lieutenants and captains, gold stars for higher ranks. Patrol cars were blue-and-white, with POLIS stenciled on the hood and doors. The cops were armed, and in a pinch could call on Turkish SWAT teams. Outside city limits, law enforcement fell to the green-clad paramilitary Jandarma, schooled in suppression of terrorism.

"They will respond, of course," Halloran granted, "but we have two points in our favor. First, the district's crime rate keeps them fairly busy. Second, Custodes Foederis is unpopular in Turkey, with the huge Muslim majority. Police may drag their feet to rescue members of the cult."

"Or hurry over, hoping for a bust to shut them down," Bolan replied.

"That's possible," Halloran acknowledged.

"So, we're still trying to bag a bishop?" Bolan asked.

"Indeed. Although this Mehmet Akdemir may be what you would call a tough nut, eh?"

"That's what we call it," Bolan agreed. "Among other things."

"If nothing else, perhaps we can interrogate a lesser member of the church, to learn if those we seek have visited the temple and, if so, obtain a time frame."

"Knowing where they're going next would be a help," Bolan observed. "Or we could always skip ahead to Rome and meet them there."

Halloran frowned and shook his head at that. "Allowing them to reach Vatican City is a grave risk. Even if we take for granted that the Ark is powerless, or a manufactured hoax, the very fact of an assault upon the Holy See might well be catastrophic. At the least, it would encourage other members of the cult to strike worldwide."

"From what I'm hearing," Bolan answered, "that's already happening."

"I understand. But picture the remaining members of the cult—say, even half the thirty thousand that they claim—waiting for a specific sign to tell them that the moment has arrived. Picture the damage they could do."

"I'd rather not," Bolan replied, but images of mayhem

were already spooling through his head unbidden, like the trailers for a horror film.

And he had seen it all before.

CHAPTER NINE

Vatican City, Rome

Cardinal Luis Bouchet dreaded his upcoming audience with Cardinal Bishop Jerome Saldana. As prefect of the Congregation for the Doctrine of the Faith, Bouchet was free to operate with near autonomy as long as things ran smoothly, but, like any other cleric of the church except the Pope himself, he ultimately answered to superiors.

And now he had a serious infraction to report.

The violence was one thing, not a standard tactic of the CDF in modern times, although it couldn't hold a candle to the fury of the sixteenth-century Roman Inquisition. Officially, that early purge of heretics had claimed 1,250 lives, but Protestant historians sometimes confused it with the longer, harsher Spanish Inquisition that had spanned 354 years and killed thousands, or the witch trials of 1450 to 1750 that witnessed 60,000 executions throughout Europe.

All ancient history.

Bouchet's task on this evening was threefold. First, he had to persuade Cardinal Bishop Saldana that the bloodshed was both necessary and controlled, with no risk of blowback to tarnish the church. Second, he had to assure Saldana that his agents still had time and opportunity to frustrate any headline-grabbing strike against the Vatican. And finally, he had to explain what he had learned only brief moments earlier, concerning Brother Halloran's unauthorized collaboration with a stranger to the faith.

Bouchet was expected at Saldana's office, on Viale dell Osservatorio near the Pontifical Ethiopian College. He found that ironic, given that his present troubles had begun in Ethiopia, but he found no amusement in the odd coincidence.

The prefect was formally dressed for his meeting with Saldana in a scarlet cassock with thirty-three buttons, symbolizing the years of Christ's life on earth. His skullcap and shoulder cape were likewise sewn from scarlet watered silk. The large pectoral cross suspended from a chain around his neck was another reminder, of his Lord and Savior's suffering.

A Swiss Guard met Bouchet outside the cardinal bishop's office and checked his name off a list on the clipboard he carried. Beyond the door, Bouchet passed inspection by Saldana's secretary—a young priest from Argentina, still awestruck by the trappings of the Holy See—and was shown into the cardinal bishop's private office.

Saldana was a large man, six foot four and well over two hundred pounds, most of it muscle judging from the way he moved and held himself when standing still. His face resembled something carved from marble, stained an olive hue by long exposure to the elements. His eyes were chips of flint beneath imposing, woolly brows. There was a rumor that he never smiled, and Bouchet couldn't dispute it from his personal encounters with the man.

Before he could speak, Saldana said, "I understand you've had some difficulties, Luis."

"That is unfortunately true, Your Eminence," Bouchet replied.

"The violence in Africa was…unavoidable?"

"According to my understanding, yes, Your Eminence."

"But we have nothing yet to show for it."

"Regrettably…"

"There's something else, I think." When Bouchet blinked at him, Saldana said, "No, I'm not psychic. It is plainly written on your face."

Unable to postpone it any longer, Bouchet took a deep breath and began. "It is my agent in the field. In Africa. You won't have met him."

"Brother Halloran?"

"Yes, sir. It seems he's met someone, American, pursuing the same mission as his own."

"On our behalf?" Saldana asked.

"No, sir. That's hardly possible."

"A spy, then."

"Yes, or something similar."

"When you say that they've met…"

"It seems that Brother Halloran, without informing me, has reached some kind of an accommodation with this person to proceed and function as…a team."

"I see." And for the first time in Bouchet's experience, he saw Saldana smile. "That may be helpful, eh?"

"Pardon?"

"If Brother Halloran succeeds, we are delivered. If he fails, let the American be held responsible."

"Of course!"

"And in the meantime," Saldana said, his smile evaporating, "keep a close eye on your man."

Aboard the Oceanus

CLAUDIO BRANCA SIPPED a cup of bitter coffee, scanning the southern horizon while sunset turned the waves to lapping flames. They were passing now between the Sporades and the Northeast Aegean Islands. Turkey in the distance on their left, Greece to their right, and open water dead ahead until they neared the Cyclades. Up on the ferry's bridge, Captain Anatolakis and his first mate steered the vessel, manned its radio and huddled over charts to keep the *Oceanus* on course.

Branca disliked the coffee, but at least it kept him warm to some extent, against the chill wind off the water. Huddled in a fleece-lined jacket that he never would have worn in Africa, Glock prodding him from where he had it tucked inside his belt, he wished that he possessed the gift of prophecy, as Janus and Mania did. If he could only see the final moments of his mission, know that he'd succeed and that the struggle had not been in vain....

But no such consolation was permitted to him. Branca reckoned he would have to wait and find what happened next, trusting his faith in God and his superiors to see him through whatever trials awaited him between his next stop and the Holy See. He couldn't let his courage and determination fail him, when the fate of all humankind was hanging in the balance, all of heaven trusting him to win.

Footsteps approached him on the deck. Since there were only friends and working drones aboard, he didn't bother glancing up as Franco Arieti settled on the bench beside him. He waited while the locksmith put his thoughts in order and began to speak.

"You think they're still behind us?" Arieti asked.

"Somewhere," Branca replied. "But they won't find us on the highways, eh?"

"We've beaten them," Arieti said, more as if he wanted to convince himself.

"For now, at least."

"Why don't they just go wait for us in Rome?"

"Some will, I'm sure." Branca imagined ranks of armored vehicles, soldiers with automatic weapons, and the gaudy Swiss Guards somewhere at the rear of the assembly, armed with pikes and daggers. "It won't matter, though."

"You're sure of that?"

"Aren't you?"

The challenge to his faith produced a grunt from Arieti, meaningless. He paused to light a pungent cigarette, then spoke again through little puffs of smoke. "I know I should believe that God will help us, eh? But what if He sits back and watches, just to test us? Say He doesn't activate the Ark as planned. What then?"

Almost by rote, Branca replied, "If you don't trust Him, He will certainly forsake you, Franco."

"Ah. Perhaps I should be praying, then."

"It can't do any harm."

"I'll see you later," Arieti said. He rose and shuffled off, still trailing smoke.

"Later," Branca replied, his own doubts nagging at him like satanic imps, inviting him to trade his faith for fear.

"Get thee behind me," he advised them, echoing his Savior from the gospels, and the voices in his head were stilled. At least for now.

Tomorrow, Branca thought, would take care of itself.

Çorlu, Turkey

FROM THE E80, Halloran drove south into the city proper, turning west from there through streets that seemed as scrambled as spaghetti in a bowl. Clearly, there'd been no master plan for routing traffic over any kind of grid that made the slightest bit of sense. Halloran did all right, though, navigating with a steady hand while his companion memorized landmarks and street signs that he couldn't translate, correlating his surroundings to a guidebook map that might just save their lives, in the event they had to cut and run.

Çorlu was new to Bolan, despite his previous campaigns in Turkey, but he had a near eidetic memory for battlefield terrain. And everywhere he went was a potential battleground.

A haze of pollution from Çorlu's many factories hung overhead like a permanent storm cloud, lit from below by the city's own lights to give it a hellish aspect as night fell. En route to their intended target, Halloran passed by a huge shopping center, then wound through a neighborhood that seemed foreign to the rest of the city.

"These are all Romani," Halloran explained. "You might know them as Gypsies. Though settled here, at least for now, they still confound authorities. Depending who you ask, their population in the country ranges from thirty-five thousand to nearly five million."

"That's quite a discrepancy," Bolan observed.

"Perhaps by design. You know that they were major targets of the Holocaust? It's safer for them to remain—how would you say? Below the radar?"

"Right."

"Another mile or so," Halloran said, "until we reach the Temple of the Resurrection."

Bolan watched for police cars as they tooled along, but saw none. He guessed that they would likely have their hands full in the city's red-light zone, but wondered if the global rash of terrorist attacks by members of Custodes Foederis might have placed surveillance teams around the church they sought.

That was a problem to confront when it arose, he decided, and let it go.

At least the shift to Turkey had resolved a racial issue for the moment. Bolan noted various black faces on the streets they passed along, perhaps descendants of historic immigrants from Africa, and was relieved that neither he nor Halloran would stand out like a proverbial sore thumb. If anything, the priestly garb they both wore would likely draw more notice than their skin tones, as they moved among the city's mostly Muslim populace.

But Bolan didn't plan on staying long, or mingling with the masses. He had only one goal in mind, and once that was accomplished, they would be on their way—if and when they had sufficient intel to continue their pursuit.

Where to?

Halloran had his money on Greece, and another outpost in the chain of temples they'd been following. But trying to anticipate the movements of their quarry was a risk they couldn't take. If they'd gone on to Greece and missed the Ark in Turkey, or the team they hunted chose another route, it might be too late to catch up before the Ark rolled into Rome.

And then what?

Bolan didn't buy the Indiana Jones mythology, but he agreed with Halloran that heading off their enemies before they reached the Holy See would be their best bet for avoiding panic and catastrophe. If there was any kind of real-life magic in the air, he'd be as much surprised as anybody else.

And it would be a whole new ball game for the Executioner.

International Spy Museum, Washington, D.C.

HAL BROGNOLA EMERGED from the Gallery Place Metro Station and walked south on F Street Northwest, automatically checking for tails, sadly aware that with the press of office staff and tourists in the neighborhood it would require a very clumsy follower indeed to stand out from the crowd. Besides, since he had been invited to this meet on neutral ground, security should be in place.

Established in July 2002 at a cost of $40 million, the International Spy Museum was a monument to espionage through the ages and one of the few museums in Washington that charged an admission fee. Brognola had a free pass in his pocket, faxed from Langley after he'd agreed to keep the date and find out what was agitating his sometime connection at the Company.

Officially, the CIA wasn't involved in running the museum, but several "former" agents sat on the board of directors, and critics had panned the facility for whitewashing agency blunders and generally romanticizing covert operations. That didn't bother Brognola—half of life in Wonderland was blowing smoke one way or another—but he kept in mind that every aspect of the meeting would be stage-managed by Langley.

The big Fed made it past the box office and theater-style marquee, into a lobby where the museum's layout was explained and diagrammed. A familiar face appeared at once, sparing Brognola the rigmarole of choosing a cover and proceeding through the exhibits where phony guards might stop and question him at random intervals, demanding papers or an explanation for his presence.

Jack Dillard was a deputy assistant director of the CIA's National Clandestine Service, established after 9/11 when the Company abandoned any pretense of confining its work to foreign countries. More specifically, he served with the Counterterrorism Center, where his job occasionally overlapped with work assigned to Brognola and Stony Man. He was a solid sort—six-one, about 180 pounds, dark hair neatly trimmed and going gray around the temples, with a decent sense of humor—but Brognola never forgot that they served difference agencies.

Their handshake was perfunctory. Once small talk was disposed of, Dillard led Hal back outside, to roam along the sidewalk. "Fewer ears out here," he said, half smiling.

That was disingenuous, of course. Dillard could be wired for sound himself, and any number of devices had the capability of tracking them, eavesdropping as they talked, or reading their lips.

Rather than state the obvious, Brognola asked, "So, what's the flap, Jack?"

"Cutting to the chase. Okay, then. We're getting pressure from the Vatican."

"Falling behind on tithes and offerings?" Brognola quipped.

Ignoring that, Dillard replied, "They're getting nervous, Hal. Know what I mean? These suicide attacks, this business with the Ark."

"What do you know about the Ark?"

"Just what I learned in Sunday school, a hundred years ago," Dillard replied. "And the importance that a symbol has for people all around the world. I don't have to believe it, only understand that others do. Belief makes people do some wacky things, like at Jonestown, Waco, Oklahoma City."

"Jonestown? You were where when that went down? In kindergarten?"

"Please. Fourth grade, and totally beside the point."

"Let's hear the point, then," Brognola suggested.

"Bottom line? Roman Catholics make up twenty-two percent of our national population. The number's pushing sixty-nine million. They vote, and none of them want to be blown sky-high or shot to shit in schools and churches."

"Hey, who does?"

"And if they knew about this business with the Ark," Dillard added, "they wouldn't want some kind of holy-moley superweapon pointed at the Vatican. *That's* my point."

"You buy the Indiana Jones routine?"

"Hell, no! But they could always fake it, right? Pull in a ringer—say, a dirty bomb, for instance—and pretend it was Jehovah or whoever."

Brognola had thought along those lines, as well, and hadn't liked the end result.

"I'm on it, Jack," he finally acknowledged. "That's all I can say."

Clearly dissatisfied, his contact bowed to the reality—and the deniability—of whatever covert ops Brognola controlled. "You'll keep me posted, though?"

"I'll do what I can," the big Fed said, and moved off toward the subway station that would take him back to work.

Ios, Aegean Sea

BISHOP ELIA MARKOPOULOS waited at the Port of Ios, on the rocky island's northwest shore, to greet the *Oceanus* and its passengers. They weren't staying long, barely a turnaround in fact, to stock up on supplies and fuel, but duty called on him to greet and honor them before they passed on to fulfill their destiny. And truth be told, if only in the silence of his heart, Markopoulos couldn't resist being a part of the crusade, however small that part might be.

The heroes of Custodes Foederis would be welcome at the Temple of the Immaculate Conception, and if they remembered nothing else about their time in Greece, at least they would recall the solidarity of brotherhood.

Bishop Markopoulos had brought two members of his congregation with him as a welcome party, both armed as he was, in case any problems arose. That was unlikely on an island eleven miles long and six miles wide, with eighteen hundred inhabitants. True, Ios attracted thousands of tourists each year, who flocked to its beaches, but careful observation of the harbor during recent days had noted no suspicious types arriving since the incident at Axum.

And indeed, who would expect to find the Ark on Ios, even for a day?

The bishop's cell phone vibrated against his thigh, demanding his attention. He removed it from his pocket, answered, and heard the Latin phrase: *"Omnia operare ad bonum."*

All things work together for good.

He completed the phrase from Romans 8:28. *"Ad eos quod amor Dei."*

To them that love God.

The bishop's signal meant that it was safe for the *Oceanus* to dock and deliver its passengers, leaving their vehicles on the ship, under guard, while they loaded supplies. He would have dearly loved to see the Ark, or simply know that it had landed on his island, while still concealed from mortal eyes, but the security arrangements had been laid down in advance. Ios was no more than a way station, a pit stop of convenience. His role in the unfolding cataclysm would be minuscule at best.

But still enough, Markopoulos felt certain, to assure him of his just reward.

"Be ready when they dock," he told his acolytes. "If anyone attempts to board the ship for any reason—"

"Then we stop them," both responded, speaking simultaneously.

Bishop Markopoulos was satisfied. He'd drilled the warning into them relentlessly, had personally double-checked the Skorpion vz. 61 machine pistols they carried concealed under their baggy shirts, each loaded with twenty rounds of 7.65 mm Browning SR ammunition. Now his eyes swept the docks and found no one who seemed not to fit, nothing to make him think killing was imminent.

Relaxing to the best of his ability, Markopoulos stood waiting for the ferry to arrive.

Çorlu, Turkey

BOLAN SLIPPED A 40-round box magazine into his AKMS rifle and cranked the action smoothly, chambering a 7.62 mm full-metal jacket round. Beside him, Halloran finished double-checking his Beretta submachine gun and turned to his pistol, pulling the SIG-Sauer's staggered-column mag to verify a full load.

"All set?" Bolan asked, as the pistol magazine snapped back in place.

"As ready as I'll ever be," Halloran replied.

The Temple of the Resurrection wouldn't be an easy target, most particularly if they found the raiders they were hunting still on-site, and Bolan meant to be prepared. Besides his AKMS and Beretta sidearm, he had clipped four frag grenades onto his belt, under the lightweight raincoat that concealed his mobile arsenal.

They'd parked the Fiat Stilo beside a service station that had shut down for the night, well back in shadows that would keep it hidden barring the arrival of police with spotlights, on the hunt for stolen or abandoned vehicles. Not likely, Bolan estimated, but if they stumbled into a worst-case scenario he thought they still might manage to escape on foot, pick up another car by one means or another, and elude pursuit.

Or not.

Luck had been running with them so far, on the first

two strikes, but it could turn at any moment. Bolan, while aware of every adverse possibility, refused to worry about things that might or might not happen. Every combat soldier lived with fear, assuming he was rational, but those who let it dominate them were as good as dead.

The blacked-out service station stood three long blocks from the Temple of the Resurrection, with a line of outlet shops in between. From that distance, nothing indicated that the church was anything beyond what it appeared to be, a meeting house for worshippers who didn't fit with the majority of Turks, who followed Islam. On its outer wall, facing the street, a man-size wooden cross was bolted to the bricks, the temple's name below it, in brass letters.

Modest. Tasteful. Nothing to suggest fanaticism to the casual observer.

Bolan looked for sentries, saw none on the street, then spotted movement at a corner of the temple's roof. A head popped up in silhouette, peered left and right, then ducked back out of sight.

"On top," he cautioned Halloran.

"I saw him," the brother said.

They had removed their backward collars and the rest of it for now, arriving after dark in what appeared to be a more or less deserted neighborhood, with no need for disguises. Bolan had considered leaving on the costume, thinking it might stall reaction time by his opponents for a crucial second, maybe more, but then decided that it made no difference. The Keepers would respond the same to clergymen with guns as they would with any other armed intruders.

Kill or be killed, when it hit the fan.

This time, at least, Bolan hoped they would be able to acquire some one-on-one human intelligence—what spooks addicted to their acronyms called HUMINT—that would put them closer to their quarry and the Ark.

On their right, an alley opened, deep and dark. Bolan and Halloran turned into it, picked up their pace, their weapons coming out from under cover now, as questions crowded Bolan's mind. Had they been spotted by the watcher on the temple's roof? If so, how long before he missed them on the street and sounded an alarm? What happened after that? How many men and guns would they be facing in the temple?

Never mind.

They'd come this far, and there could be no turning back.

CHAPTER TEN

Temple of the Resurrection, Çorlu

Bishop Mehmet Akdemir sipped a glass of raki, savoring the anise-flavored liquor on his tongue and welcoming its heat inside him, waiting for the alcoholic "lion's milk," as it was known in Turkey, to relieve his lingering anxiety. The bottle on his desk was nearly full, but Akdemir thought he might need another glass or two before he could relax.

He'd done his part, sending the Ark and its armed escorts on their way with fresh supplies, alerting the Sedem Illustratio once they were gone. The rest came down to waiting now for news from Rome, and possible retaliation from the infidels against his temple and his flock.

Akdemir knew that the raids in Axum and Massawa had come *after* any hope of locating the Ark in either place was gone. That told him the attacks were meant as punishment, or as a means to gain intelligence about the object's whereabouts, to intercept it and prevent its use against the Scarlet Whore of Babylon. If Bishop Sultan had been induced to speak, perhaps through torture, it was possible the enemy would come for Akdemir and his disciples next.

No time to waste, then.

Akdemir had taken special interest in the plan hatched by Janus Marcellus and Mania Justina to vanquish their age-old enemy. His ancestors, the Seljuq Turks, had been primary targets of the great Crusades after they cut off

Christian access to Jerusalem by seizing Anatolia. His homeland had been a blood-drenched battleground for some two centuries, and Akdemir had been raised to hate the popes who'd claimed divine rights to the world at large. His lifelong study of those tragic years included the collection of a thousand books or more on the Crusades, together with a host of maps depicting troop movements and battle sites.

And now, when he was helping to seek retribution for a great historical injustice, it was only natural that Akdemir would write a treatise of his own. The document would be complete with maps, of course, depicting how the Ark was transported from Ethiopia to Rome by a select cadre of heroes and delivered to the very doorstep of their enemies. And if he did say so himself, the hand-drawn illustrations weren't half-bad. He had a flair for illustration that would certainly impress a host of readers in the years to come, once the corruption of their adversaries had been purged by holy fire.

But if it fell into the wrong hands while the Ark was still in transit...

As he poured a second glass of raki, barely conscious of draining the first, the bishop experienced a new pang of concern. Destroying all his hard work was unthinkable, but he could hide it, certainly, where no intruder could discover it. There was a vault concealed within the temple's basement, nothing grand, but stout enough to weather fire and flood with no loss to the articles inside. A simple stroll downstairs, and Akdemir could hide his work from prying eyes until such time as it was safe and he could write the final chapters in his epic saga of global salvation.

But first...another glass of raki.

It was curious, he thought, how each mouthful tasted a little better than the last. The ninety-proof liquor no longer burned going down. It simply made him feel mellow. A few more sips, a few more moments, and he would carry the crate filled with his literary and artistic labors to the vault. No one else in the temple even had to know. It would be Akdemir's little secret.

He was smiling, satisfied with his decision, when the first shots echoed from outside.

BOLAN WAS STILL expecting shouts of warning as he cleared the alley, turning left to reach the Temple of the Resurrection's small back door. In fact, the lookout on the roof had still done nothing, had to have missed the enemies approaching, but another stood before Bolan and Halloran, blocking their way.

Or, rather, he was slouched in front of them, half dozing on his feet, slumped back against the stucco wall. Whether imbalance or a premonition of impending danger woke him, they would never know. Bolan squeezed off a silenced round from his Beretta, drilled the sentry's left eye socket with a Parabellum bullet, and dropped him like a sack of laundry to the pavement.

Where the automatic weapon carried by the dead man suddenly discharged a 3- or 4-round burst.

The bullets posed no threat to Halloran or Bolan, angled backward, ripping through the lookout's lifeless legs and feet before they struck the back door of the church, but the reports were loud enough to wake the dead.

Well, almost.

Bolan heard a muffled curse from Halloran, but saved his own breath for a rush to kick the door in, smashing through it with minimal resistance from the simple keyed lock in its knob. The dead bolt, he supposed, was left open to let the sentry come and go, convenience taking precedence over security. Across the threshold, with Halloran behind him, Bolan scanned for targets and saw no one, but heard voices drawing closer, barking inquiries and orders that he couldn't understand.

No matter. Their intent was obvious, and so was his response.

He met the first three shooters with his AKMS set on full-auto, stroking short bursts from the piece with a precision touch. The first one around the corner took his in the chest and vaulted backward, slamming into number two, the bullets ripping through him, taking both men down. The third tried to retreat, but wasn't quick enough, half turning to become a profile target, framed by light behind him, dropping in a haze of crimson mist as Bolan's next rounds found him.

More voices, footsteps pounding toward them over concrete floors, and Bolan went to meet them, Halloran staying close. Stepping around and over corpses, Bolan reached the corner, risked a glance around it, then ducked back before a spray of automatic fire blazed down the corridor.

"Four more," he cautioned Halloran, already reaching underneath his raincoat for a frag grenade. He palmed the RGD-5, pulled its pin and lobbed the bomb in a sidehand toss around the corner, more shots crackling at him as his arm was visible to his assailants for a fraction of a second.

With that racket, Bolan couldn't hear the RGD-5 bouncing over concrete, but the Keepers had to have seen it coming. They were shouting suddenly, still firing as they scrambled to get out of range, but how far can a person scramble in three seconds and change, on slippery concrete?

Not far enough.

The warning shouts turned into screams, then were eclipsed by thunder as the fragmentation grenade exploded in the narrow corridor. Bolan heard shrapnel plinking into walls and ceiling tiles, and wet slapping sounds where razor-edged fragments of sheet steel met flesh. Easing around the corner, he found his four opponents down, two of them lying sprawled and silent, while the writhing pair drew bloody abstract patterns on the floor.

Bolan gave each of them a mercy round at point-blank range, heard Brother Halloran mouthing what might have been a prayer, and moved on past the dead in search of living prey. None of the young men they had met so far matched the description he'd been given of the temple's master, Bishop Mehmet Akdemir. The man he hoped to find and take alive, this time, in hope of bringing a conclusion to their quest ASAP.

But first, he thought, there'd be more guns to face.

More blood to spill.

BROTHER JOSEPH HALLORAN was torn by mixed emotions as he followed Matthew Cooper along the hallway strewed with bodies, sprayed and smeared with blood as if a psychopathic artist had been called to decorate the place. He felt revulsion at one level, witnessing—and joining in— the desecration of a church, misguided and fanatical as its parishioners might be. But on the other hand, Halloran also felt exhilaration in the heat of combat, something he'd experienced before and felt compelled to mention in confession.

His Beretta M12S weighed seven pounds without its 32-round magazine, but it felt featherlight to Halloran just now, as if he'd brought along a plastic replica by accident. Adrenaline was singing through his veins, making him almost giddy, while the smell of burned gunpowder filled his nostrils, mingling with the sharp metallic tang of blood.

In front of him, Cooper raised a warning hand, but Halloran had heard the enemy approaching, voices lowered

to a whisper now, after their shouting friends had come
to bloody grief. From the sounds, they were collected in
a room ahead and to his left, the door ajar, light spilling
forth. Some kind of meeting hall, perhaps, where they had
gathered for their prayers or social discourse, then had
found themselves besieged.

Halloran edged to one side of the tall American, leveled
his SMG and moved ahead with cautious steps to meet the
next wave of defenders. When they spilled from hiding, he
was ready, dropping to a crouch beside Matt Cooper and
firing short bursts to conserve his ammunition, marking
targets as they came in turn, putting them down.

Counting was pointless, numbers totally irrelevant.
There was no keeping score in battle, only fighting on
until no enemies remained a living threat. The stutter-
ing of his Beretta was eclipsed by Cooper's Kalashnikov
and the responding fire of Keepers rushing to eliminate
them, bullets singing overhead and gouging scars into the
walls on either side. Halloran's magazine ran empty, and
he drew his SIG in lieu of fumbling in his pockets for a
fresh one, squeezing off in rapid fire at strangers bent on
killing him, excited and repulsed to see them screaming,
lurching, falling. Down and dead.

Halloran hardly knew it when the screaming stopped,
his pistol's slide locked open on an empty chamber, but
his mind cleared faster than the gunsmoke in the corridor.
He dumped the SIG's spent magazine, replaced it, stowed
the sidearm in its holster and reloaded the Beretta SMG.
Matt Cooper, already on his feet and moving, snapped another magazine into his carbine, cocked it and moved out
to find more enemies.

The brother followed Cooper into the charnel house,
prepared for anything.

THE TEMPLE HAD gone as quiet as a tomb. Its occupants lay sprawled in graceless attitudes of death, none of them looking much like candidates for resurrection at the moment. Bolan wasted no time pondering the disposition of their souls, if such things did in fact exist. Only the living threatened him, and he was off in search of more.

One living target in particular.

It stung to think they might have missed the bishop, that he could have missed the party quite by accident and might be on his slow way back home right now, stopping for coffee and a pastry, maybe window-shopping. It could happen, Bolan knew. Sometimes your life turned on a dime.

Before he wrote off the temple's honcho, however, Bolan meant to search the place. And time was wasting, with the hellish noise they'd made. Even in the city's textile outlet district, with shops closed for the night, there had to be *someone* in the neighborhood who'd notice racket from machine guns and grenades. Whether that person would alert police or not was something else again, but Bolan couldn't trust a simple case of apathy to save his life and Halloran's.

They had a job to do, and quickly, searching high and low before the law arrived.

Either way, he couldn't leave before a thorough effort had been made.

Halloran had briefed him on the temple's floor plan. It was single-story, with a basement below. They'd cleared approximately half the ground-floor rooms already and proceeded on their way with caution, one man covering the other as they darted in and out of doors, meeting no further opposition as they whittled down the unexplored remainder of the temple. Bolan felt odd, treating a church like any other hostile hardsite, but he didn't let it slow him.

Most days, he didn't care what faith a group of people

chose to follow. If they went mainstream or deified some character from third-rate science fiction, it was all the same to Bolan. But when faith came down to violating others, *killing* others, his tolerance evaporated like a raindrop on a desert highway in July.

Two rooms remaining, one of them a spotless kitchen, the other its pantry. Both were well-stocked but deserted when Bolan and Halloran reached them, with no stragglers hiding in the corners or behind appliances. The soldier tapped on the pantry walls and satisfied himself that none gave access to a hidden room or corridor. He paused then, listened for the cry of sirens, and heard nothing yet.

"Downstairs," he told Halloran.

"This way," the brother replied, and led him to a door that might have opened on a closet, but actually hid a flight of steep stairs. Below, a bare bulb in a ceiling-mounted cage lit their way.

That could mean someone had preceded them down, or simply had forgotten to switch off the light last time around. There was no way of telling until they committed and went underground.

Bolan went first, letting Halloran watch his back. The wooden steps were solid, but creaked softly under his weight. When he was back on concrete, looking at an empty corridor with more rooms opening on either side, he covered his partner's descent.

They were below street level now and insulated from the city's sounds. They might not hear police arriving, could be trapped down there like gophers in a hole, but Bolan had to forge ahead. Holding his AKMS ready, he began to move along the corridor.

BISHOP AKDEMIR WISHED he had skipped the second brimming glass of raki. Even though the sounds of death and battle had a sobering effect, he still felt fuzzy, as if there were cobwebs wrapped around his brain, and he was on his third fumbling attempt to open the vault's old combination lock. It was pathetic, shameful and humiliating.

Worse yet, terrifying.

It was quiet on the ground floor now, the gunfire and explosions silenced. Akdemir surmised, since none of his parishioners had come to fetch him, that they'd lost the fight and been annihilated. He supposed that they were better off than he was, in the Lord's eyes, since they'd gone down fighting for the cause, sober and dedicated to their faith.

But what of him?

Though armed, he hadn't fired a shot so far, nor had he managed to secure the documents that now began to strike him as a strange, potentially disastrous self-indulgence. If the enemy was searching for him, Akdemir knew he might have only moments left. And if the combination lock continued to defy him...

He could always burn the papers, though it pained him to destroy them. Akdemir had matches in his pocket. Simply pile them up—or better, shred them first—and light the heap before the infidels discovered him. Before his hubris ruined everything.

Breathing slowly, trying to collect himself, the cleric made one last attempt to beat the stubborn combination lock. A full turn to the right before he stopped on 3, then left to 17. He stopped there when his hand began to tremble, frightened that he'd overshoot the next number in line, as he'd already done repeatedly. The lock had no time limit, but it was completely unforgiving if he missed a stop and tried to double back.

A whispered prayer, before he turned the calibrated knob back to his right, stopping on 9. Two digits left, and *left* was the direction that he had to twist the dial this time, stopping on 21. From there…

Was that a sound of footsteps on the basement stairs? He hesitated, moved his right hand from the combination lock, in the direction of his pistol, then stopped short. If enemies were coming, were already in the cellar, then he had no time to shred his papers and ignite them. He could only forge ahead and try to get them in the vault before the hunters overtook him. Then, if there was time, he could die fighting like the heroes of his congregation in the temple overhead.

Akdemir bit his lower lip until it bled, hoping the pain would help him focus on the task at hand. Clutching his right wrist with his left hand to prevent a tremor from betraying him, he eased the combination dial back to his right, creeping toward 35. The click wouldn't be audible to ears ringing with the effects of too much raki, but he strained to listen for it, anyway.

And heard, instead, the sound of footsteps coming closer, unmistakable this time.

One final half turn of the dial, one digit left, then he could fling his work inside the vault and slam the door, trust someone else to find it later and release it to the world, though incomplete. An inside view of how Custodes Foederis had rescued humankind from the long dark night of mortal sin.

A shout behind him made the bishop turn, the combination lock forgotten as he clutched his pistol, raising it. Two strangers stood before him, black and white, with automatic weapons in their hands. The last thing Bishop Mehmet Akdemir beheld was their twin muzzle-flashes blinding him, propelling him headlong into a darkness without end.

"THIS ISN'T TURKISH," Bolan said, showing Brother Halloran the manuscript he'd lifted from the floor.

"It's Latin," Halloran replied.

"With maps," Bolan observed, impressed by the apparent skill of whoever had done the work by hand, painstakingly. "If these are right, they track the Ark from Axum all the way to Rome."

"We ought to wait and read the rest of it another time," Halloran said.

"Agreed." He couldn't let a lucky break—assuming that was what they had in hand—delay them at the scene until police arrived. It would be all for nothing then, a total loss.

Evacuation of the temple went without a hitch. Bolan was half expecting gunfire from the sentry on the roof, but when it didn't come, he figured that the guy had either joined the battle in the church and died there, or had bolted from the site in panic. Either way, they cleared the building without any further opposition and were rolling in the Fiat Stilo moments later. Still no sirens, making Bolan wonder what it took to rouse the cops in Çorlu.

When they had put a mile behind them, Halloran spoke up. "If we can trust the maps, they give us an advantage."

"If we trust them," Bolan echoed.

"Why take time to draw them, otherwise?" the brother inquired.

"I'm more concerned about who knows the maps exist," Bolan replied. "If someone on the transport team suspects their route's been compromised, it wouldn't be that hard to find another route."

"The manuscript may help us there," Halloran said. "If Akdemir prepared it on his own, let's say his bid to be a part of history, the thieves won't know the maps exist."

"In which case, there's a chance that we could jump ahead of them," Bolan suggested.

They were due to catch a break, he thought—but was this it? Mehmet Akdemir's attempt to hide his manuscript and maps confirmed Bolan's impression that they must have some significance. He couldn't think of any reason why the cleric would waste time preparing bogus documents, then die defending them.

Assume they were important, then. If they could chart the Axum raiders' movements from the maps prepared by Akdemir, there was indeed a chance to head them off, but crucial variables still remained unknown. How long ago had the raiders left Çorlu? Had they reached their next stop yet, or were they still en route? What means of travel were available to Halloran and Bolan for the next leg of their journey? Could they fly ahead to meet their quarry, or would they be forced to travel overland?

Unanswered questions.

Bolan hoped that Halloran's translation of the Latin manuscript would fill in certain blanks, but it would not foretell the future. Moving targets on the battlefield were tricky in their own right. Zeroing in on a group of runners with a week's head start was infinitely harder and might prove to be impossible, even with maps and notes.

A thousand things could change the route of travel chosen by his targets, Bolan realized. Police activity, terrain, the weather, even something whimsical could alter the game board drastically. Worst case scenario: if they believed their route was known to enemies, the Ark transporters might abort their mission and attack some secondary target still unknown. Bolan and Halloran could wait in Rome until doomsday while the raiders veered off course and scored their hit a hundred miles away.

But Rome would be their first choice, clearly. Bolan

thought they'd grasp at any chance to strike the Vatican. And if he couldn't stop them sooner, he would be there when it happened.

Laying down his life if need be, to avert catastrophe.

CHAPTER ELEVEN

Las Vegas, Nevada

From the action on The Strip, you wouldn't know Americans had ever heard of a recession, unemployment or the gridlock paralyzing Congress. It was still a business to do pleasure with you in Sin City, name your poison, with an emphasis on flushing hard-earned money down the crapper in casinos. Neon ruled the night along Las Vegas Boulevard, beginning at Sahara Avenue and running south to Tropicana.

Trudging north along The Strip, sweating inside his baggy jacket, Lucius Porter had already passed Mandalay Bay, the Luxor and Excalibur, New York-New York, the Trop and MGM Grand. He turned east on Harmon, crossing against the light with blaring horns on every side, daring some infidel to run him down, some guardian of so-called law and order to detain him. Porter knew God wouldn't let it happen.

Not this night. Not when he had a job to do.

Promoters of Las Vegas as a "family town" liked to say that the city had more churches than casinos. Porter didn't know if that was true, though there were plenty to be found. Only one of them was faithful to the scriptures, though, and he'd been fortunate enough to find it in the Temple of Enlightenment.

Custodes Foederis had changed Porter's life. Now he was going to help change the world.

Two blocks east of The Strip he saw the lights of Saint Columba Church. No competition for the searing neon he had left behind, but it was Porter's beacon on this last night of his earthly life. Befitting its locale, the church was holding bingo night to raise funds for remodeling. Its members almost certainly believed that they were gambling for "a good cause," heedless that they were engaged in Satan's work.

Or did they know? If so, did any of them care?

Beneath his loose, unseasonable jacket, Porter had a sawed-off semiautomatic shotgun dangling under his right arm on a loop of slender nylon rope. He'd drilled the gun's stock near the pistol grip, after he'd cut off most of it and wrapped the portion that remained in friction tape. Without its plug, the weapon held six shells loaded with double O buckshot. He could empty it in three seconds flat, putting three dozen .36-caliber pellets in flight before his prey knew Death had come to visit them.

Porter had filled his pockets with more shotgun shells, not bothering to count, mixing some double O and rifled deer slugs with the triple O, just for variety. Beneath his belt, pressing against his spine, he'd wedged a .44 Magnum Colt Anaconda revolver, its four-inch barrel prodding the cleft of his buttocks with every step Porter took. It was uncomfortable, granted, but he liked the extra weight back there, knowing he had a backup weapon when he'd used up all the shotgun rounds.

A nice surprise for the police.

People were laughing as Porter entered Saint Columba's fellowship hall through an open door on the church's west side. A few looked up from bingo cards, one total stranger smiling at him as if they were lifelong friends, but when he brought the twelve-gauge out it definitely changed their mood. The priest was moving toward him, one hand raised as if in blessing, his face gone pale, and Porter shot him in the chest before he had a chance to speak. The triple-aughts propelled his rag-doll figure backward, airborne, crashing into the bingo cage filled with white ping-pong balls.

"It's Judgment Day!" Porter announced, before the screaming started and the infidels began to scatter. He was singing "Onward Christian Soldiers" as he set to work.

Amsterdam, The Netherlands

ALDO DRIESSEN RODE the Metro from Amsterdam Centraal to De Clarcqstraat and disembarked there, hiking northwest along the street and crossing one canal, approaching Nassaukade and his final destination. It felt strange to know that he would soon be dead, yet satisfying that his death would count for something.

And he wouldn't be alone.

Driessen had stopped to boost his courage at a hash bar, washing down a "space cake" with a cup of strong black coffee. He supposed it was a sin, and had already offered up a prayer asking the Lord's forgiveness as he rode the Metro, but he wasn't sure he could have forged ahead without the cannabis to bolster his resolve.

Around him, most pedestrians had their umbrellas out and open, warding off a drizzling rain from leaden skies. Driessen himself had come outfitted in a wide-brimmed hat and knee-length slicker, doubling as concealment for the pistols wedged under his belt. It might have seemed excessive to a stranger, but he carried three: a Belgian FNP from Fabrique Nationale d'Herstal, chambered in 9 mm Parabellum with a 16-round magazine; a Glock 20 in 10 mm Auto with a 15-round mag; and a snub-nosed Taurus

Model 85 revolver in .38 Special. Together, their weight threatened to drag down his trousers, but Driessen wore suspenders with his belt to spare himself embarrassment.

It wouldn't do for him to be a bare-assed martyr and become a public laughingstock.

Not that the city would be laughing when his work was done.

Outside the Church of Saint Gerlach he paused to idle in the rain, content to nurse the secrets that he carried underneath his coat and in his heart. A wedding was in progress in the church, and while he could have interrupted it, Driessen felt generous this day. Why not allow the priest to finish, and the groom to kiss his bride? It was the closest they would come to their intended honeymoon. Let them enjoy the moment while it lasted, brief as it might be.

Driessen had spent last night rehearsing every move he planned to make before a full-length mirror in his small flat on Retiefstraat. While it was impossible to know exactly how his targets would react, he now had every confidence that he could draw and fire his weapons in turn, without mishap. He knew which pockets of his raincoat held spare magazines for both the FNP and Glock, so there would be no awkward mix-ups.

He was ready, down to the cotton wadding stuffed in his ears.

A pair of police constables, male and female, passed him in their bright yellow slickers. Neither gave Driessen so much as a second glance, as there was nothing about him to arouse suspicion in this neighborhood. He let them go, hoping that they would be well out of earshot when the wedding ceremony ended and the celebrants emerged.

Earshot. A term he'd never really thought about till now.

Five minutes later, with the yellow slickers lost to sight, an usher opened up the double doors of Saint Gerlach and braced them so they wouldn't swing back on the people trooping through. Guests left the church before the bride and groom, lining the steps outside to offer them applause that would have been unseemly in the nave. Driessen moved up to join them, still unnoticed as he halted at the bottom of the steps.

Here came the happy couple, herded by the pastor, all three smiling broadly at the friends and relatives arrayed before them. If they noted Aldo Driessen in the mix, it didn't seem to register.

He drew two of his pistols, FNP in his right hand, Glock in the left, and raised them both together. Almost whispering, he offered up a final prayer: "My life for you, dear Lord."

And opened fire.

Çorlu, Turkey

HALLORAN TRANSLATED BISHOP AKDEMIR'S manuscript from Latin while reading it aloud to Bolan, skipping over parts that rambled into cult theology, seeking the bits that might assist them in locating the Ark and its Keepers. Bolan listened in their parked car while he scanned the maps that Akdemir had drawn by hand. No travel routes were depicted by dotted lines, but temples of Custodes Foederis were marked and labeled.

"He believed that they would stop at Ios, in the Cyclades," Halloran said. "I can't say whether he was told that or surmised it on his own."

"No way to drive there," Bolan said. "They'd have to fly or sail."

"A ship, then," Halloran declared. "They couldn't find a cargo flight to carry vehicles, or risk being observed with their peculiar cargo at an airfield."

And if they traveled overland, driving along the east coast of the Adriatic Sea, then doubling back toward Rome, it meant driving the width of Greece, then passing through Albania, Montenegro, Bosnia and Herzegovina, Croatia and Slovenia—five countries in all, with seven border crossings, before they reached Italian soil.

Too much. Too far.

"Okay," he said. "They've got a ship and a head start that we can only estimate. But why Ios, when they could keep on going through the Med to Italy?"

"They may do that," Halloran said. "In fact, it would be logical. The better choice. But I suspect that they are on a pilgrimage, as well as a crusade. Compare it to the stations of the cross, perhaps."

"Even if it turns out to jeopardize their mission?"

Halloran could only shrug at that. "I won't pretend to fully understand their thinking," he replied, "but if we grant that they're sincere believers, then we must expect a fair amount of ritual in this, their effort to evoke the End of Days."

"That's good for us, then, if it slows them down," Bolan observed.

"If we're correct in estimating where they will 'touch base,' as you might say."

"But if we can't catch them at one of their pit stops, we're still just playing catch-up," Bolan said.

"Correct."

"Ios won't have an airstrip, I suppose?" Bolan asked.

"No. A seaplane could deliver us, but it would also draw a great deal of attention."

Meaning greater likelihood of fighting that would place civilian lives at risk.

"Fly to another island, then," Bolan suggested. "Catch a charter boat from there. At least we'd save some time."

"That's good," Halloran said. "The local airport only serves AnadoluJet and Germania commercial flights, but we should find private pilots somewhere in the neighborhood."

"More bribes," Bolan said.

"No doubt," the brother agreed.

"In for a penny, in for a lira."

"And a euro, when we land in Greece."

"Sharing the wealth," Bolan replied.

And maybe, in a short while—if their luck improved—sharing the pain.

Paris, France

MARCEL HARNOIS WASN'T a tall man, nor a heavy one, but he was strong. While serving terms for larceny in each of three Parisian prisons there had been ample time for him to build his upper body strength by lifting weights, and several opportunities to use his muscle against the people who thought he'd be an easy conquest.

They were wrong. But Harnois still had much to learn.

His true enlightenment hadn't begun until his third incarceration, when he'd met a chaplain unlike any other in his personal experience. The priest had opened Harnois's eyes to facts about the world and universe at large that had eluded him throughout his thirty-seven years. Harnois had been amazed to learn that *he* wasn't to blame for his pathetic life of crime. In fact, his parents and their rotten church had set him on a course that led inevitably to a courtroom and a prison cell.

Once carefully explained, it was as clear as day.

He had promptly pledged his life to Jesus and the One True Faith. And as with many midlife converts to religion or some other cause, Harnois displayed a gratifying zeal.

Why else would he be chosen when the moment came to strike Notre Dame de Paris?

That morning he had gone for one last walk along the Seine, mixing pleasure with duty, enjoying sunshine on his face while he scouted the Île de la Cité. From shore, on the river's south bank, the Gothic cathedral looked invulnerable, unapproachable, but that was an illusion. Harnois crossed the river on the bridge supporting Rue Lagrange and made his way on foot to stand before the church that harbored the official chair of the Archdiocese of Paris.

Inside, he knew, there was a reliquary said to house the very crown of thorns Christ wore when he was crucified. Harnois presumed that was a fictional embellishment, on par with Victor Hugo's famous novel of the hunchbacked bell-ringer, advanced to awe a flock of sheep who worshipped things they couldn't see or touch. And if the crown *was* hidden somewhere in the church, what of it? That just meant it had been stolen and defiled, along with so much else, by the malignant Scarlet Whore of Babylon.

And that would end today.

Notre Dame had suffered major damage—"desecration," as the bishops termed it—at the hands of rioting Huguenots in 1548, and again from revolutionaries in 1793, but each time it was rebuilt at the expense of parishioners who valued the edifice more than their own humble abodes and families. Marcel Harnois didn't suppose that he could do more damage than a mob, even with forty kilos of Semtex strapped beneath his raincoat, but it hardly mattered.

His action this day was only part of something greater, an attack on all fronts that the Scarlet Whore couldn't resist. Although he wasn't privy to the details, Harnois understood that something extra-special had been planned for Rome, a lesson for the Vatican that no one drawing breath on earth would soon forget.

It was a privilege to play his humble part in something great, and thereby ensure his seat in paradise. What more could any true believer hope for?

Harnois approached the cathedral with a straggling group of tourists, striding toward the central set of double doors, each pair beneath a looming archway crowded with saints carved from stone. None of the supplicants and gawkers paid the least bit of attention to him as he passed among them, right hand in the pocket of his raincoat, wrapped around the detonator that would send his soul to heaven while the rest went hurtling to their individual rewards or punishment. They meant no more to Harnois than a stream of ants bustling across the pavement, seeking crumbs.

His lips moved silently, one final prayer. "My life for you, dear Lord."

Amen.

CHAPTER TWELVE

Tekirdağ Çorlu Airport, Turkey

It was a stretch to call Tekirdağ Çorlu an international airport, although Germania's once-daily flight would carry passengers to Düsseldorf. Bolan and Halloran had better luck with a private pilot, Ekrem Arikan, operating as Aegean Tours.

Arikan's one and only aircraft was an Italian-made Piaggio P.136, a twin-engine amphibian last manufactured in the early 1960s. It seated five and had a range of nine hundred miles, powered by two Avco Lycoming GSO-480 flat-six piston engines mounted on its overhead gull wings. Cruising at 208 miles per hour, with a service ceiling of 25,000 feet, the Piaggio could drop them on Sikinos, southwest of Ios in the Cyclades, in something under two hours.

Halloran handled the negotiation with their flyboy, Bolan handing over the equivalent of seven hundred dollars in Turkish lira. The Piaggio was fueled and ready, waiting only for a clearance before Arikan taxied onto the airport's lone runway and sent them hurtling skyward. The Piaggio seemed to be straining at first, but once off the ground, with its landing gear retracted, it was smooth enough. The noise from its engines and rear-mounted pusher propellers vibrated through the passenger compartment, making conversation iffy, but Bolan was happy to sit back and think without having to talk for a while.

They'd picked Sikinos as the island nearest Ios. It harbored two villages, one at the harbor where they would be landing, with a total year-round population of 238 inhabitants. Halloran took for granted that they'd find at least one local sailor who would either carry them to Ios or rent a boat to them to make the journey on their own, and Bolan had no reason to dispute it. Living off the sea made people happy to collect a little money on the side, even though they were prone to viewing strangers with suspicion.

Traveling by water, Bolan and Halloran would avoid the notice that attended landing at Ios itself, where spotters might report their arrival to the Temple of Immaculate Conception. Even so, the word of new arrivals on the island might precede them, as it often did in tiny insular communities, but there'd be less time for the Keepers to prepare a welcome if they didn't know trouble was coming until it set foot on the beach. Another dicey problem was the presence on Ios of two small police outposts—one for Port Police, the other for Tourist Police. Given the reputation Ios carried as a "party island," there would likely be at least a dozen officers in residence at any given time, and they would not have far to travel from the port to any other point on the island's forty-two square miles of rocky soil.

A challenge, then, to hit the temple, see if they had come in time to catch the Axum raiding party still ashore, and either take it out or get a pointer to its next stop on the way to Rome, while managing to duck the cops. Their pilot had agreed to wait for them at Sikinos and take them on from there to anyplace within his flying range, not bothering to inquire about their business in the Cyclades. He likely figured them for smugglers, but was disinclined to jeopardize his fee by asking any questions.

Skimming over the Aegean, Bolan was reminded of the Greek myths that he'd read in school, tales of heroes, gods

and monsters battling in an ancient world where magic
was accepted as the norm. No demigod himself, he sym-
pathized with Hercules and his appointed labors. Bolan's
enemies were like the fabled Lernaean Hydra, sprouting
two fresh heads for every one he severed, and his battleground resembled an extended version of the Augean
stables, packed with filth from a thousand cattle left un-
tended for decades. Bolan spent his life hacking and shov-
eling, hoping for light at the end of the tunnel, with no
break in sight.

But he kept on, because he *could*. And when he thought
about it, Bolan knew he wouldn't have it any other way.

Custodes Foederis Headquarters, Rome

UGO TROISI USED a small brass key to unlock the lower
right-hand drawer of his spacious mahogany desk. Inside
the drawer, behind a rack of hanging files he'd filled with
office correspondence, lay an Olympus WS-700M digital
audio recorder with four gigabytes of internal memory,
permitting Troisi to record more than one thousand hours
of conversation. Its battery's life was a maximum twenty-
five hours, but that was actual recording time, when its re-
mote "intelligent" microphones transmitted human voices.

From Mania Justina's bedchamber.

Troisi had planted the tiny mikes last week, racked by
guilt but compelled by suspicion. He still wasn't sure, precisely, what had driven him to mount this audio surveillance on his lover—and the reigning Reginae Matris of
Custodes Foederis. He couldn't say her attitude toward him
had changed, exactly; she was still both energetic and explosive in their couplings. But there had been something:
darting glances, worried little frowns that vanished when

he caught her at it and was too afraid to ask what might be preying on her mind.

This day, as usual, Troisi used an earpiece to review the night's recordings in perfect privacy. None of his aides would dare to enter without knocking, and even if Marcellus barged in uninvited he would simply see his second in command transcribing figures from the sect's far-flung accounts. Nothing suspicious about that.

Technology spared Troisi from dead-time hissing static. The first thing that he heard was Mania greeting someone, clearly male, who answered in a voice Troisi didn't recognize. Who could it be? Access to Marcellus and his wife was by invitation only, strictly limited. Contributors, reporters and the like were never welcomed into private quarters—and they certainly wouldn't have said the things that set Troisi's cheeks aflame with jealous rage, sparking a pain that throbbed between his eyes.

The couple wasted little time on small talk, and said nothing that would help Troisi name the man. Not Marcellus, that was clear; Troisi would recognize his voice immediately. This was someone else who knew Mania intimately and was taking pains to please her, even as he taunted her with gutter language, which she didn't seem to mind.

Sickened, Troisi switched off the recorder and removed the earpiece, shoving the equipment to the far side of his desk. He'd thought to pick up private conversations between Marcellus and Mania, maybe learn if either one of them had grown dissatisfied with him in any way, or if there was some plan afoot from which he'd been excluded. He'd expected that they might engage in sex from time to time, although he had Mania's word that such events were few and far between.

But this! To learn that she'd betrayed Troisi *and* her husband with another man? The thought had never crossed his mind.

This meant that he had never truly satisfied her. Worse, he could no longer trust a single thing she'd said to him while they lay tangled in her sheets or stood beneath the warm spray of her shower. Every word out of her luscious mouth had been a filthy lie.

What could Troisi do about it? That required some earnest thought. He craved revenge, but not if it rebounded on himself.

He stowed the digital recorder in its drawer and settled back to think.

Over the Aegean Sea

MACK BOLAN CHECKED his watch and saw that they had roughly half an hour left before their touchdown at Sikinos. Halloran had given him a rundown on the Temple of Immaculate Conception: twenty-five to thirty members, kept under loose surveillance by a Catholic pastor who tended his own flock on Ios. Keepers came and went on errands that could only be surmised, but they'd been quiet, peaceable so far, and kept to themselves for the most part.

Halloran had called his spotter midway through their flight from Çorlu, but there'd been no answer at his church. Peculiar, since he should have been on high alert the past few days—guarding against attacks, if nothing else—and Bolan saw that Halloran was worried. If there'd been an incident like those still making news around the world, Bolan supposed it would have been reported. But with mayhem like the Paris bombing and the shootings in Johannesburg, would Ios even rate a mention for a missing priest?

"I wish that we had time to check on him," Halloran

said, as islands passed beneath them, flecks of color in the azure offshore water indicating vessels.

"Not likely," Bolan said, meaning, no way at all.

They had to focus on their targets first, and once they'd tangled with the Keepers there'd be no time left for anything but mopping up, dodging police and getting back to Sikinos as soon as possible. They couldn't count on Ekrem Arikan to hang around and take a fall on their behalf. Missing their charter flight meant being stranded, cut off and caged, if they were even taken in alive.

"You're right, I know," Halloran said. "Priorities. He was a good man. Father Pananides."

"Maybe still is," Bolan said. "Don't write him off until you're sure."

"He knew that we—or, rather, *I*—was coming. He'd have tried to update his intelligence on what the Keepers have been doing. Possibly he had new information on the Ark."

"No point in speculating," Bolan said. "We'll have to run with what we've got."

Halloran was silent for a moment, then pressed on. "Perhaps I shouldn't ask this, but do your people have some contingency in place? In case we fail?"

"I don't get into that." In fact, while failure was a possibility on any mission, Bolan rarely let it cross his mind. "*Your* team must have a backup plan in place," he said.

"Oh, yes. There is security, of course. Even before the failed attempts to murder John Paul II, the threat of terrorism was assessed and measures taken. It's mandatory in a world that hovers on the brink of madness."

"So you're covered."

"Ah. That's something else. It would depend upon the weapon, naturally."

"Something supernatural about the Ark, you mean?"

Halloran shrugged. "As you must know, sincere belief in God dictates that there must also be an adversary. Satan, Lucifer, Beelzebub, Satariel—select your name of preference. That doesn't mean that I expect to meet him on our present journey."

"Let's hope not," Bolan replied.

"As to the Ark, *if* it exists, how can a true believer think God would allow His enemies to wield it as a weapon to destroy His holy church?"

"No problem, then," Bolan said.

"But, as we've discussed, some earthly weapon *masquerading* as the Ark could still wreak havoc, both in Rome and through the world at large, if wrongly taken as a symbol of God's wrath."

"The PR isn't my department. I try to tackle one thing at a time."

"You won't mind if I pray, then?"

Bolan turned back toward his window as he said, "It couldn't hurt."

Aboard the Oceanus

CLAUDIO BRANCA WATCHED a spray of flying fish explode before the *Oceanus,* silver flashes there and gone within a fraction of a second. Pelicans swept overhead, pursuing, swooping with their jaws agape to snare a meal. Branca heard someone coming up behind him at the rail and turned to see it was the ferry's skipper, Nikolaos Anatolakis.

"We're all right," the captain said without preamble, speaking heavily accented English. "Nothing on the radar that appears to follow us."

"You'll keep a sharp watch, though," Branca replied.

"Certainly. And if something appears?"

Branca had wondered about that himself. Travel by ship had been intended to save time and difficulty with successive border crossings, while eluding the pursuers who had followed them belatedly from Axum. The reverse side of that coin involved a risk of being trapped aboard the *Oceanus,* still at sea, with no means of escape if they were overtaken.

No means but the Ark, perhaps.

In Branca's estimation that would be a dreadful waste. Assuming he could activate the sacred weapon—and he had no manual to work from, nothing but some texts from scripture vowing death for anyone who touched it—what would be the net result? Perhaps the *Oceanus* would disintegrate with all aboard her, or the sea might boil. And then what?

Abject failure where his mission was concerned.

He was supposed to wield the Ark in Rome, against the Vatican, not spend its force and sink it in the midst of the Aegean Sea. In that event, the Scarlet Whore of Babylon would be unscathed, free to manipulate the media and wipe out any trace of Branca's failed crusade. Branca wasn't a scientist, but all Italians knew that the Aegean and the Med had dozens of volcanoes slumbering. In the event of a mysterious explosion, was the media more likely to accept an explanation drawn from science or accept that God had touched the earth with fire?

And did it even matter, if the Holy See emerged unscathed?

Branca considered praying, but his nervous agitation kept him from it, worried that the Lord would hear his ego and his agitation talking, rather than his heart. Prayer should be undertaken thoughtfully, if not in relaxation, then at least from some semblance of inner peace.

Not possible today.

If need be, Branca was resolved to go down fighting on the *Oceanus,* sink the ferry and the Ark, to keep it out of hostile hands. Retrieval at some future date might still be possible—he thought of the *Titanic,* sunken for three-quarters of a century before six thousand of its artifacts were raised from a depth exceeding two miles—and then another, more proficient hero would be starting closer to his target, making good on the crusade.

But I won't fail, he told himself. Acceptance of defeat ensured it, and he wouldn't let himself be sucked into that trap. They could still outrun their enemies, reach Rome and turn God's cleansing fire against the infidels who had usurped His name.

Two stops remaining for the *Oceanus,* then his team would be back on the road. Once they were rolling on Italian soil, in Branca's estimation, they would be invincible. If he knew anything of scripture, if he hadn't been deceived by Janus Marcellus and Mania Justina, victory was guaranteed. Satan, his minions and their earthly followers were all condemned to burn.

If Branca closed his eyes and concentrated, he could almost smell the smoke.

Custodes Foederis Headquarters, Rome

JANUS MARCELLUS FACED his wife of fourteen years across a dining table built for twenty guests. They were alone this evening, as usual, since they broke bread with others only on specific ceremonial occasions. More particularly, Marcellus wished to speak with Mania Justina in private about certain things that had been preying on his mind.

She beat him to the punch, though, with a question: "How goes Branca's progress with the Ark?"

Marcellus laid down his fork, considering the best response. While he and his wife had planned and organized their church together, building from the ground up to its present shining moment in the sun, Marcellus wasn't convinced that she still shared his zeal and dedication to their common goal.

"The team is still intact and moving forward," he replied. "There's been another incident along their route, however. In Çorlu."

"The Temple of the Resurrection," Mania Justina said, almost whispering. "And Bishop Akdemir?"

"Martyred, with at least a dozen members of his congregation."

"Figli di puttana! Cazzo!"

Marcellus nearly smiled at that. When Mania was angry, cursing, she reminded him of how she'd been when they had met, a fiery thing who could entrance and capture any man. He seldom saw or felt that fire these days. But was she warming someone else, behind his back?

Clutching her silverware so tightly that her knuckles blanched, she asked, "Is there nothing we can do? No way to intercept the people who are chasing Branca and his men?"

"If we knew who they were—"

"Who do you *think* they are?" she challenged, interrupting him. "Who but the CDF?"

Marcellus considered that. He had no doubt the Congregation for the Doctrine of the Faith would try to stop the Ark from reaching Rome, might even kill him at his own headquarters if the opportunity arose, but could the CDF track Branca from East Africa, through Europe to his final target, without help from the inside? Had someone from the inner circle of the Sedem Illustratio betrayed them?

And if so, who could it be?

Not Mania herself, Marcellus decided. She had grown

addicted to her affluence and power in the church. Destroying it would no more occur to her than cutting up her stack of credit cards. Unless, that was, she had a reason. If she thought their holy quest was bound to fail, and she devised some way to save the church while blaming her husband for the Axum raid and all that followed, leaving her in charge…

No. Mania enjoyed her luxuries, but seldom evinced any interest in daily operations of the church. She would require another mate and leader for the sect if Marcellus was deposed. He cast about for candidates, considered several, then focused on the man he trusted most. Perhaps his Brutus, as it were?

Ugo Troisi.

Janus possessed no evidence of any impropriety between his first lieutenant and his queen, but if they *had* been dallying behind his back for any length of time, securing that evidence shouldn't be difficult. First thing tomorrow, he would speak to Marco Gianotti, security chief for the Sedem Illustratio, to arrange covert surveillance. Not on Mania, which might produce destructive gossip, but on Troisi and a handful of his aides. No reason given or required for a directive from the Pontifex Rex.

Feeling better already, Marcellus took up his fork and dug into his pasta con sarde, while asking Mania, "How was your day?"

Sikinos, The Cyclades, Aegean Sea

EKREM ARIKAN BROUGHT the Piaggio P.136 in at wavetop level, throttling back its twin engines, and touched down at the port of Alopronia, on the southeast shore of Sikinos. As if he had performed the act a hundred times before, Arikan taxied toward a concrete pier protruding seaward on the north side of the harbor, his aircraft stabilized by pontoons mounted underneath its wings. When they were close enough to dock, he killed the engines and a grizzled islander ran out with rope in hand to secure the plane's nose.

It was bright and warm as Bolan stepped out of the plane, a soft breeze carrying the smells of fish and brine common to every seaport in the world. For most, it would evoke vacation memories, perhaps of a fishing trip or sailing, but the images that came to Bolan's mind were of military landings, dodging customs agents, flaming cargo freighters packed with contraband.

Speaking of customs, he spied an officer in uniform approaching just as Halloran emerged from the Piaggio P.136. Bolan let the cleric deal with the now-familiar dickering, produced the sum that Halloran and the official agreed upon, then waited while the customs man considered Halloran's request for pointers to a boat for hire. Another tip produced a name—Yiorgos Kallis—and directions to the tavern where he was most likely to be found.

Unlike its neighbors Sikinos hadn't grown wealthy from the tourist trade. Its two established villages—Alopronia, the port and Sikinos, sequestered in the island's hills—were small and relatively quiet, while the island claimed but two paved roads, neither in great repair. Plans to build a lavish beach resort had stalled repeatedly, leaving the island's 230-odd inhabitants to earn their living from the sea, or by their wits.

Yiorgos Kallis, Bolan thought, had likely managed some of both. He spoke four languages, including English, and owned two boats: the *Argus,* used for fishing charters, and the *Sybaris,* which he agreed to rent for the equivalent of forty bucks per hour, plus a security deposit large enough to replace the boat if it never came home.

Bolan agreed, doled out the cash and listened to a series of detailed instructions on the vessel's proper handling.

Ekrem Arikan had already agreed to wait and fly them on from Sikinos to their next stop, wherever that might be, with the proviso that he could depart at once and leave them flat if the police appeared and started asking questions. In that case, he had provided Halloran and Bolan with his cell phone number, which would let them call him back or redirect him for a pickup out at sea, and they'd agreed to instantly forget his name and contact information if they were detained.

No problem there, since dead men told no tales.

The *Sybaris* was thirty-odd feet long, a onetime fishing trawler, probably as old as Bolan and, like him, still seaworthy. Its Perkins T-6-354-MGT diesel engine took some coaxing to start, but once they got it running it had kick to spare. Halloran took the wheel and pointed them toward Ios, angling toward landfall at Manganari on the island's southern tip, their nearest point of access to the Temple of Immaculate Conception.

"It's a smaller port, as well," Halloran said, "although still popular with tourists. Watchers are more likely to expect us at the ports of Koubara or Milopotas."

Maybe, Bolan thought. But he'd be ready for a hot reception when they landed, just the same. If it went down that way, they would have trouble getting to the temple, much less finding time to grill its bishop or whoever was in residence, but they'd still have to try.

That was the nature of the game, and Bolan didn't plan to fold.

CHAPTER THIRTEEN

Custodes Foederis Headquarters, Rome

Marco Gianotti read the list of names hand-printed on the slip of notepaper he held, then raised troubled eyes to meet the gaze of Janus Marcellus.

"Ugo Troisi, Your Grace? And his three closest aides?"

"A mere precaution," Marcellus said, putting on a smile that stopped short of his eyes. "Consider it a spot check, for my peace of mind. You understand how critical security must be during these final days."

"Of course, Your Grace. If there is anything specific I should watch or listen for...?"

"Nothing particular," Marcellus replied. "Use blanket coverage, within the limits of discretion. By the day after tomorrow, be prepared to tell me everywhere they've gone and what they did there. Everyone whom they've communicated with by any means."

"Outside the Sedem Illustratio, Your Grace?" Gianotti asked.

"Anywhere at all," the Pontifex corrected him. "Within, without, it makes no difference."

"And privacy..."

"Is not an issue in this case. If Ugo speaks to me, I will expect a transcript all the same."

"Of course, Your Grace. It will be done as you command."

"Starting immediately."

"Yes, sir."

"Then you'd best begin, Marco."

Dismissed, Gianotti left the royal apartment without further comment and headed off to make arrangements for covert surveillance on the Dextera Dei and his three top aides, collectively known as the Concilium. Gianotti had no clear idea of what inspired the order, but it troubled him. Not so much for Troisi's sake or any of the others, but for Mania Justina.

And himself.

Surveillance on Troisi would expose the man's visits to Mania. Gianotti took for granted that the Pontifex was unaware of what went on behind closed doors when it was just the pair of them together. Gianotti knew about their trysts because he was a trained observer—and because Mania had informed him of their dalliance.

That information had been shared in bed.

Which was the crux of Gianotti's new dilemma. If surveillance of Troisi turned a spotlight on Mania's chronic infidelity to Janus Marcellus, what might be the end result? Ugo Troisi's fall from grace—and possibly from life itself—was the most obvious. And what would be Mania's punishment? If she was pressed for a confession, would she give up Gianotti's name in turn, together with the details of their ongoing affair?

Perhaps.

With that in mind, he started searching for solutions. Breaking off his dalliance with Mania today, in a preemptive strike, might tip her over into rage and sabotage his own best interests. Certainly, it wouldn't stop her from exposing him if she was cornered by her husband. Tipping off Troisi and any of the others to his orders from the Pontifex was pointless, short of hoping for a mutiny or exodus of the entire Concilium. Which left...what?

He could warn Mania, since she wasn't a selected target of surveillance, trusting her to put off any further meetings with Troisi for a time—but *could* he trust her? Was she not as likely to brief Ugo on the plan, thus jeopardizing Gianotti in his turn?

The final option was to forge ahead as ordered, shadowing Troisi and the members of his council day and night. When he reported back to Marcellus, Gianotti could omit whatever information he decided was too volatile. And if abridging the reports placed his own life at risk, if he was caught at it? What then?

It was a partial plan at best, and faulty. Gianotti knew he had to do better still, in order to survive.

And be the last man standing if it came to that, on Judgment Day.

Manganari, Ios

ONCE THE MEDITERRANEAN'S undisputed spring-break party capital, Ios had lost much of its teen and twenties crowd in recent years to rowdier resorts, such as Faliraki on Rhodes and Ayia Napa on Cyprus. The kids still came and drank themselves into oblivion, albeit in reduced numbers, but most of the action these days was confined to Chora, the island's largest settlement and its adjacent beach.

The island's next-most popular beaches—Kalamos, Milopotas and Theodoti—saw roughly half the traffic of Chora. The remainder of Ios, by and large, offered a traditional Greek experience for older, more sedate tourists, including the tomb of Homer, author of the classic *Iliad* and *Odyssey*.

There were no drunken, naked legions waiting to receive the *Sybaris* at Manganari, therefore, when it docked and Bolan went ashore with Brother Halloran. Customs didn't appear to be an issue, either, since there were no uniforms in evidence. A sleepy-looking harbormaster greeted them with fish and ouzo on his breath, relieved them of a minor docking fee and steered them toward a tilting shed with three cars parked around it, marked for rental.

The lot's proprietor was a round-faced man who introduced himself as Nikos, smiling through a thick, untamed mustache. Two of his teeth had gone missing in action, but he didn't seem to mind. Upon presenting driver's licenses, Bolan and Halloran were welcome to their choice of vehicles: a native Greek NAMCO Pony Super resembling an oversized golf cart; a supermini Citroën C2; and a Peugeot 206 about the same size. They took the Peugeot, since it was the newest of the three and seemed less likely to break down on their short journey to the Temple of Immaculate Conception.

"Why not *the* Immaculate Conception?" Bolan asked, once they were on their way, the Peugeot's one-liter straight-four Renault engine muttering under its hood.

"I haven't got a clue," Halloran answered. "Possibly because there's only one on record. Or perhaps they're hoping for another one someday."

"That's something else," Bolan continued, while he checked the weapons in his tote bag. "Say this business with the Ark was true from start to finish and they make it to the Vatican. Here comes the big reveal. Flash, bang, they win. What are they hoping happens next?"

"According to the cult's own literature, when the Scarlet Whore of Babylon is overthrown, a wave of retribution will sweep the planet."

"Retribution?"

"Against the Roman church, of course, for all its sins—

as viewed by Janus and Mania. The Catholics with souls worth saving will repent and join the One True Church—"

"Meaning Custodes Foederis?"

"What else? Those who are unrepentant face God's faithful on the field of Armageddon, which they claim will be in the Sahara Desert, for a battle to the death. And in the midst of that, you have the Second Coming as foretold in Revelation. Christ returns and leads his army to resounding victory, with Janus as his field commander."

"That's in Revelation?" Bolan asked.

"They've made a few adjustments and interpolations," Halloran replied. "After the battle, Christ restores Earth to its original condition from the early days of Genesis. He leaves Janus and Mania in command of a virtual Eden, reigning benevolently over Armageddon's survivors, while souls of the fallen return with Him to heaven."

"And the Keepers buy that?"

"By comparison to some other creeds arising in the past half century or so, it isn't that outlandish," Halloran replied. "Rastafarians believe Ethiopian emperor Haile Selassie was God incarnate. In the United States, your Nation of Islam claims whites are devils created by a mad scientist named Yakub. The Seedline cult claims Eve had sex with Satan and produced Cain, the first Jew, who in turn fabricated 'mud people.'"

"I get it," Bolan said. "No crazy shortage all around."

Myrtoan Sea, aboard the Oceanus

CLAUDIO BRANCA HAD never cared much for geography in school, but he had learned more from necessity while planning his crusade to liberate the Earth from Satan's grasp. It was peculiar how the human mind could focus on details once deemed irrelevant, once it had fastened on a sacred cause.

He'd never heard of the Myrtoan Sea, for instance, but was now aware of its significance, although most modern maps failed to identify it. Lying between the Cyclades and the Peloponnese peninsula of mainland Greece, it granted access from the Aegean Sea to the larger Mediterranean and beyond, to the Atlantic Ocean, if he sailed west as far as the Strait of Gibraltar. That was not the plan, however, not this time. Branca was traveling approximately half that far, call it 550 miles.

To sunny Sicily.

How long before they landed? Branca had done all the calculations in his head. Captain Anatolakis boasted that the *Oceanus* had a top speed of thirty-seven knots, translating to forty-three miles per hour. Reaching Sicily, therefore, would take the better part of thirteen hours—two of which were already behind them. Branca had arranged for a reception on arrival at Catania, on the Ionian Sea, and for an escort on the Autostrada A18 to Messina. From there, another ferry would convey them to the Italian mainland, at Villa San Giovanni, and they could embark on the mad race toward Rome.

Geography. It was a marvel how the pieces fell together with a solid plan in place.

Branca had certain qualms about the aid he had enlisted for their brief passage through Sicily, and it had cost him dearly, but the bargain proved that even abject sinners had a role to play in earth's final redemption. He hadn't informed his Pontifex that they were dealing with the Mafia. Why burden Marcellus with another problem, when he had so much to think about already? It was strictly cash for services rendered, no questions asked by the Sicilians. Had not Christ himself been known to sup with whores and lepers?

Of course, the mafiosi claimed allegiance to the Vatican, if it was even possible to view them as religious, and the irony of that didn't escape Branca's attention. It delighted him, in fact, using one of the Scarlet Whore's own factions to bring her down. What better way to prove the maxim that all things work together for those who love God?

Michele Sansovino joined him at the ferry's forward rail, staring away toward Crete before he voiced a question. "Do you trust these people where we're going, Claudio?"

"Trust doesn't enter into it," Branca replied. "They've been well paid."

"They're bandits," Sansovino said. "I know their kind."

Indeed. Sansovino had involved himself with the Camorra, a kind of mainland Mafia based in Naples, before a brush with death had led him to Custodes Foederis. This day, the skills he'd learned as a felon served the Lord, and all was forgiven.

"You can watch them for us," Branca said. "At the first sign of a betrayal, be prepared to act."

"We'll be outnumbered and surrounded," Sansovino said.

"But we still have the Ark," Branca replied. "And God is with us."

"Amen," Sansovino said, then muttered something to himself that sounded like, "I hope so."

Branca watched him go, then turned back to the open sea, thinking, I hope so, too.

Temple of Immaculate Conception, Ios

BISHOP MARKOPOULOS SIPPED from his glass of retsina, enjoying the flavor of the resinated wine. He had earned a few moments of relaxation, Markopoulos believed, and there was nothing in the scriptures that forbade a soothing taste of alcohol.

Having settled that, he allowed himself to think once more about his recent visitors. They had moved on, were miles beyond his humble parish now, and he had done his best for them. Whatever happened on the road to Rome, no one could say the Temple of Immaculate Conception had not done its part for the crusade. Markoupolos hadn't been privileged to glimpse the Ark, of course, but he hadn't expected to. If one thing could be said about him without fear of contradiction, it was that he knew his proper place.

The atmosphere was more relaxed, now that the Dei Legatus had moved on with his soldiers and their cargo. Hosting them had been an honor and a burden, all at once, particularly with the bishop's knowledge of the violence that had trailed them from the dusty wastes of Ethiopia. Markoupolos had been prepared for trouble on his own turf, but it hadn't come to pass.

At least, not yet.

He still had sentries posted, watchers idling in the island's capital and on the beach at Chora to forewarn him of a raiding party, but there had been no alarms so far. Perhaps, Markoupolos allowed himself to hope, they would be spared the mayhem that had claimed their brethren in Addis Ababa, Massawa and Çorlu.

If not, Markoupolos had guns and ammunition, had disciples who would spend the last drops of their blood to hold the temple against any infidels who sought to desecrate it. Each had sworn a solemn oath to God that they would die before betraying Him. Their afterlife in paradise depended on fidelity to that vow and the church itself.

Not that Markoupolos was in a hurry to depart this earthly life. With the retsina's flavor on his tongue and sunlight streaming through his window, there could be no doubt that life was sweet. A gift from God, in fact. But gifts could be surrendered to the greater need, the greater good. Again, Christ was the ultimate example, facing death for all the sinners of the world, in knowledge that the vast majority of them would finally reject his sacrifice and plunge headlong into the fires of hell.

No longer relaxed, Bishop Markoupolos reached out for the retsina bottle and refilled his glass. Another wouldn't make him drunk, by any means. And if he grew a little tipsy, what of it? Flesh was weak, divine forgiveness infinite. Markoupolos strove for perfection, but had yet to reach it.

He closed his eyes, imagined sailing on the blue Aegean. Not for Sicily and Rome, but simply traveling to parts unknown, with the whole world spread before him, ripe for exploration. So it would be when the final battle was concluded and the smoke cleared to reveal a new earth, freed from dominance by Satan and his imps. Markoupolos hoped he would live to see that golden morning break, and would stand among the victors, crying Hallelujah to their Lord.

THE PAVED ROAD running north from Manganari, following the stony spine of Ios, petered out after they'd driven about a mile. From there on, following a dirt and gravel track that raised a rooster tail of dust behind them, Bolan thought they'd have been better off to rent a Jeep. Their Peugeot 206 hadn't been made with off-roading in mind, and Bolan didn't know how well the car had been maintained or whether it was good for the round-trip.

Of course, there hadn't been a Jeep available, and Bolan couldn't say if he and Halloran would make it through the round-trip to their target, either. War was all about the calculated risks, weighed against their potential rewards. Sometimes you couldn't draw and were compelled to play a shaky hand, against the odds.

One good thing about the awkward lurching drive was that they met only a couple of civilians on the way. Most of the island's year-round residents were found in Chora, with the rest clustered in smaller, scattered settlements. To Bolan, that meant there would likely be no innocents hanging around the Temple of Immaculate Conception, getting in their way when trouble started.

And if prior experience was any indicator, that would be as soon as they arrived.

A half mile from their destination, with the temple still concealed behind a lumpy range of hills, they stopped and nosed the Peugeot into a rest stop, cautiously maneuvering the car until they had it pointed back downhill, toward Manganari and their rented boat. If things went badly and they had to flee with shooters on their heels, the seconds wasted on a clumsy three-point turn could make the difference between survival and a shallow grave.

When he was satisfied with the Peugeot's position, Bolan spent another moment with his weapons. He was carrying the AKMS and the Uzi SMG, hoping that some degree of stealth could be preserved, but wanting to be ready with an autorifle if it went to hell. He had grenades for backup, if the opposition forced them to abandon all hope of a quiet probe.

If they got lucky, found the team from Axum at the temple catching up on rest, whatever, they could finish it on Ios, but he wasn't counting on that kind of break. If there was any kind of comm link between Bolan's quarry and their leadership, the Ark gang had to know that they were being hunted. Even if they *didn't* manage to communicate with Rome, that just came down to common sense.

He wasn't selling any of the opposition short on smarts, simply because he didn't buy the basic tenets of their faith.

One thing the Executioner had learned from grim experience: he didn't have to share the views of any given cult, sect or denomination to accept that others were sincere—even fanatical—in their beliefs. If any individual or group proclaimed that they were killing in the name of Allah, Yahweh, Jesus, Satan, or the Easter Bunny, Bolan took them at their word and did his best to stop them in their tracks.

To stop them dead, before their madness claimed a higher body count.

Sincere belief could wreak no end of havoc when it graduated from discussion into action, spilling blood. That was the world where Bolan lived, and every predator received some variation of the same response. The universal language understood by thugs and terrorists from California to Calcutta, from Tasmania to Tokyo.

Hot lead, cold steel or cleansing fire.

"Ready?" he asked, and got a nod from Halloran.

With Bolan leading, they began to climb the final hill.

Custodes Foederis Headquarters, Rome

"I'M ONLY SAYING that we need to be more careful," Marco Gianotti said. "*You* need to be more careful."

Mania Justina glared at him with a look of petulant confusion. "I don't understand why he is doing this," she said. "Does he suspect something? Does he *know* something?"

"I've already told you everything he said to me," Gianotti replied. "He's worried about the Concilium, not you. But with surveillance on Troisi—"

"Yes, yes. It comes back to me. But why? What can I do? You say I can't warn Ugo."

"Absolutely not," Gianotti confirmed. "Who knows what he might do? If he confronts the Pontifex, it will be obvious the warning must have come from me or someone on my team."

"Why did this have to happen now?" she asked him, almost whining. "We're so close to changing everything. Rewriting history."

Gianotti knew what she meant to say, and didn't bother trying to correct her. Why waste time and breath explaining that, while it was possible to change the course of history, events already in the past could not be altered?

"Tomorrow or the next day," Mania Justina exclaimed, "after the Ark arrives in Rome, it won't make any difference what Janus thinks of Ugo. Will it?"

"Well…"

"I mean, the sinners will be swept away!"

Gianotti had no response for that. Should he remind Mania that she had, herself, been sinning most egregiously on a daily basis, with Troisi and with him? Clearly, her thoughts were focused on a different set of sinners, infidels and servants of the Scarlet Whore. It seemed that she was making no allowance for the possibility of failure.

If the Ark was intercepted short of Rome, or if it had no power when the moment of unleashing came…what happened next?

Asking that question, even harboring the smallest doubt of God's almighty power, was an act of blasphemy, but Marco Gianotti couldn't shake his nagging fear of failure. Even though his faith was strong, he knew from history that many End Time prophecies had fizzled out on the appointed day. From Saint Clement's prediction of the Second Coming in AD 90 to the "Great Disappointment" of October 1844, on to Y2K, dozens of predictions for the day of Christ's return had fallen flat. If faith alone was enough to save the world, the job would have been done two thousand years ago.

But he could hope, offer an earnest prayer and watch his back where Janus Marcellus was concerned.

"I'll see what I can do," he said, and kissed her pouting lips. "Try not to worry."

"Do you love me?"

Marco smiled. "Who wouldn't?"

CHAPTER FOURTEEN

Temple of Immaculate Conception, Ios

The Twenty-third Psalm kept running through Brother Halloran's mind as he trailed Matt Cooper between two stony crags and got his first view of their target.

The Lord is my Shepherd; I shall not want. He maketh me to lie down in green pastures: He leadeth me beside the still waters.

No pastures here, of course. No visible water, either, unless you counted the Aegean, two miles off to their right, or east, three miles away to the west. Their chosen battleground would be a sun-bleached rocky hillside, where the blood of fallen men would simmer in the unrelenting rays and bake onto the stones.

His blood? Perhaps.

Cooper stopped in front of him, crouching, and turned to catch his eye. Halloran knelt beside him, conscious of the prayerful pose and hoping that it wouldn't be interpreted as mockery.

"The aerials you showed me indicate two exits," Bolan said. "North and west. We need to cover both of them, so nobody gets out and slips away. You have a preference?"

"It makes no difference to me," Halloran said.

"Okay. I'll circle to the north, then. You go east. Ten minutes and we go."

Halloran synchronized his watch to Cooper's, reminded

of a scene from some commando movie that he'd watched in childhood. Had it been *The Guns of Navarone,* which also had been set in Greece? Was this how fragments of a life returned to haunt a dying man?

I'm not dying, Halloran thought. At least, not yet.

His exit on the east was closer than the northern door Cooper planned to cover, so he stayed in place and watched the tall American move out. It still surprised him that a man so large could move so swiftly, gracefully, almost without a sound. Beside him, Halloran felt like a plodding amateur who had been dropped into a deadly game light-years beyond his capability.

But he'd survived this far, and wasn't finished yet. Not while an ounce of strength or faith remained.

When it was time, Halloran moved off to his right, winding between more boulders, careful not to let his sub-machine gun tap or scrape against the stones. He wished there had been time and opportunity to pick up a sup-pressor for the M12S, but he would do his best with what he had.

Who was around to register the sound of gunshots, any-way?

On Ios, you could never tell. The noise might echo for a mile or more, though likely not as far as any of the tourist beaches. Say a villager got curious, decided to alert police. How long would that take? Could they even pinpoint the location of the shots without triangulating gear? And then how long before an officer arrived? Words of the psalm came to him unbidden: *Thou preparest a table for me in the presence of mine enemies.*

And the feast was about to begin.

TOO MUCH RETSINA, Bishop Markoupolos thought. He'd nearly tipped the bottle over, reaching for it to refill his

glass, which would have made a mess and brought at least
one of his people on the run. Still, if his reflexes were quick
enough to catch the bottle and retrieve it, could he really be
intoxicated? And regardless, was there any harm in that?

Everyone needed to relax sometime, even a bishop of
a church engaged in bringing on the Great Apocalypse.
Perhaps he, most of all.

And what about the young men traveling to Rome,
where some of them at least would almost surely die? What
prospect did *they* have for any rest and relaxation on the
road? Little to none, he thought, and poured himself another glass of wine on their behalf.

"Ad vitem et victoria," he told the empty room. To life
and victory!

The glass was at his lips when one of his brethren burst
in, wide-eyed, gasping as if he'd run a mile instead of ten
or twenty yards. "Intruders on the grounds, Your Grace!
Inside the temple!"

"What?" Markoupolos wasn't aware he'd dropped his
glass until it smashed and splattered on the concrete floor
beside his swivel chair. "What did you say, Stefan?"

"Intruders! Armed! Hurry, Your Grace!"

Markoupolos absorbed the warning, oddly conscious
of the way Stefan preserved his formal manner of address
despite his panic. Only as he bolted upright from his chair,
half staggering, did he observe the pistol Stefan clutched
in his right hand.

The sight of it reminded Markoupolos to grab his own
weapon, ripping open the lower left-hand drawer of his
desk to retrieve the Heckler & Koch MP-7 submachine
gun resting there. It was a marvel of technology, scarcely
sixteen inches long with folding stock collapsed, weighing
barely five pounds with a 40-round magazine in place. Its
revolutionary HK 4.6 mm rounds could penetrate standard

body armor but yawed on impact with soft tissue, causing greater damage than most other pistol and SMG rounds. With a full-auto cyclic rate of 950 rounds per minute, the MP-7 was a certified man-breaker.

Which would help Markoupolos only if he survived to use it.

Stefan teetered in the open doorway, shifting restlessly from foot to foot, anxious to be away. Markoupolos turned toward him, gun in hand, and ordered, "Show me the intruders!"

"Yes, Your Grace. This way!"

The bishop emerged into the corridor, still without any enemies in sight. It crossed his mind that Stefan might be tricking him somehow, but why? To what end? Then his nostrils caught the first faint whiff of gunsmoke and he frowned.

Shots without sound? If that were true—

A second later, gunfire echoed through the temple and Markoupolos felt his heart lurch, kicking into double time. There was no trick, and no mistake. They *were* under attack.

He mouthed a silent prayer of thanks that Branca and the rest had left already, with the Ark. Whatever happened here, from this point onward, it wouldn't affect their mission. If Markopoulos could stall the enemy and hold them here, increasing Branca's lead toward Rome, it would be beneficial. And if he could stop them, kill them here, so much the better.

End it, and God's lieutenant could proceed without another worry on his mind until he reached the Vatican. Whatever might await him there, it was beyond Markopoulos to sway the final outcome. Each man was responsible for his own part of God's great master plan, no more, no less.

The force of an explosion seemed to rock the floor beneath his feet, but still the bishop kept moving forward. If the only thing he could accomplish now was dying for the cause, so be it. He would give that much to serve his Lord.

Clutching his submachine gun, he began to run, anxious to join the fight.

BOLAN APPROACHED THE north-facing entry to the Temple of Immaculate Conception with his AKMS slung, holding the Uzi with its sound suppressor attached, its fire selector set for semiauto. He was gambling with his life, doing his best to get in close and personal without alerting anyone inside the church, but risk was something that he faced every day.

It was a handicap, not having any kind of solid fix on numbers in the church as they approached, but the uncertainty was also commonplace in Bolan's world. Prolonged surveillance of intended targets wasn't possible, nor could he always manage to approximate the numbers that he faced from markers at a given scene. Most times—like now—he had to forge ahead using the tools at his hand, preparing for the worst and hoping for the best.

When he had almost reached the door, it opened and a pair of smiling, suntanned men emerged. They took one look at Bolan and the Uzi in his grasp, then sealed their fate by groping underneath their long, loose shirts for hidden weapons. Bolan shot the closer of them first, a muffled *chug* of sound that punched the gun backward into a collision with his comrade. Round two drilled the second Keeper through his forehead and they both went down together on the threshold, their bodies holding the door open.

Bolan stepped over them, scanning the darker space inside the temple's entryway. A third man was approaching with his head down, fanning money in his hands and counting it, speaking in rapid Greek as if explaining something to his fallen comrades. By the time he noticed what was going on and dropped the bills in favor of a fumbling attempt at a fast draw, his time was up.

A third round from the Uzi caught him in the chest, staggered the guy and dropped him to his knees. Bolan was on the verge of giving him another when the Keeper's eyes rolled back in his head and he collapsed, hitting the concrete floor facedown with force enough to break his nose.

Precision work so far, but how long could it last?

The answer to that question came about ten seconds later, when another pair of men dressed almost identically—a sort of uniform, it seemed—rounded the corner fifteen feet in front of Bolan. One let out a yelp and bolted, gone before the Executioner had time to tag him, while the other went the hopeless hero route and took a Parabellum mangler through the left eye socket for his trouble, splashing gray and crimson on the wall behind him.

Bolan reached the spot where number two had disappeared, but the guy was gone, the echoes of retreating footsteps clearly audible. He hadn't started shouting yet, which was a wonder in itself, but how long could it be before he found his voice?

Not long enough.

Letting the Uzi dangle from its shoulder sling, Bolan unhitched his AKMS, flicked the safety switch to the middle position, for full-auto fire. He could control the weapon, milking short bursts from its magazine, but Bolan also wanted the capacity to let it rip if he ran into a mob.

He moved on, hoping Halloran had reached the temple and could make his way inside, then focused on the task ahead—hunting a bishop in a bloody game of chess.

THE BISHOP HAD met a number of his people gathered in a hallway near his study, ten or twelve armed men, four women, all abuzz with nervous conversation. They were spoiling for a fight, he thought, though none of them was taking the initiative. At sight of him, they flocked around, still shooting anxious glances back in the direction of the temple's major entrance, to the north.

"Quiet!" he snapped at them, demanding full attention. "Raise your hand if you have seen the enemy."

A single hand went up—Stratos Sedaris, pale and trembling.

"Tell me," Markopoulos commanded.

"We were going into Chora," Sedaris said. "Myself, Minas, Georgios—"

"Yes, yes. Get on with it!"

"Minas and I were running late, Your Grace. We hurried to catch up and met a stranger. With a gun. Bodies behind him."

"Only one man?"

"That I saw, Your Grace. There may be more."

"And then?"

"I ran to warn the rest of you," Sedaris said, nearly sobbing, suddenly uncertain whether he should be ashamed for fleeing or feel proud that he'd been clever.

"What of Minas?"

"I don't know, Your Grace. He didn't follow me."

"You heard no shots?"

Sedaris lowered his eyes, shaking his head.

"All right. You women, get into the pantry and conceal yourselves as best you can. The rest of you—"

Before Markopoulos could finish giving his instructions, gunfire hammered through the temple, an assault upon his eardrums as it echoed down the brick and concrete corridors. One of the women gasped, then they were moving to obey him, while his men stood facing toward the sounds of battle, their weapons ready.

"Go, then!" he commanded. "Find the infidel intruder and destroy him!"

Several of them looked back at Markoupolos, frowning. He raised his MP-7, telling them, "I'm with you! Lead the way!"

Reluctantly, it seemed to him, his men moved out and toward the sounds of gunfire, which were drawing nearer at the same time. Markopoulos stayed at the rear of the pack, saw no reason to push ahead when they were all headed in the same direction, anyway. Surely the lot of them could overcome one man, no matter who he was or where he'd come from. If they did—

He had a sudden mental image of himself exalted for achieving what the bishops of three other temples hadn't. Where they had fallen to the infidels, Markopoulos could triumph and be venerated as a hero. Not a huge thing, in these final days before the Ark was used to slay the Scarlet Whore of Babylon, perhaps, but it would still rank as a major contribution to the effort. Possibly, he'd be promoted.

Or did such things even matter in the new world that was coming?

And then it struck Markopoulos, a sudden inspiration, that he ought to warn the Sedem Illustratio that he was under siege. Rome couldn't help him, obviously, but headquarters *could* alert Claudio Branca's team to exercise more caution on the last lap of their journey. Since he didn't have a contact number for Dei Legatus programmed on his own sat phone—a matter of security, completely understood—Markoupolos would do the next best thing, which meant returning to his study for the phone.

An act of cowardice, or a fulfillment of his duty? Hesitating for only an instant more, the bishop turned and scuttled in the direction he had come from, frightened to look back and see if anyone had noted his departure from the ranks.

Apparently, one of them did. He heard someone call out behind him, "Wait, Your Grace! Don't go! We need—"

And then more gunfire, closer than before, its hellish racket following Markopoulos along the corridor.

BOLAN WAS FOLLOWING the runner who'd eluded him, when gunshots from a hallway on his left told him that Halloran had joined the fight. No sound suppressor on his Beretta SMG, or on the handguns popping back in answer as the brother made his appearance on the scene. Three shooters, by the sound of it, or maybe four.

Instead of keeping up the chase, Bolan veered off to see if he could help. It was another calculated risk, but he was stronger with a backup than alone, against uncertain odds. As for the one who got away, he likely wasn't going far. Just down the hall to round up reinforcements and return to finish what the Executioner had started.

Or to try that, anyhow.

Bolan came up behind the shooters who'd met Halloran and blocked his access to the inner temple. He'd dropped one of them before they pinned him down, but now it wasn't going well at three on one. The soldier took stock in nothing flat and raised his AKMS, putting two rounds in the nearest gunman, scarlet geysers bursting from between his shoulder blades as he went down, stone dead before he hit the concrete floor.

Startled, the other two were turning to confront the latest threat, but Bolan had them covered, triggering a 3-round burst that ripped across the second shooter's chest and bounced him off a nearby wall, smearing the bricks with blood as he went down.

The last surviving Keeper gave a little squeal then, but couldn't very well surrender in the circumstances. Rising from his crouch, holding his pistol in a two-handed grip, he rapid-fired toward Bolan, hasty jerking on the trigger causing him to miss initially, still driving his adversary to the deck with bullets snapping overhead. To fire the AKMS, Bolan had to turn it to one side, since its magazine was too long for aiming from a prone position, while—

The pop-pop-pop of lighter automatic fire issued from behind the standing gunman, Parabellum shockers ripping into him as Halloran cut loose from his position in the open doorway. Bolan saw the Keeper topple, drop and shiver once before the life fled from his prostrate form. Halloran hustled past the corpses, reaching Bolan just as he vaulted to his feet.

"So much for quiet, eh?" the brother remarked.

"Don't sweat it," Bolan answered. "I already missed a runner. This way."

He doubled back with Halloran beside him, heard the brother snapping a fully loaded mag into his SMG, and quickly reached the point where he'd diverted to engage the Keepers at their temple's eastern door. The voices he'd heard earlier were definitely closer now, advancing toward the battlefront. Bolan tried to gauge the distance, signaled Halloran to stop at the next corner, then unclipped and primed a frag grenade.

Say, thirty feet between himself and his approaching adversaries now. He ducked and stretched an arm around the corner, set the grenade rolling on its wobbly way along the corridor, and drew back out of range before the enemy had time to fire. With recognition of the danger came a chorus of alarm, stampeding feet and then a blast that stung his ears, pushing a cloud of smoke and dust toward Bolan from ground zero.

"Ready?"

Halloran responded with a silent nod, raising his SMG.

The Executioner stepped out into another smoky scene from hell.

TRAILING THE BISHOP was easy, once his fighting men were down and out. The frag grenade had killed some, wounded more, and muffled shots from Bolan's Uzi finished those, while Halloran moved on ahead. Bolan caught up with him to find the brother outside an open door, and four women cringing in a crowded pantry while he covered them.

"They don't seem to be armed," Halloran said.

"A lot of guns out here," Bolan observed, "and no lock on that door. You want to hold them here while I go on, or…"

Lowering his voice to whisper level, Halloran replied, "I can't just shoot them."

Bolan nodded. "Keep them covered, then."

He left Halloran to it, moving on in the direction that his quarry had to have taken, clearing rooms along the way until he reached the far end of the corridor. That door was locked from the inside, and Bolan took the knob off with a 3-round Uzi burst, then went in low and rolling to his left.

Markoupolos was waiting for him, more or less. He had a telephone in one hand, pressed against his ear, not speaking. It wasn't clear if he was listening or waiting for his call to connect, and Bolan didn't have much time to think about it as the submachine gun in the bishop's other hand sprayed bullets through the doorway he'd just cleared.

Another burst from Bolan's Uzi silenced it and left the cleric draped across his desk, gasping his life away through sucking chest wounds. Rising, Bolan shouted through the open door to Halloran, "All clear! Stay where you are!"

The bishop was still gargling blood when Bolan reached

him, but he obviously didn't have much time. The soldier reached past him for the sat phone lying by the cleric's outstretched hand, raised it and listened to a male voice on the other end.

"*Ciao? Salue?* Hello?" A fleeting silence, then the voice inquired, "Who is this?"

"Someone who'd love to meet you," Bolan said.

Another hesitation. Then, "Perhaps you shall."

"Just tell me where and when," the Executioner replied.

Soft laughter now. "Piazza San Pietro, eh? As to the when…"

The line went dead, a hiss of static mocking him. Bolan took the sat phone with him, guessing that the numbers it had logged in its memory would match those lifted from the first phone they had captured, at Massawa's Temple of the Guiding Light. In any case, Bolan assumed Aaron Kurtzman could point him toward the stranger he'd just spoken to.

A man Bishop Markopoulos had died trying to reach.

That had to count for something, right?

Bolan retraced his steps along the corridor, found Halloran still standing watch over the women in the pantry. "The bishop's out," he said, then raised the liberated phone. "I had a word with someone else, though."

"Traceable?" Halloran asked.

"Should be. But just in case, he told me where to find him," Bolan said. "Saint Peter's Square."

"We need to get a fix on him as soon as possible," Halloran said.

"Agreed. You think of any way to keep these four from arming up and coming after us?"

"Perhaps deadweight," the brother replied, eyeing the bodies of their recent victims.

Bolan nodded, moved to drag the first corpse over to

the pantry door while Halloran was closing it. They used four bodies altogether, better than six hundred pounds, stacked up against the door like sandbags, calculating it would stall the women long enough for the two of them to reach the Peugeot and escape.

While they were hiking back, Bolan raised Stony Man and patched through to Kurtzman.

"Same number," Kurtzman said, two minutes later. "And it's on the move."

CHAPTER FIFTEEN

1600 Pennsylvania Avenue, Washington, D.C.

Once upon a time, Americans could stroll or march in protest on the White House lawn. President Rutherford Hayes had ordered the property fenced in 1877, following his hotly disputed electoral victory over rival Samuel Tilden. In 1995, after the Oklahoma City bombing, Secret Service agents barred all vehicular traffic from passing near the White House, a "temporary" policy made permanent in the wake of 9/11. These days, cars and trucks detoured onto Constitution Avenue or H Street, while pedestrians and bicycles were still permitted access.

This day, they'd come in thousands to protest the mayhem that had ravaged sacred sites across the nation and worldwide. Chants and placards called for action to prevent further attacks and punish those responsible. Some demonstrators knelt to pray, while others massed along the traffic barriers lined with Capitol Police and Metro officers in riot gear. Two fellows from Saint Louis dragged a twelve-foot cross complete with a papier-mâché Jesus down the middle of the avenue, trailed by pallbearers with a casket labeled with a sign reading Religious Liberty.

Tyrone Dubois loved all of it.

When he'd been chosen for the mission—what an honor!—he had worried that security might foil whatever plan he hatched before he had a chance to prove himself and earn his wings. That fear had vanished when the demonstration was announced, including blanket invitations for concerned Americans of all denominations to participate. Delighted, he had grinned and told the smiling blonde on Channel 9 to count him in.

It didn't take much preparation after that. Despite some fairly strict controls on guns within the District of Columbia, Virginia, just across the river, welcomed anyone with cash in hand. Gun dealers were required to file reports of pistol sales to out-of-staters with the police, but that was no encumbrance for a buyer heading back to D.C., New York City or wherever else there was some heavy shooting to be done.

Tyrone Dubois had plunked his money down for two secondhand TEC-9s, together with a dozen 32-round magazines. Chambered in 9 mm Parabellum, the semiautomatic pistols hadn't been converted to full-auto fire, like those favored by street gangs in D.C. and elsewhere, but it hardly mattered to Dubois. As for the fifty-yard effective range, who cared? Roaming a crowd of demonstrators pressed together on the avenue, he wouldn't have to aim at all. Just point and blaze away.

Good times.

It pleased him in particular that he could teach adherents of the Scarlet Whore a lesson while they clamored for attention in the nation's capital. They wanted airtime, right? Now they would have it, only not the way they'd planned. He wondered if the Antichrist himself would watch some of the footage, maybe even sitting on his golden throne at the Basilica of Saint John Lateran in Rome.

Dubois hoped so. It would be fitting, as a foretaste of the fire to come.

Moving among his enemies, Dubois sang softly to himself. Not one of *their* songs, but "Onward Christian Soldiers." He felt strong, invigorated, even knowing that he'd never walk away from Pennsylvania Avenue alive. The cops or Secret Service watchers on the fringes of the mob would see to that.

All part of the design. A movement needed martyrs to inspire the masses, right?

Reaching beneath his jacket, hauling out the TEC-9s in their homemade shoulder harnesses, Dubois was grinning like a kid on Christmas morning.

He thanked Jesus for the moment as he opened fire.

Alopronia, Sikinos

"But why Sicily?" Halloran asked, as they were docking, tying up the boat and jogging back to where their pilot waited with the freshly fueled aircraft. "The Keepers have no temple there, as far as I know."

"Maybe that's the reason," Bolan said. "To throw us off. Or maybe they decided it's a safer way to reach the mainland, if the major ports are covered."

Bolan was already thinking ahead as Ekrem Arikan revved the engines and taxied away from the dock, nosing seaward and gathering speed. There'd been no sign of police so far, no warnings via radio to interrupt their takeoff. No one back on Ios would have recognized the seaplane. If they managed to get airborne, he believed that they were in the clear.

For now.

But Sicily…

He couldn't think about that island—rocky football that it was, to the Italian boot on maps—without recalling that it spawned the Mafia and still remained in thrall to brutal godfathers of the so-called Honored Society. Successive waves of prosecution, from the Fascist era of the 1920s to the "Maxi Trial" six decades later had done little to break Cosa Nostra's grip on the island. Of 470 defendants charged in the 1980s show trial, 360 were convicted. Nineteen received life terms, with the remainder drawing sentences that totaled 2,665 years, but only sixty remained in prison two years after those sentences were pronounced.

And how had that happened, while law-abiding Sicilians demanded an end to the Mafia's rule? A judge suspected of collusion with the Mob, nicknamed "The Sentence Killer" by reporters, threw out some of the convictions based on technicalities, then ceded control over the remaining appeals to Salvatore Lima, ex-mayor of Palermo, widely regarded as a Mafia associate. That judgment was confirmed by Lima's drive-by murder in March 1992, *after* he granted early release to most of the defendants convicted at the Maxi Trial. Why kill him, then? According to the mafioso who confessed to giving the order, Lima hadn't overturned the verdicts fast enough to please some of the mobsters who had greased his palm.

And once again: why Sicily?

Had Custodes Foederis, based in Rome, reached some accommodation for safe passage with the Mafia? Most mafiosi made a point of showing off their dedication to the Catholic Church, but Bolan chalked that up to lip service, a hypocritical facade. To him, Sicilian gangsters were no more "Christian," whatever that entailed, than members of the Russian Mafiya were true Eastern Orthodox worshippers or Japanese Yakuza soldiers were spokesmen for Shintoism. Religion masked their crimes without absolving them or cleansing the accumulated filth from rotten souls.

So, would the Mafia be willing to assist the Keepers in transporting their illicit cargo, for a price? Of course. And would they even bother asking what was in the van, beyond negotiation of a fee based on the risks involved? Hell, no.

Which meant, if it was true, that Bolan could be facing opposition that was more determined, more experienced and deadly, than the members of Custodes Foederis had proved themselves so far. How many men and guns, in theory? That depended on the Family and its commitment to the job, which would in turn be measured by the money paid up front.

It was something to think about, while they were airborne.

And to live or die with, when they touched down on Sicilian soil.

Custodes Foederis Headquarters, Rome

UGO TROISI SPOTTED Marco Gianotti walking toward the cafeteria, his head down as if he was immersed in thought, and called out to him, "Marco! May I steal a moment of your time?"

Turning to face him, Gianotti seemed distracted—or was that a flicker of annoyance in his eyes? Troisi forced a smile, refusing to be snared and led astray by supposition when he needed facts. Besides, if his suspicions were correct, he needed to tread softly in his dealings with the man in charge of church security.

"How may I help, Your Grace?" Gianotti asked, answering Troisi's smile with one that seemed a trifle strained.

"No need for such formality between us," Troisi said. "We're alone here, after all."

"In that case, Ugo, how may I assist you?"

"It's a matter of some delicacy."

"Ah. My specialty," Gianotti replied.

"Indeed. And you would be aware, no doubt, if there were any problems with security surrounding the Concilium?"

"Of course."

Troisi frowned, lowered his voice another notch and said, "Perhaps it's nothing, but I have to ask. Salvo believes that he may be under surveillance."

Meaning Salvo Deodato, a Concilium member and the sect's treasurer. He was a little ferret of a man, with shifty eyes and lobeless ears, whose wiry, thinning hair resembled a moth-eaten fright wig.

"What sort of surveillance?" Gianotti asked, all innocence.

"It's difficult to say," Troisi answered. "It may be a suspicion of surveillance. He's excitable, you know. In fact, I might have called it paranoia, if it weren't for Federico."

Federico Comencini, secretary of Custodes Foederis and another Concilium member. He was the very opposite of Deodato, corpulent and florid-faced, with straight hair slicked back from a high forehead.

"He has the same suspicion?" Gianotti asked, concerned about the clumsiness of his appointed watchers. Lord, if two of their three targets had already tumbled to the fact that they were being watched, he needed new investigators.

"Not the same, exactly," Troisi said. "He thinks he's heard a clicking on his office phone line that suggests a tap in place."

Gianotti feigned shock, blinking twice for effect. "A wiretap?"

"So he thinks," Troisi said.

He had assigned the bugs and taps to Corradino Noli, and would certainly be ripping him a new one before another hour had passed.

"It's most improbable, but I'll look into it at once," Gianotti said.

"And report to me if anything is found?"

"To you, and to the Pontifex. This matter, if substantiated, will most certainly concern him."

Troisi glanced around, as if confirming they were still alone, then said, "I thought he might already be aware of it."

"How so?"

"If he had ordered the surveillance, let us say. No doubt he would have reasons for whatever actions have been taken. All I ask is to be kept informed of any matters that affect my closest aides."

"And so you would be, Ugo," Gianotti lied, "if such an order had been given."

"Then I have your word?"

"On what?"

"That you are not investigating the Concilium."

A prompt reply was critical. "You have my word," Gianotti said without missing a beat.

Troisi seemed relieved. "It may be nothing, after all," he said. "The pressure of our progress toward the Final Days, tension before the Ark arrives in Rome. It's only natural."

"Find strength in faith and rectitude," Gianotti suggested.

"Sound advice, brother. I'll pass it on."

"And I'll check on the phones," Gianotti said. "Just in case."

Catania, Sicily

TO CLAUDIO BRANCA, all seas looked alike. He knew from charts when the *Oceanus* had left the Aegean and entered the Ionian Sea, but nothing in the water's hue, the sky above or on the distant rocky shores that he could see through his binoculars suggested they were making any progress. He'd grown anxious near the end of their pro-

tracted journey, and was now relieved as Captain Anatolakis brought them into port beneath the shadow of Mount
Etna.

That volcano, Branca knew, was Europe's tallest and
still active, growing sixty-nine feet higher in the past three
decades, with accumulated lava from its various eruptions.
A full-scale detonation could destroy Catania at any time,
engulfing the metropolitan area's 750,000 inhabitants in
smothering ash, yet life went on from day to day as if the
threat didn't exist. High-tech industry thrived in Catania,
earning it a reputation as "Europe's Silicon Valley."

All for nothing, Branca thought. None of the infidels
bustling around their hive like insects were aware that Fate
had dealt the death card in their endless game of chase-the-
euro. Who among them realized that life as they knew it
would be ending in another day or two at most, their lust
for wealth and adoration of the Scarlet Whore consigned
to ashes?

Not a one.

He watched his team securing their vehicles, preparing for the moment when they disembarked. The *Oceanus*
would be docking in the company of cruise ships, fishing
boats and pleasure craft of all varieties, with nothing to
distinguish it from any other vessel in the harbor.

Not unless the infidels were waiting.

Strike that. *Some* would certainly be waiting, if the mafiosi he'd employed were waiting to perform the function
they'd been paid for. He had specified a dozen men, which
meant at least two cars, more likely three. All armed, of
course, like any self-respecting gangsters. They should
have the wheels of customs greased before the *Oceanus*
docked, the normal fees and bribes paid. From there, it
ought to be a routine drive along the Autostrada A18, no
more than fifty miles to reach Messina in the north.

Routine, if they weren't ambushed along the way.

And it could happen, Branca knew. Aside from being hunted by commandos of the Scarlet Whore, in Sicily he had to think about the rivalries that split the Mafia into a dozen warring factions, not to mention generations of hostility with the Camorra, based on the Italian mainland. If the Family that he'd recruited sprang a leak, and rivals learned that something valuable was under escort from Catania to Messina, they might try to hijack Branca's cargo on the highway. Maybe hold the Ark for ransom, or destroy it just to irritate their enemies.

Just what he needed as they neared their goal: more threats to guard against, further distraction for his soldiers as they carried out their duty to their Pontifex and to Almighty God.

As they approached the dock, the *Oceanus* slowed to a crawl, its captain starting the maneuvers that would bring them safely to a pier. Whatever waited for them there, or once they got back on the road again, Branca promised himself that nothing would prevent the execution of his duty. He had come too far and sacrificed too much to let the Scarlet Whore or anybody else defeat him now.

CHAPTER SIXTEEN

Over the Mediterranean Sea

Ekrem Arikan advised remaining over water as they exited
Greek territory, and Mack Bolan didn't argue with the pilot's judgment. From his window seat, the soldier watched
Crete appear and pass below them to his left, six hundred
thousand people on the largest and most populous of all
Greek islands unaware that death was winging overhead,
westbound in search of other prey.

Including their diversion to avoid the Greek mainland,
he estimated that the flight from Sikinos to Sicily should
take about three hours. Twenty minutes out, there'd still
been no attempts to call back the Piaggio seaplane, nothing on Arikan's radio news channel about the firefight on
Ios. The boat they'd rented would be found, of course, but
no ID had been demanded when they hired it, so the trail
might end there, with descriptions of what cops back in
the States once called a salt-and-pepper team.

One white, one black. No longer quite politically correct.

There was a chance that someone would connect Arikan's plane to the events, but was it likely anyone had
memorized its registration number? And if so, what could
be done about it once the Turkish pilot had returned to
Çorlu? Greek police could make inquiries, seek permission
for an interview with Arikan, but centuries of diplomatic

conflict would obstruct them, as would Turkish bitterness at ostracism from the European Union. Even if an interview *was* granted, it would be on Turkish terms, and Arikan could simply, honestly, plead ignorance of where his charter passengers had gone, and what they'd done, while he was fueling up at Sikinos.

Case closed.

But Sicily…that might be something else entirely.

If the Mafia had signed on to provide safe passage for his targets, Bolan knew the risks he'd face with Halloran would increase exponentially. Mobsters aside, he'd also have to think about police, bearing in mind that Italy employed twice as many law-enforcement officers as all of Great Britain, boasting the highest number of lawmen and women of any EU nation. Contenders included the Arma dei Carabinieri, the Polizia di Stato and the Guardia di Finanza, with specific anti-Mafia and antiterrorist units on tap.

Bad news all around, if they turned out in force.

This wouldn't be Bolan's first visit to Sicily, and each time he stepped onto its soil he stretched his luck a little thinner. He'd begun his private war fighting alone against the Mafia, and now he was returning once more to the monster's birthplace, not with any plan to challenge a specific godfather, but ready to include them on his hit list if they meddled in his business.

Would it have made a difference if he'd had someone to contact in the councils of the Mafia, alerting them that his intended targets wanted to annihilate the Church of Rome? Would any ranking mafioso lift a hand to save the pope, if there was money to be made from sheltering his enemies? It was a moot point, since Bolan had no such connections to the Syndicate, and likely would have balked at asking for their help in any case.

What he needed was a starting point. Someplace on Sicily's 9,927 square miles where he could start his search with a reasonable prospect of success. Assuming that the Keepers he was tracking meant to cross at the Messina Strait and thereby reach the mainland, he could narrow down the hunt to eastern Sicily, but where exactly would they be when he and Halloran arrived?

Bolan's best hope for pegging that location was Kurtzman, assuming that the runners had their sat phone up and running when he closed to striking range. If not…well, then, he'd have to improvise.

And hope they weren't too late.

Acireale, Sicily

CLAUDIO BRANCA'S CONVOY reached Acireale, at the foot of Mount Etna, in good time after clearing the toll barrier at Catania Nord. The city, he'd been told, was famous for its churches, including Saint Peter's Basilica, Saint Sebastian's Basilica and the Acireale Cathedral, but none of that interested Branca. He had come to destroy the Scarlet Whore of Babylon, not praise her temples of Mammon.

Their Mafia escorts were rough men of few words, dressed like low-rent ambulance chasers, disinclined to fraternize with Branca's soldiers. It was just as well, since being in proximity to them made Branca feel unclean, but he was satisfied to use them for the moment, when it served his purpose. Two cars traveled out in front of Branca's van, a third behind his other vehicles, four men in each. All came equipped with submachine guns, shotguns, pistols, but their foremost weapon seemed to be their attitude and reputation, which made people look away, some even reaching up to cross themselves as the convoy passed by.

They would lose the escort at Messina, and Branca had

made no similar arrangement for protection on the mainland, trusting speed and his own men to protect the Ark on its last lap to Rome, northbound on Autostrada A22, also known as the southern portion of European route E45. Stopping for petrol only, or to change drivers along the way, Branca hoped they could cover the final 465 miles in under eight hours, arriving in time to find Saint Peter's Square packed with pilgrims and tourists.

It was too much to hope that The Beast himself would make a personal appearance, perhaps, but once the power of the Ark had been unleashed, there would be nowhere in the Holy See—or on the globe—for him to hide. Judgment would find the man no matter where he scurried to conceal himself.

Branca wondered how the Ark would channel God's almighty wrath, and whether he'd survive to see its work completed. Granted, scripture warned that any man who touched it would immediately die, but Janus Marcellus and Mania Justina claimed a later revelation from the Holy Spirit, granting leave for dedicated soldiers of the Lord to wield His weapon in defense of the abiding One True Faith. It felt like blasphemy to think they might be wrong, but Branca had prepared himself to die in Rome, a sacrificial lamb.

Or lion, as the case might be.

And if the Ark did nothing? If its power had evaporated somehow over the millennia…then what?

Branca had planned for that eventuality as well. He was prepared to lead his team against the Scarlet Whore without God's help, if He denied them aid. In that case, Branca knew, they'd likely be cut down before they breached Vatican City, but at least they would have seen their mission through, against all odds. Success was sometimes measured by a warrior's courage and determination, rather than the outcome of a given battle.

Someday, somehow, Branca's fellow Keepers would taste victory and share the bountiful rewards laid by for them in paradise. They would be honored for their valor, for their sacrifice on God's behalf. That much, at least, was certain.

Otherwise, why even try?

As for the hunters coming on behind him, if they hadn't lost his trail yet, Branca hoped that he would have a chance to meet them, too, before the end. He felt invincible today, perhaps a vain conceit, but it was still uplifting for the moment.

There'd be time enough tomorrow to lie down and die.

Washington, D.C.

HAL BROGNOLA'S PRIVATE line to Stony Man rang twice before he picked it up, distracted by the images that CNN was beaming to his office from the latest atrocity scene. He snared the receiver without taking his eyes from the TV screen, where grim-faced ambulance attendants carried sheet-draped stretchers across blood-slick pavement.

"Brognola."

"It's me," Aaron Kurtzman advised.

"What's the word?"

"Well, the sat phone's in use—or it *was,* briefly, five or six minutes ago."

"Sicily?"

"That's affirmative. It's on the A18 Motorway, north-bound between Catania and Messina."

"Like you figured."

"Right. How's Striker doing?"

"Hanging in there," Brognola said. "Should be getting close to touchdown at Giarre."

"Cutting off some highway mileage," Kurtzman noted.

"That's the plan. I guess he thought a straight shot to Messina would be pushing it. Too many watchful eyes."

"Police and otherwise."

"Hey, don't remind me."

"One good thing," Kurtzman observed.

"What's that?"

"At least they don't know who he is."

Meaning from Bolan's *other* one-man war, when it was personal between him and the Mafia, repaying debts of blood in kind.

"Small favors."

"I'll be in touch if we can track them on the mainland," Kurtzman said. "Till then…"

"Till then," Brognola echoed, cutting off the link.

Okay, so he was bothered by the thought of mafiosi meddling in a job that was already dangerous enough. So what? After the hell they'd wreaked in Bolan's life, and all he'd gone through to repay them for it, anytime Bolan came up against the Mob it had to push some buttons. Even with the iron control he'd demonstrated from the first time the big Fed had met him, Striker was still a man. He wasn't made of steel, and likely couldn't close his eyes without at least a fleeting glimpse of ghosts.

Make it the friendly ones, at least, Brognola thought. Not quite a prayer.

What could he do to help in Sicily? Say nothing, in a nutshell. Justice had connections to Italy's various national police forces, particularly the Guardia di Finanza, but what was Brognola supposed to do? Call Rome, maybe Palermo, and explain that he was trying to avert disaster at the Vatican, so could they turn a blind eye just this once to any killings that his agent might be forced to do along the way? Pretend that nothing was happening?

Sure. Try selling that to the attorney general, the State Department, or the magistrates in Sicily who risked assassination daily, building legal cases they could file against the Mafia. Who wouldn't take a deal like that and toss it back to Brognola, maybe with a demand that he be cut loose and replaced with someone sane.

Stony Man operated covertly to cut through red tape and secure results where all routine efforts had failed. Or in cases like this one, when urgency ruled out the usual foot-dragging process of investigation, indictment and trial. Terrorists couldn't be fought with writs, injunctions or restraining orders. Action was required, and that meant closing one eye to the law—hell, *both* eyes—while the job got done.

And there was still the possibility, on any given job, that they would fail. Which, in the present case, could mean a tragicomic fizzle in the heart of Rome, or a fullbore catastrophe.

Brognola, though prepared for either, almost wished he was a praying man.

Custodes Foederis Headquarters, Rome

UGO TROISI TURNED on the SCI-SC1 radio frequency scanner and studied its seven-digit liquid crystal display. The device was slightly larger than a pack of cigarettes, with a directional antenna sprouting from its top. It was designed to pick up frequencies emitted by wireless audio or video surveillance devices, while microprocessor filter circuitry prevented nuisance alarms from random noise frequencies. None of which concerned Troisi, as long as the damned thing worked.

He started at his desk, aiming the scanner at his telephone, then at the intercom, and finally running the antenna randomly around the desk and underneath it, deep into the knee well. Nothing registered, leaving Troisi torn between relief and…what? Confusion? Disappointment?

He'd been half convinced that he was under some sort of surveillance, after hearing the suspicions of his fellow Concilium members. It seemed like something Janus Marcellus might do, and bland denials from Marco Gianotti meant nothing. The church's security chief would bug his own mother if Marcellus decreed it. And if Marcellus suspected Troisi's secret relationship with Mania…

Troisi wasn't techno-savvy, not what Americans labeled a geek, but he knew there were ways to tap phone lines without planting transmitters at the source. Headquarters had a switchboard downstairs, and Gianotti—or Marcellus himself—could order the operators to eavesdrop on anyone using a phone on the premises. Cell phones were even more vulnerable, Troisi knew, since their signals could simply be plucked from thin air.

Perhaps the scanner was a waste of time, then, but since he'd obtained it he might as well finish sweeping his office. Working outward from the desk, Troisi circled counterclockwise, moving slowly, feeling slightly foolish, as if he were a superstitious peasant dowsing for water in a barren field. At least no one was there to see him going through the fruitless ritual.

Halfway around the room he stopped, feeling the scanner vibrate in his palm, its LCD window revealing a hit. He moved the antenna back and forth, up and down, watching the sixteen-section bar graph rise and fall until he zeroed in. He moved closer to the bookcase on the east wall of his office, following the scanner's lead—and found it.

Not a wiretap, obviously, but a tiny bug, attached by

means of some adhesive to the underside of a shelf at chest height, lined with reference books. Kneeling to study it more closely, he confirmed that it was the size of a small coin, matte black, presumably some kind of plastic casing with the microworks inside.

His first impulse was to remove it, smash it, maybe flush it down the toilet in his private bathroom, but Troisi quickly recognized that that would be a rash response. Why tip his hand and let whoever placed the microphone know he had found it? It should be a relatively simple thing to censor any comments made within the office. He might even turn the bug to his advantage, find some way to trick his adversaries with it, if the opportunity arose. Marcellus or Gianotti? Both? Or someone else?

He'd have to finish covering the office, look for any other listening devices, cameras, whatever, then decide on his next action. Warning Mania could be a problem, if her quarters had the same kind of equipment tucked away, but he would manage somehow. And from there? What next?

Troisi realized that he had no idea what his next move should be, but he would have to think of something. And he'd have to do it soon.

Before the Ark reached Rome and altered everything, forever.

Autostrada A18, Catania Province, Sicily

NINO RICCOBONO TOOK a last drag on his cigarette and pitched it out the window of his black Lancia Thema. In his wing mirror, he saw the second carload of his soldiers, and the van behind them keeping pace, its driver and its front-seat passenger concealed by sun glare on the windscreen. Behind that, three more vehicles, the last in line more of his soldiers, bringing up the rear.

It was a shit job, Riccobono thought, but he'd been ordered to perform it by the Family's underboss and he couldn't refuse. Seen in another light, it was a kind of paid excursion through the countryside, though he would have preferred to stay at home, working the streets and earning money for himself.

Basta! he thought. They would be in Messina soon enough, and he could drop his party at the ferry docks, put this obnoxious babysitting chore behind him and get back to normal business. Riccobono didn't know what sort of cargo was concealed inside the van, but it was certain his *padrino* had been paid, and handsomely, for furnishing a dozen armed escorts.

So far, they'd served no purpose other than intimidating peasants in the towns they passed through, glowering at faces on the sidewalks and in slower vehicles. Riccobono kept a sharp eye out for police, cruising the autostrada in their Alfa Romeo 159 Panteras or crouched atop their Moto Guzzi Falcone motorcycles.

Riccobono assumed that the van he'd been assigned to escort had to be hauling contraband. What kind? He neither knew nor cared. If its occupants were terrorists, it made no difference. They would be on the mainland soon, free to conduct whatever bloody business suited them without disrupting Nino's life or interfering with his business. If they killed a dozen or a thousand strangers, what was it to him? Perhaps, by chance, they'd take out some Camorra thugs, and do the Mafia a favor.

Thinking that made Riccobono smile. He wouldn't mind if they wiped Naples off the map, now that he thought about it. The Camorra had been putting feelers out toward Sicily, trying to poach his drug customers, meddle in some of its construction and extortion schemes. A war was brewing, and he'd welcome anything that thinned the opposition's ranks before the shooting started.

Meanwhile, he would sit back, enjoy the ride and hope they met no opposition during the remainder of their journey north. It had been smooth running so far, but with the tension simmering between organizations, a mafioso never knew when he might stumble into danger without warning.

Thus, the arsenal they carried with them. Each man had at least one pistol on his person, backed up with Beretta AR70/90 assault rifles, Franchi SPAS-15 combat shotguns, and MP-5 K submachine guns. Riccobono had considered bringing hand grenades, but thought they were a bit too much for a simple ride in the country.

With any luck, none of the weapons would be needed. If they were, however, Nino and his hand-picked crew were all veteran killers. Nothing fazed them, least of all police or members of some rival syndicate. If anyone got in their way...well, it would be the last mistake the bastard ever made.

Giarre, Sicily

THEY CIRCLED ONCE over the seaside town before Ekrem Arikan got his amphibian aircraft lined up for landing. There was no airfield at Giarre, but he didn't need one, gliding in much as he had at Sikinos and touching down on the aircraft's pontoons. Taxiing toward the nearest dock, he called back from the cockpit, "Safe and sound! Thank you for flying with Aegean Tours!"

Despite the smile that brought to Bolan's face, he kept a sharp eye on the pier and shore beyond it, watching for police or any other kind of welcoming committee. There was no reason to think they'd be expected here, but this was Sicily, where nothing ever was precisely as it seemed to unfamiliar eyes.

Bolan and Halloran removed their own bags from the plane and paused to settle up with Arikan, before he topped the tanks and started back for home. Their pilot eyed the wad of currency that Bolan handed him, frowning, and said, "It is too much."

"Consider it a bonus," Bolan said. "You've been a great help."

"Now I get what you call the amnesia?"

"It's the safest way to go," Bolan agreed.

"Good luck to you!" the pilot said. "Long life!"

"Back at you."

Bolan and Halloran rode in a taxi to the car rental agency on Via Don Luigi Sturzo, showing up without a reservation but with credit cards aplenty. Twenty minutes later they were rolling in an Alfa Romeo Giulietta five-door hatchback, heading up the A18 to seek their quarry.

"Have you seen the advertisements for this car?" Halloran asked from behind the wheel.

"I don't think so," Bolan answered.

"One says, 'I am Giulietta, and I am such stuff as dreams are made on.' Another says, 'Without heart, we would be mere machines.'"

"I can't argue with that," Bolan said. "But this isn't a dream."

"No, a nightmare," Halloran replied. "If we don't catch them on the highway to Messina…"

"Then we push on to the mainland. Since we're this close to Rome, have your people got some kind of backup plan in place?"

"You mean, in case we fail?" Halloran nodded. "You may rest assured that measures have been taken. The inspector general of the Corpo della Gendarmeria will have spoken to headquarters of the Polizia di Stato in Rome. All possible precautions will be taken—without upsetting visitors, of course."

"The show must go on?"

"It is more than a show to the pilgrims who turn up each day, seeking miracles," Halloran said. "Even those who just snap photographs or patronize the gift shops come away with something that may comfort them, something they'll cherish in their hearts for the remainder of their lives."

And Bolan's job—or one of them, at least—was to prevent those lives from being cut short by a terrorist attack. If it came down to confrontation at the Holy See, he didn't know how many adversaries they'd be facing or what kind of weapons they were packing for the knockout punch. It strained credulity to think an ancient relic posed any threat to modern Rome, but he was conscious of the various alternatives available on open markets in the world today.

A suitcase nuke, for instance. Or a Semtex charge that would disperse virulent pathogens and let the wind make its deliveries of death. The Keepers could have planned their move for months, or years, waiting until the opportunity arose to slip their lethal calling card inside an envelope with ritual significance.

In this case, Bolan was the guy assigned to interrupt delivery.

And he was running out of time.

CHAPTER SEVENTEEN

Giardini Naxos, Sicily

Fabio Gravina lit another cigarette, hoping the nicotine would calm his nerves. It wasn't working so far, and he wished he'd brought some marijuana to chill out with, but that would be the end of him, if he got high and botched the job. No second chances this time. If the mafiosi didn't kill him, worse would happen back in Naples.

As a soldier of the Camorra, it was forbidden for Gravina to show fear. What would the men serving under him think if they knew he felt apprehension over their impending clash with mortal enemies? They had a job to do, and every man had to play his part without exemption.

The five men riding with him in the Fiat Scudo van were all accomplished killers and survivors of the long, running war between Camorra and Mafia. If he had to guess, Gravina would have said they had some fifty kills among them, with his own fifteen the highest number. By the time the sun went down this day, that total would have been substantially increased.

The call from Naples had been urgent, although short on details. Word had come from Rome that something big was in the offing, not a Cosa Nostra project in its own right, but supported by the Sicilians, and thus worth disrupting. Gravina was the soldier closest to the crossing at Messina, so the task fell to him. He'd grabbed the best men available on short notice, and here they were, waiting for a convoy of sorts to appear, bearing its unknown cargo northward along the A18 Motorway.

Their mission: first, to stop it at all costs, then to discover what the cargo was. If possible, obtain it for the profit of their own Family; if not, destroy it and deny that profit to their enemies. Dispose of anyone who tried to interfere, including witnesses who could betray them to police.

Simple.

They had come well armed for the assignment. Gravina himself would man the Belgian FN Minimi light machine gun, belt-feeding 5.56 mm NATO rounds from a 200-round polymer ammunition box attached to the base of its receiver. With a cyclic rate of 700 rounds per minute, it alone could ventilate any civilian vehicle and the unlucky passengers. Bearing in mind the odds that they might face, though, Gravina's men also carried a variety of small arms: Heckler & Koch G41 assault rifles, Spectre M-4 submachine guns, a Benelli M-4 Super 90 shotgun and various pistols.

By all rights, it should be a massacre.

Of course, there was a possibility that they would find themselves outnumbered by their adversaries. Surprise and firepower would help them in that case, but they'd still need ample nerve to pull it off. Whatever one might think of mafiosi, most were brave enough when it came to fighting, and some fanatically so. Best to kill them outright and be done with it, if they could manage.

"I wish they'd get here," Tito Grassi muttered, from the driver's seat.

"We haven't missed them," Gravina said. "They'll be coming."

"Still."

"Just be prepared to block them, eh?"

"We should have brought a second car," Ennio Fracastro suggested, from the rear.

"One van's enough," Gravina said. "We won't be taking any passengers."

"I meant for blocking them. Or chasing," Ennio replied.

"We stop them here," Gravina answered. "Stop them dead."

"We may upset the tourists," Mario Tartaglia remarked.

"To hell with them," Gravina said. "To hell with anyone who interferes."

Fiumefreddo di Sicilia

"THAT'S A MOUTHFUL," Bolan said, as they approached and passed the sign announcing the next commune on the northbound A18 Motorway.

"It means 'cold river,'" Halloran translated. "The Fiumefreddo gets its chill from snowmelt on Mount Etna. Did you know they filmed most of the Sicilian scenes from your movie *The Godfather* here?"

"Good to know," Bolan said. "But it wasn't *my* movie."

"Of course. I only meant—"

"We need to keep an eye out for the real-life Mafia," said Bolan, interrupting, with another quick glance toward his outside mirror. No tails yet. "They shouldn't know we're coming, but they haven't lasted this long by letting people surprise them."

"We have no business with them, eh?" Halloran asked.

"Unless they make our business theirs."

The Alfa Romeo Giulietta was fast, for a family car. Halloran was a skilled and confident driver, whose taking the wheel left Bolan's mind and hands free for emergencies along the way. He'd also make a better spokesman if they happened to be stopped by the police, though Bolan had seen no patrol cars on the A18 so far. Was that unusual? Or was it possible someone had made a call to clear the way?

If so, it meant the Mafia had to be on board, at least for the Sicilian portion of the journey, since Custodes Foederis would have no pull with Italian police. Word was out, however quietly and classified, about the Axum raid, and no lawman with any self-respect or fealty to his religion would allow the Ark convoy to pass unless the wheels were greased, a cover story fabricated.

On the other hand, they might be used to going blind when mafiosi moved their contraband, a longstanding tradition on an island where *omertà* and the vendetta had ruled life for at least a hundred fifty years. Police who stood against the Mafia were killed, along with prosecutors, judges, jurors who returned convictions, journalists who wrote the truth—most anyone, in fact, who dared oppose the Families. Conversely, those who played along and took the bribes without complaint would either be promoted or, at least, allowed to live in peace.

"We're gaining on them," Halloran said, out of nowhere. "Don't you think we must be?"

"Should be," Bolan granted. "Anyway, we know they're still in Sicily."

So far. That knowledge coming courtesy of Stony Man, where Aaron Kurtzman's team was shadowing a sat phone carried by the Axum team, accessed so far by two of the cult's bishops they were sure of. It had been some forty miles ahead of Bolan when he landed at Giarre, and doubtless gained some while they hassled with the rental agency. But even with the Ark on board, the runners still were bound by all the laws of physics. They could drive only so fast on planet Earth, and Bolan had a chance—however slim it was—of overtaking them before they reached Messina.

Maybe.

Would they recognize the target when they saw it? For the Ark or whatever it was, they'd need some kind of van or truck, but there would also likely be at least one escort vehicle. He didn't know how many raiders were involved at Axum, whether all of them were still on board, or if they'd picked up reinforcements somewhere on the way from Ethiopia to Sicily. None of that mattered now.

He had to find the Ark, whether it had two escorts or two hundred. And he had to stop it cold.

Or…what?

Bolan was tired of speculating, wasted no more time on thinking about what could happen if a given hypothetical chain of events occurred. His job, as usual, was relatively simple: find the target, isolate it, then detain it or destroy it, as the situation might demand.

And anyone who tried to stop him was expendable.

Giardini Naxos

"Shit! It has to be them, right?" Excitement hummed in Tito Grassi's voice. "So many cars?"

So many cars.

That was the problem. Fabio Gravina counted five cars, plus the cargo van, with four men in the first sedan. Extrapolating, that meant he and his five soldiers were outnumbered four to one, at least. But maybe, with the critical advantage of surprise…

He lowered the binoculars and snapped, "Get ready!" Stepping from the Fiat Scudo van, he took the FN Minimi with him, leaving its bipod folded and bracing the machine gun's fifteen-pound weight across the joint where his open door met the van's frame. Around him, his men were scattering for cover at selected points around the highway rest stop, cocking weapons as they ran. Peering through the Minimi's sights, his index finger on its trigger, he left them to it and concentrated on his own part of the ambush.

Stop the lead car, and the rest would halt—or, at the very least, be slowed enough to riddle them with bullets. Failing that...

Failing that, he was as good as dead.

Gravina opened fire when the lead car was sixty yards out, strafing its hood and windscreen, instantly aware that his bullets weren't having the proper effect. Paint flaked from the target vehicle's hood, its windshield sprouted misty splotches, but the slugs weren't penetrating.

Bulletproof!

Cursing, Gravina shifted his aim to the grille and the tires, his troops already firing at other vehicles in the speeding convoy. And they were taking fire in return from gun ports in some of the escort cars. Unless Gravina stopped the lead car soon, blocking the motorway...

Incoming bullets struck the Fiat Scudo, shattering its windshield, spraying him with pebbled safety glass. Eyes narrowed to slits behind his Valentino sunglasses, Gravina held his place and kept on firing, heedless of the blood that streaked his face from shrapnel slices. He could live with pain and scars, but not with failure to complete his mission.

Counting rounds expended in the midst of battle was impossible, but at a cyclic rate of thirteen rounds per second, Gravina knew the Minimi was close to running dry. He let it rip until the bolt locked open on an empty chamber, then lunged back into the van, groping for the athletic bag filled with SureFire casket magazines, each loaded with another hundred rounds. There was an awkward moment while he removed the polymer ammo box, snapping a magazine into its place, then Gravina ducked back into firing position, raising the light machine gun—

A bullet slammed into his shoulder, spinning him, the Minimi chattering skyward, spent brass cascading to the pavement around Gravina's feet. He felt himself falling, concrete rushing up to meet him with a jarring impact that wrenched the light machine gun from his grasp. Around him, his soldiers kept firing, and one of them cried out in pain as dizziness swept over Gravina in waves.

He found the strength to reach his cell phone, rip it from his pocket, turn it on and hit the top number he had on speed-dial. Three rings seemed to take forever, with the gunfire drumming in his ears and consciousness evaporating, then a voice came on the line, demanding, "What?"

"Help!" Gravina blurted out. "We're getting killed here!"

"Where are you?" the voice demanded.

"Giardini Naxos," Gravina gasped. "Hurry! They're getting away!"

Custodes Foederis Headquarters, Rome

"WHAT'S THAT THING?" Mania Justina demanded.

"Shh!" Ugo Troisi hissed at her, feeling the anger warm his cheeks. Why did she think he'd entered her apartment with a finger pressed against his lips, if not to signal silence?

"But—"

A long step brought him almost kissing-close to her, and he clapped his hand over her mouth. Before she could escape, he leaned in closer still and whispered in her ear, "Quiet, for God's sake! It's a scanner. I must check for hidden microphones."

Troisi withdrew his hand an inch, and two, then clamped it back over her mouth as she said, "Mic—"

Enraged by her stupidity, he cautioned her in urgent whispers. "Do. Not. Speak!"

At last she nodded. He removed his hand and started sweeping the apartment with his scanner. Painfully aware of passing time, Troisi made a thorough job of it, finally satisfied that there were neither hidden cameras nor listening devices to be found within the bedroom or adjoining bathroom.

"Clean," he said, the first word he had spoken in a normal tone since entering.

"You hurt my lips," she told him, pouting.

"Better that than the alternative," he answered.

"Oh? And what's this about microphones? Why would you even think—"

"I found one in my office," Troisi interrupted.

"Oh?" Not quite the tone he had expected.

"Someone's spying on me," he explained, in case she was too dense to understand. "And on the rest of the Concilium, I think."

"And why would anyone do that?"

"Security is Marco's area, of course. He does as Janus orders."

"Have you asked him? I mean Marco?"

There was definitely something in her tone. Troisi frowned and answered, "Not about the microphone. Only an idiot would dare confront him with it. When I told him Deodato and Federico thought their phones were tapped, he denied it, of course."

"Well, then."

"Are you not listening? I *found* a microphone inside my office."

"But does that mean Marco put it there?"

"One of his sneaks, more likely."

"And," she said, "you thought the wisest thing to do was rush straight here? With people watching you?"

As stunned as if she'd slapped him, Troisi said, "I came to warn you, Mania. I obviously couldn't trust the telephones."

"But as you've proved yourself, no one is watching *me*. Unless they trailed you here, that is. In which case you've endangered me."

"I was not followed!"

"Are you certain? What if there are cameras along the hallways?"

Christ! He hadn't thought of that, had been content to satisfy himself that no one followed him to Mania's apartment. But if she was right…

"The wise thing, I believe," she told him, "is for you to stay away. For the time being, only. When you've settled this unpleasantness, perhaps…"

"Perhaps?"

"We can't take foolish risks now, can we? Not when we're so close to having everything."

Mania's logic, for the first time in Troisi's memory, seemed unassailable. He dipped his head, not quite a bow, and answered, "As you wish, Your Grace."

"Not as I wish," she said. "As it must be."

Troisi left without another word and softly closed the door behind him, his mind awhirl with questions and emotions that collided, ricocheted and left him feeling dizzy. There'd been no discernible regret from Mania as she announced the moratorium on their relationship. No, state it plainly: she'd discarded him. To save herself from scrutiny attached to him? Or was there something else?

Obviously, since he had heard a voice, it was *someone* else.

Not Janus. But then…who?

Rushing along the corridor, Ugo Troisi was determined to find out.

Autostrada A18, Province of Messina, Sicily

"POLICE BEHIND US."

Bolan saw the flashing lights in his mirror a split second before Halloran spoke. The squad cars—two of them, he realized—were racing northward, only switching on their sirens when they came within sight of the Alfa Romeo Giulietta.

"Well?" Halloran asked.

"Pull over," Bolan said. "No guns."

Halloran sighed and did as he instructed. They sat waiting for a moment, engine idling, then the two police cars passed them in a blur, continuing along their northward route. Bolan watched them dwindle with distance, riding a wave of relief.

"Somebody else's problem," he remarked.

As soon as they were rolling, Halloran switched on the Giulietta's radio and found a news broadcast. None of it was clear to Bolan, until Halloran began to translate. "It's a special bulletin," he said. "There's been a shooting up ahead of us, at Giardini Naxos. The announcer says it's Mafia-related. Several men are dead."

"Nothing about our guys?" Bolan asked.

"Not yet. If they *were* involved—"

"Your troubles could be over," Bolan said. "Game, set and match."

"But who would try to stop them here?" Halloran asked. "Unless you called for help…?"

"You know I didn't, " Bolan said. "But what about buddies from the CDF?"

"Impossible," Halloran replied. "I would have been alerted, at the very least."

"So, someone else, then," Bolan said. "And if it's not about the Ark…"

"Coincidence? That seems improbable, to say the least."

"Agreed. But if the Mafia's involved, they'd bring all kinds of baggage to the job."

"An underworld vendetta?"

"Maybe, if they're on somebody else's turf, or enemies found out that they were escorting a convoy."

"Just a few more miles," Halloran said. "If I can speak to the police—"

"Don't even think about it," Bolan warned him. "Make one cop suspicious, and we're both in custody before you know what hit you."

"But—"

"If you believe the CDF can help, phone in and have somebody else touch base with the police, through channels. If they've got the Ark secured, then I'll call home and see if that's a wrap. But if the Axum team got through, we still have work ahead of us."

"Agreed."

Ten minutes later they were rolling into Giardini Naxos by the sea. Passing the checkpoint where police were steering traffic past the scene, Bolan could see it hadn't happened long ago. A burned-out van, still smoking, sat on melted tires beside a service station where the windows had been blown away, stucco facade pockmarked with bullet holes. A team of firefighters was foaming down the wreckage and surrounding pavement. Funny that the fuel pumps hadn't blown like rockets launching, but the flames couldn't have reached them. Cops were photographing bodies where they'd fallen, other uniforms pushing the tourists back. They would have gathered quickly, once the shooting stopped and there was no more danger, rubbernecking sudden death.

"You think that is the van?" Halloran asked.

"I don't know," Bolan replied. "But while we're trying to find out, I think we ought to keep on heading north."

Taormina, Sicily

THE CONVOY STOPPED outside town, directed to a farmhouse off the highway by the leader of their escort. There, concealed from scrutiny by passing drivers, they assessed the damage to their personnel and vehicles.

All the cars had taken hits, scarring the armored Mafia machines and ventilating Branca's vehicles, which weren't bulletproof. An oversight, of course, but who could have envisioned being ambushed by a pack of Camorra on the open road? Two of his men were hit, one seriously, with the black blood oozing from a wound between his ribs proof positive of lethal damage to the liver.

"Do you want to take him with you?" Nino Riccobono asked.

Claudio Branca shook his head. "He won't last long. Better to leave him here, and first make certain that he cannot speak. I'll take care of it myself. About the vehicles…"

"I've called someone. He'll send more cars, another van, but it takes time."

"How long?"

"An hour, ninety minutes." Riccobono shrugged. "I can't be sure."

"Police may come by then," Branca said.

"If so, I'll deal with them. They'll find us quicker on the highway, driving shot-up cars. You couldn't board the ferry at Messina with these wrecks, regardless."

"You're convinced that it was the Camorra?" Branca prodded.

"Who else? We've been at war for twenty years."

"And so they pick today, of all days, to attack?"

"It is the nature of an ambush to be inconvenient," Riccobono said. "The main thing is, we killed them."

"And if there are more?"

"We deal with them, as well."

"I'm trying to *avoid* attention," Branca told him, "not invite it."

Riccobono shrugged. "Things happen."

"That is all you have to say?"

"It's a fact. There's no use stewing over it. You can't change what's already done."

"And you expect full pay for this fiasco, eh?"

"Why not? Your cargo's still intact. Most of your men are fine."

Branca reviewed his narrow range of options. Pressing on with bullet-punctured vehicles invited the police to stop his team, and after what had happened in Giardini Naxos, they'd be out in numbers, fully armed. He was compelled, therefore, to wait for the replacement van and cars. But once they arrived...

Should he allow the mafiosi to profane the Ark by watching while his soldiers transferred it from one van to another? Would they even move away when asked, or would he have to force them? And if trouble started, with the two sides nearly matched in numbers, could his people win?

Perhaps, if they were ready when the moment came.

"You're right," he said at last, reluctantly. "I should be thanking you for all your help."

That put a smile on Riccobono's face. "Damn right,

you should. And I accept your thanks, as I'll accept your money."

Branca forced his own smile, nodding. "While we're waiting, I just want to brief my people on the change of plans."

"Of course. Relax them, if you can. It won't be too much longer now."

"I hope there will be no more *camorristi* waiting for us when we leave," Branca said.

Riccobono made a rude, dismissive noise. "Don't waste another moment fretting over those pricks. We'll take care of anyone who tries to interfere with our parade."

CHAPTER EIGHTEEN

Chianchitta, Sicily

Giardini Naxos was crawling with cops and coroners, forensic teams and journalists. Mack Bolan couldn't wait there for a bulletin from Stony Man, nor could he tolerate the thought of pulling back to Fiumefreddo di Sicilia or Giarre if his enemies were still alive and rolling northward with the Ark. His compromise was driving on a mile or so farther to the village of Chianchitta and idling there until Kurtzman called back.

It took the computer genius fifteen precious minutes from the time of Bolan's call to come back with the intel. The soldier raised the phone and said, "Let's have it," skipping the amenities.

"The phone we're tracking was in operation and still moving as of five minutes ago," Kurtzman declared. "Still north of you, but stationary when it made a forty-seven-second call to Rome."

"Headquarters?"

"Right," Kurtzman confirmed. "That phone stays on around the clock. It doesn't leave the compound."

"So they've checked in since the shooting," Bolan said.

"Somebody did. Same phone, for sure. Of course, I can't say who was using it or what they talked about."

Bolan considered that. Suppose the Ark or whatever it was *had* been inside the burned-out van at Giardini Naxos.

Say, one of the Keepers guarding it had managed to escape the ambush and report the mission's failure. Bolan's job was to prevent the Ark from reaching Rome, not chase a straggler or two around the countryside after his target was destroyed.

"Coordinates for where they called from?" Bolan asked. Kurtzman replied with digits he could use to find the spot by GPS.

"Okay, thanks," the soldier said. "If you find out any more—"

"I'll be in touch. So long."

He turned, found Halloran just closing up his cell phone. "Someone in my prefect's office called a friend with the police. It's not official yet, but he was told that officers found nothing in the van like stolen icons or objets d'art. That's the cover, incidentally. A theft of gold and art belonging to the Church."

"No Ark, then."

"No. Nothing even close."

Bolan relayed his news from Stony Man, closing with, "So they're still in motion. Or at least they got away from here. I can't say why they stopped to make their last call, or how long they stayed at the coordinates we have."

"Some damage to their vehicles, perhaps," Halloran suggested. "If they're disabled, they may still be trying to procure replacements."

"Giving us a chance to catch them," Bolan said. "Let's roll. We're burning daylight."

"Burning—?"

"Never mind," Bolan said. "I was channeling John Wayne."

"Ah, yes. *The Shootist*."

"Close enough."

Another moment found them burning up the A18, their

vehicle's 1.4-liter turbo multiair engine pushing the hatchback from zero to one hundred kilometers per hour in seven seconds flat. Bolan programmed the dashboard GPS device to home on the coordinates that Kurtzman had provided, then sat back to watch the countryside stream past his window, keeping one eye on the mirror for police.

Was it too much to hope that unknown enemies might stall the Ark in Sicily and let him overtake it there, a safe three hundred miles and change from Rome? It seemed unlikely, given all that Bolan and Halloran had endured so far, but he was never one to look a gift horse in the mouth if opportunities arose to make a tough job easier.

And if the Ark had already moved on, at least he knew where it was going, and he had a spotty means of tracking it, dependent on who used the sat phone Stony Man had monitored.

It wasn't much, but he had worked with less.

And told himself that this should be enough.

Taormina, Sicily

THE HARDEST PART of switching vehicles—and the most dangerous—was moving the Ark from its old van to a newer Volkswagen Transporter with blacked-out windows on the sides and at the rear. Claudio Branca balked at letting any of their escorts help shift it, fearing that some inappropriate behavior might force him to kill them, or worse yet, set off a chain reaction that would leave them all reduced to smoking piles of ash. He wasted precious time convincing Nino Riccobono that his men should move away and keep their eyes averted while the Ark was being moved, demands that virtually guaranteed they would attempt to peek at it when Branca's back was turned.

At last the job was done and they were ready to depart

in fresh, undamaged vehicles. The drivers who'd delivered them would take the other van and cars somewhere, to have them fixed or just dispose of. It made no difference to Branca, but he wondered whether any residue of the divine remained inside the old van to surprise the mafiosi who'd be moving it.

It was no longer Branca's problem. When the wrath of God was finally unleashed, all infidels and sinners would be punished in His own good time. What difference did one pathetic gangster, more or less, make in the cosmic scheme of things?

Half of their Sicilian journey was behind them now. Another thirty-five kilometers remained before they reached the next toll barrier south of Messina, and their escorts would be leaving them there, making certain that they weren't followed or harassed while waiting for the ferry to Villa San Giovanni on the mainland. Whatever happened after that was in God's hands—and Branca's, too. He wouldn't trust in faith alone, if fighting was required to bring on the Apocalypse and Second Coming.

It pleased him in a strange way, knowing that the vast majority of people inhabiting the world might think he was insane, but Branca reckoned he would have the last laugh when they realized their fatal, irrevocable mistake. How stunned and terrified they would be on that day, summoned for battle unprepared, against a righteous host whose victory was guaranteed by scripture.

Branca knew he might not live to see that day in mortal form, knew that his flesh and bone might be consumed at the unveiling of the Ark, and he was ready for that sacrifice. Although some might believe he was offending God by using the Ark as a weapon, revelations granted to Janus Marcellus assured Branca of his just reward. He silently pronounced the verse from 1 Corinthians 15: *O death, where is thy sting? O grave, where is thy victory?*

This time tomorrow, maybe sooner, Branca would be a hero—or a martyr—for the ages. One way or another, he would be remembered and rewarded on the Day of Reckoning.

And any sinners who opposed him would go down like weeds before a scythe, their broken bodies trampled underfoot.

Branca wondered if the other Keepers were prepared, if those selected from the temples overseas had done their part. He hoped so, but if they had failed for any reason, it didn't affect his mission or its outcome. He and his men had overcome all obstacles so far and were proceeding toward their final goal. The world would ultimately know their names and marvel at their bravery.

Before it all burned down.

Furci Siculo, Sicily

TWO WEEKS IN HIDING, now this. Cosimo Di Lauro hated rude surprises, but the thing he hated worst of all was being called out on a rush job without knowing all the necessary details. Like the great emergency he'd been asked to handle, scrambling to gather weapons, load them in the car and tear away from Pagliara, their safe haven, on a moment's notice.

For two weeks, going on a third, they'd been staked out in the commune southwest of Messina, waiting for their target—Don Adolfo di Mazzanti of the Corleonesi clan— to show himself. Invulnerable on his home ground, as the last four teams of *camorristi* had discovered to their sorrow, di Mazzanti had a weakness by the name of Gloria Kanakis, an aspiring model whose career the mafioso was "assisting." Even so, she wouldn't live with him in Corleone, insisting that they stay out of the public eye and enjoy their monthly visits in her modest hometown.

It may have rankled Don Adolfo or amused him. Who could say? With time and patience, it would certainly have killed him, but the chance was lost now, thanks to the great emergency that had flushed Di Lauro's team from hiding.

And for what?

A group of fellow *camorristi* had been slaughtered in a firefight with some mafiosi at Giardini Naxos. Now Di Lauro and his four men had been ordered to pursue and punish the offenders. Five men, chasing unknown numbers, who had killed six of his fellow *napoletani* already.

Madness? Possibly. But when an order was received…

At least, Di Lauro thought, they were well armed, including an RPG-7 antitank weapon for stopping Don Adolfo's armored limousine. Once they had cracked it open like a sardine can, their backup weapons would have proved effective: three 5.56 mm Beretta ARX 160 assault rifles, two Uzi submachine guns and various personal sidearms. More than enough for one old mafioso and three or four bodyguards.

But for a larger force? Who knew?

"How many of them did you say there are?" Patricio Zaza asked.

"I didn't say," Di Lauro replied.

"Well then?"

"You know what I know. A shooting. Six of our brothers dead. It calls for a response."

"Not like this."

"Oh, no?" Di Lauro said. "Why don't you call up Don Cesare, then, and tell *him* that. Tell *him* that you're unhappy with his orders, eh?"

That silenced Zaza, but it didn't make the others happy,

nor did it relieve Di Lauro's own anxiety. It was a half-assed order, any way you looked at it, but they were still required to follow through and carry out the task.

Or die in the attempt.

"Do you at least know what we're looking for?"

"Something in a cargo van, with escort vehicles," Di Lauro said. "Don't ask how many. I have no idea."

"Should we just take out the first van that we see?" Pupetta Mallardo interjected.

"The first with mafiosi guarding it," Di Lauro answered. "Can you tell the difference?"

"I hope so."

"So do I," Di Lauro said. "You've staked your life on it."

And that was true for all of them. They were on hostile ground, diverted from the job they'd come to do, and sent into the field to find—and then annihilate—a killer team of unknown size. It was ridiculous, but Cosimo Di Lauro didn't call the shots. He simply pulled the trigger.

And this day he would be hoping that he got it right the first time, for there'd be no second chance.

Taormina

AARON KURTZMAN'S GPS coordinates led Bolan to a farmhouse south of town. Halloran drove past once, then doubled back, with no waiting vehicles in evidence. Preferring not to waste more time on parking, hiking overland and trying to surprise their quarry in broad daylight, Bolan told the brother they ought to drive straight in, ready to fight, and see what happened.

The answer: nothing. They had come too late.

Cars *had* been here, and recently, according to the many overlapping tire tracks. Bolan guessed the Keepers and whatever escorts they'd acquired had stopped to swap out damaged cars for others that wouldn't attract undue attention on the highway. In support of his hypothesis, he noted scattered pills of safety glass that might have dropped from window frames as doors were opened and reclosed.

Not proof, but close enough.

"We've missed them," Halloran said, stating the obvious.

"Probably with new wheels," Bolan said. "It isn't likely they'd have prearranged for backup cars, so they'd have lost time calling out and waiting for delivery."

"There's still a chance, then."

"As long as we get moving in a hurry."

And they did. Halloran still wanted to drive, and Bolan didn't argue. He'd been doing fine so far and showed no signs of perilous fatigue. With less than twenty miles to go before they reached Messina, and their targets still somewhere ahead, Bolan couldn't see his driver dozing off behind the wheel.

It was a true race now, to overtake their quarry without carrying the fight into Messina, Sicily's third-largest city and home to a quarter-million year-round residents. Toss in five million tourists visiting Messina each year, en route to the offshore Aeolian Islands, and you'd have a recipe for disaster if a firefight erupted in the streets.

But would they have a choice?

"My phone," Halloran said, in explanation of a muffled humming from one of his pockets. He answered with his surname, listened for the best part of a minute, then said *"Grazie"* as he cut the link. To Bolan he stated, "The dead men back at Giardini Naxos were *camorristi*."

"Feuding with the Mafia as usual," Bolan suggested.

"And forewarned somehow about the convoy," Halloran replied.

It wasn't hard to figure that one out. Crime families,

by definition, were conspiratorial, simmering hotbeds of intrigue. Supplying information to an adversary would mean execution for a member of a Mafia Family, but that wouldn't stop some greedy mobster from cashing in when opportunities arose, if he could hide his tracks effectively. Somebody heard about a shipment passing through and dropped a dime—or maybe let it slip in pillow talk to an unreliable mistress. Whatever, the leak led to scheming, and later to killing. The story was almost routine.

And if one group of *camorristi* knew about the convoy, if they'd died trying to hijack what it carried, would a backup team be standing by? That might be helpful, slowing the targets Bolan sought, but on the flips side of that coin was a potential second massacre. How many times could mobsters clash in public places without claiming innocent lives?

And would an intervention by the Executioner make matters worse?

On top of that, there was the ferry schedule Halloran had checked on his cell phone. Two separate companies— the government-run Ferrovie dello Stato, and the privately owned Caronte & Tourist line—made a total of forty-three crossings per day from Messina to Villa San Giovanni. If their timing was right, and Bolan got snarled up in town, the Keepers could be seaborne again before he ever caught a glimpse of them.

"Does this rig go any faster?" he asked.

"I think it might," Halloran replied, and pressed the pedal to the floor.

Roccalumera, Sicily

CLAUDIO BRANCA, RIDING shotgun in the new van, with a guidebook open on his lap, knew they were roughly seventeen miles southwest of Messina. Rolling into town along the A18, they passed a white rectangular sign informing them that Roccalumera's population stood at 4,145. A beach slid past, to Branca's right, and cruise ships that resembled great hotels set afloat. The town's main street had shops and homes, mostly two-story, painted in a wide range of contrasting colors, the commercial windows topped by metal screens that could be drawn down overnight. On hills behind the downtown district, larger, mostly older buildings looked down on the peasant class with fine disdain.

All typical of towns whose history had been submerged and lost while its inhabitants toadied to foreigners on holiday. Branca regarded all the frenzied chasing after euros with contempt, the worship of Mammon elevated almost to an art form, making him more glad than ever for his part in bringing on the Final Days. The people passing in their cars, on bicycles, afoot, would likely never know his name, much less his role in speeding up their march to hell, and that was fine. Branca served his Lord and Savior, not the masses of a world mired in corruption.

His escorts, minions of that reeking cesspit world, had served him well enough so far, but he would soon be parting company with them, once they were safely in Messina. From there on—

"Son of a bitch!" Branca's driver blurted out the curse as something roared across the open ground in front of them to strike the point car filled with mafiosi. A fireball, detonating as it struck the vehicle and peeled its hood back, drove the engine back into the laps of the startled front-seat occupants, then set the fuel tank off in roiling waves of flame.

"A rocket!" Branca snapped. "Drive on around the wreckage, quickly!"

As the van accelerated, lurching, Branca snatched his cell phone from its holster on his belt and keyed a single speed-dial number that would reach phones in his two remaining cars. In each, one of his soldiers answered, Branca speaking over them, issuing orders.

"Leave the escorts! Let them do the fighting! Hurry and catch up with us!"

"Affirmative," Elio Fontana answered, from the nearer of the cars.

"Right!" Michele Sansovino said from the other.

Passing the point car, all in flames, Branca spared a quick glance for its passengers, trapped in their seats, already blackened by the fire. Behind them, as his other soldiers broke formation to pursue the van, Branca saw gunmen on both shoulders of the highway, no great number of them, but with automatic weapons blazing. Whether the surviving escorts understood what Branca had in mind or not, their vehicles were slowing, swerving and returning fire.

Buying the time that Branca needed to escape.

"Hurry!" he commanded.

"This thing isn't built for racing," Arieti, his driver, answered through clenched teeth. "We've hit its top speed now."

"Do better, for the love of God!"

"You think He'll give us more horsepower?"

"Drive! Don't blaspheme!"

"Mea culpa," Arieti said, cutting a quick glance toward his mirror. "Do you see? They're catching hell back there."

"A little early, then," Branca replied. "See to it that we don't wind up along with them."

Santa Teresa di Riva, Sicily

THE VILLAGE CAME and went almost before it had a chance to register in Bolan's mind, another place where they wouldn't be stopping to admire the scenery. Nine miles past Taormina, they were burning up the highway, racing on ahead toward—what? Another disappointment? Or the culmination of their long pursuit?

It would depend on how long Bolan's targets had been stalled in picking up replacement vehicles for those shot up in Giardini Naxos, and perhaps on whether they had suffered any casualties. They couldn't stop to bury any corpses, obviously, but they wouldn't want to drag their dead aboard a ferry to the mainland, either. Any small delay would play in Bolan's favor now, against his enemies.

Halloran's lips were moving silently, praying perhaps, which couldn't hurt as long as he kept both eyes on the road ahead. Bolan watched out behind them, with his mirror, constantly alert for flashing lights or any other indicators of pursuit. Aside from cops, there was a possibility of mafiosi on patrol, after their clash with the Camorra, looking out for other trespassers and seeking payback. Bolan didn't want to get caught up in that game, but he was prepared for anything the highway threw at them from this point on.

To play it safe, he placed another sat phone call to Stony Man and got through to Kurtzman. "Too late on those coordinates," he said. "Looks like they traded cars and kept on going."

"Figures," Kurtzman said. "Unfortunately, there's been no more action on the phone since we got our last fix."

"Okay. What kind of preparations are they making on the mainland?" Bolan asked.

"Low-key, but thorough. Nothing's leaked yet to the

mainstream media. Word's out along the fringe, but there's a lag in publication for the loopy newsletters. Some rumblings on the web, a few occult and paranormal sites, but nothing that's created any public agitation. Well, besides the various attacks worldwide, of course."

"Still going on?" Bolan asked.

"Two more, so far," Kurtzman replied. "Some kind of chemical-biological warfare agent was released at a cathedral in Caracas. Seven dead, the last I heard, with something like a hundred more exposed. The Center for Disease Control has got people flying down to check it out, hoping it's not ebola or whatever."

"And the other?"

"Lisbon," Kurtzman said. "A screwball with a bag of automatic weapons crashed the installation ceremony for their new archbishop. The Public Security Police acknowledge thirteen dead, but they're still counting."

"Okay, thanks. If you get any action on that phone—"

"You'll be the first to know," Kurtzman said.

"Two more attacks," Bolan told Halloran, when he'd switched off the sat phone. "Lisbon and Caracas."

"I've been wondering if it will end, after we've stopped the Ark from reaching Rome."

Still thinking positively, not suggesting they might fail.

"I couldn't tell you what they're thinking," Bolan said. "It's more your area than mine."

"I understand their hatred of the Church," Halloran said. "But as for calculating what they may do next—"

His cell phone hummed again, cut off whatever Halloran had meant to say. He answered, listened briefly, then clicked off, turning to Bolan with a stark expression on his face.

"There's been another ambush," he reported. "Just ahead of us, in a town called Roccalumera."

"Says who?"

"We have our eyes and ears," Halloran said.

"All right," the Executioner replied. "What are we waiting for?"

CHAPTER NINETEEN

Roccalumera

Another scene of carnage, but they nearly beat the cops this time. One car was on the scene—a blue-and-white Alfa Romeo 159 "Panther"—with two dazed-looking highway patrolmen surveying the battleground. They couldn't keep the rubberneckers back, some of them literally walking through the blood that pooled on concrete and asphalt, already starting to dry in the afternoon's heat.

To Bolan's practiced eye, it seemed the fight had been a brief one, but ferocious. Someone had to have taken out the lead car with a rocket or grenade launcher, since its front end was crumpled with no evidence of a collision, and the rest was a burned-out hulk. Three other cars were shot to hell with automatic fire, the patterns unmistakable, their occupants and drivers either still inside or sprawled where they had gone down fighting in the street. On both sides of the road, stray rounds had shattered windows, scarred the walls of shops and punctured cars that had been parked before the shooting started.

Bolan counted bodies as they passed, came up with twelve and knew he could have missed a couple with the cars and gawkers in his way. The dead all looked like standard-issue mafiosi, but although he'd never seen the Axum crew—wouldn't have known them if they crossed the street in front of him right now, in fact—one thing stuck in his mind.

"No van, and they had to have had one," he said.

"They got away somehow," Halloran agreed. "Despite all this."

"Unless you think the Ark could fit inside one of these cars."

"No, no. According to the measurements from scripture—"

"That's the *real* ark," Bolan interrupted. "We don't know what they might be carrying, in fact."

"It still required a van at Axum," Halloran replied. "I think we must assume that they've escaped."

"No point in loitering around here, then."

"Agreed."

Whoever had arranged the ambush, it had failed—at least, to the extent of hijacking the convoy's cargo. Bolan didn't know if any Keepers had been killed or wounded in the firefight, and it didn't seem to matter if the Ark was rolling on toward Rome. Camorra, Mafia, what difference did it make? Whether his quarry's numbers had been whittled down or not, the team was still in play. Still carrying their so-called mystic weapon toward ground zero at the Vatican.

There had been moments during the pursuit when Bolan thought the whole thing was ridiculous, a waste of time. Assuming that the Ark was mythical, maybe some pseudo-relic fabricated by the church in Axum to increase its own prestige, why shouldn't he stand back and let the final act play out in Rome? There'd be enough Swiss Guards, caribinieri and police on hand to smother any normal threat, with force to spare.

Why not?

Because he couldn't say it was a fake for sure.

Forget about the wrath of God erupting from an ancient wooden chest like something on the SyFy Channel. You could find blueprints for the construction of a suitcase nuke online these days, or purchase deadly toxins with a minimum of difficulty if you managed to acquire—or forge—a research license. Others could be cooked up in a simple lab at home, again, using directions from the internet. Weapons of mass destruction had eluded searchers in Iraq, but they might well be lurking in suburbia.

Or in a van, en route to Rome.

That was the reason Bolan couldn't quit, stand back and treat Custodes Foederis as a pack of harmless loons. Their lone-wolf strikes in recent days had proved the cult's propensity for mayhem against Roman Catholics. He couldn't take for granted that their final grandstand play would be a flop.

Unless the Executioner was there to bring the curtain down.

Messina, Sicily

"WE COULD GET lost here," Franco Arieti said, steering the van through traffic along Via Giuseppe La Farina, toward the waterfront.

"That's the idea," Branca said. "As long as *we* know where we're going, eh?"

"The other car's still with us," Arieti said.

One out of two, that was. The other had been damaged in the second ambush. Only slightly, and it was still operable, but they couldn't risk driving a vehicle with bullet holes around Messina, much less taking it aboard a ferry. Six men occupied the trailing car now, the remainder of their party packed into the van and trying not to touch the Ark, which they'd covered with a mover's blanket.

"It's a miracle that any of us made it," Enzo Vanvitelli chimed in from the rear.

Instead of adding an *amen,* Branca told Arieti, "We must catch the first ferry available. You understand?"

"I understood the first four times you told me," Franco answered.

"Nobody likes backtalk," Branca warned him.

"Excuse me."

"Forget it. We all have a case of the nerves, eh? And still far to go."

Far indeed. Another 450 miles from Villa San Giovanni to Rome, once they had made the ferry crossing from Messina. That included passage through Naples, the heart of Camorra territory, but Branca thought they should be safe enough without a crew of mafiosi in attendance, setting off alarms. In retrospect, he cursed himself for the decision to hire gangland escorts for the Sicilian leg of their journey, but it had seemed like a good idea at the time.

And nearly ruined them when it went bad. Not once, but twice. Perhaps it was a miracle that they had managed to survive.

Well, *most* of them. He still regretted losing Rocco Conte in the first attack, being compelled to personally end his suffering. The other wounded member of their team, Romano Craxi, was more fortunate. The round that pierced his arm hadn't disabled him to any serious degree, though he would have to fight one-handed if they met more enemies along the way.

And that was still a possibility, Branca admitted to himself. Aside from any opposition they might face in Rome, the same pursuers who had dogged their tracks from Africa to Greece might still be following them, momentarily forgotten in the midst of the Sicilian madness.

My mistake, he thought, but not a fatal one.

Not yet.

Branca considered that the *camorristi* might have phoned ahead with a description of their vehicles, posing another threat before they got to Rome, but he would have to deal with that problem when it arose. *If* it arose. Their mission, at its root, was based on faith: in God, in Janus Marcellus and Mania Justina, in the creed of Custodes Foederis. If that faith meant anything, had any basis in reality, there was a point where Branca had to trust his Lord for help with problems that exceeded his own capacity to cope.

And then what? Lightning bolts out of a clear sky, striking down his enemies? It seemed preposterous, but so did much of scripture, to the nonbeliever. If the Lord had truly chosen Branca and his men to save the world, why wouldn't He protect them on the road to Rome? Or would each mile still ahead be yet another test of Branca's faith and fortitude?

If so, he was determined not to fail.

Custodes Foederis Headquarters, Rome

JANUS MARCELLUS WATCHED grim images unfolding on Rai News, updating the reports of bloodshed from the killing grounds of Sicily. He normally wouldn't have spent ten seconds studying the mayhem between rival gangsters, but this violence was a result of his advice—his *order,* if the truth be told—to Claudio Branca.

Granted, he had been advised in turn, by Mania and Ugo Troisi, both Sicilians, that the Mafia could be of service in their time of need. Now, that had nearly blown up in his face, complete disaster foiled only by Branca's quick wits under fire. And Janus Marcellus wondered if the bad advice he'd taken might have been deliberate, a means of undercutting him and his authority, for reasons that he didn't fully understand.

His first report from Marco Gianotti had revealed no solid evidence of treason within the Concilium. But what did that prove? Was he growing paranoid as they approached the Final Days, or was he right to think that something evil and corrupt had taken root beneath his very nose? It wasn't something that he wanted to believe of Mania, or Ugo Troisi, or his other close advisers, but Marcellus knew from history that every prophet had a Judas waiting to betray him.

Sometimes more than one.

From Sicily, the news broadcast jumped to Caracas, then to Prague, where Marcellus had unleashed God's wrath against the Scarlet Whore of Babylon. He wasn't claiming credit for the raids—not yet, at least—but a contact with the Guardia di Finanza had warned him of questions raised and scrutiny directed toward his church. Why not, when he'd been so outspoken in condemning every aspect of the papacy?

In this case, as it happened, the suspicions were correct. But *proving* it would still take time, and that was a commodity his foes didn't possess. It commonly took weeks, or months, to build a case that might succeed in court, but only hours now remained before his soldiers brought the enemy's corrupt house tumbling down in ruins. When the smoke cleared, nothing would remain of his opponents but an ugly, fading memory.

A rapping on his office door distracted Marcellus from his train of thought. "Enter!" he called out, relieved to see that it was Marco Gianotti on his threshold, carrying a briefcase.

"Pontifex," Gianotti said with a quick dip of his head.

"What news from your investigation?"

"Nothing yet, Your Grace."

"Nothing?"

"It's early yet, Your Grace. Traitors don't expose themselves on any certain schedule. Duplicity demands a certain level of discretion, and—"

"You have transcripts for me?"

"Yes, Your Grace." Setting the briefcase on an ornamental table, Gianotti opened it, removed a sheaf of documents and handed them to Janus. "Conversations between Ugo and his aides on the Concilium. Nothing I deemed to be incriminating."

"I shall be the judge of that."

"Of course, Your Grace."

"And you're prepared to act at once, if I find something that you've missed?"

"Yes, sir."

Riffling quickly through the transcripts, barely skimming, Marcellus said, "I don't see anything pertaining to my wife."

"No, sir. I didn't understand your order for surveillance to include the Queen Mother."

"Quite so. But I thought…" Marcellus caught himself, paused, then said, "Never mind. We're close now, Marco. I can feel it."

"As do I, Your Grace."

Their eyes met for a moment. There was nothing there except devotion and obedience, as far as Marcellus could discover. Could he be mistaken, even now?

No, surely not.

"We'll speak again when you have something more for me," he said. "Leave these with me for now."

A final bow from Gianotti as he left, and Marcellus sat at his desk, the transcripts stacked before him. He would read each one in turn, dissecting them until he found his Judas hiding there, perhaps between the printed lines.

And when he knew the traitor's name, his vengeance would be merciless.

Messina Toll Barrier, Autostrada A18

BOLAN WAS READY for trouble as they rolled up to Toll Gate 1 on the southern outskirts of Messina. Any soldier—or dedicated filmgoer, for that matter—could tell you that highway toll gates and construction sites made ideal ambush points, with traffic bottlenecked and slowed down to a crawl. And if police had laid the trap, it made things even worse, since Bolan's vow prevented him from fighting back.

It hadn't come to that, so far, but he'd wondered more than once how it would feel. Facing a wall of guns intent on killing him, with no intention of resisting. Would he act in self-defense, reflexively, before he even recognized his killers as police? If they were plainclothes officers who didn't bother to announce themselves, how would he even know?

The question wasn't tested this time, as the jowly, middle-aged attendant in the toll booth palmed Halloran's money and muttered, *"Buongiorno"* with something less than conviction. They passed through the gate, mounted cameras tracking their progress, but no one attempted to stop them.

The A18 split off at that point, becoming the A20, looping westward toward Palermo. They continued on a new branch of the E45/E90, locally named Via Giuseppe La Farina, passing through Messina's southern suburbs, making their way toward downtown and the waterfront beyond. To their right lay railroad tracks and industrial wasteland, beyond that the sparkling blue Strait of Messina. To their left and dead ahead, the city was unfolding for them, welcoming two unexpected visitors as it had welcomed countless others in times past.

Messina, Bolan knew from high school history, had seen its share of battles, from the Punic Wars of Rome and Carthage through Spanish invasion, civil war that liberated and united Italy, on through the Second World War. It had been shelled and bombed, demolished by successive earthquakes and ravaged by plagues. Always, it survived and rose again, celebrating its endurance through construction of elaborate cathedrals, fountains, botanical gardens and other landmarks that drew tourists from around the globe.

Bolan wasn't a tourist, but he recognized both the beauty of his surroundings and the irony of his circumstances. Traveling incessantly, he'd seen the world and then some, but he had to stop and think about it to recall a time when he'd gone anywhere for pleasure, to relax, simply take in the local sights. How many years ago had that been? During some high school vacation? On a fleeting hitch of R & R between campaigns? Messina had his full attention now, but as a warrior, not an idle traveler on vacation.

Halloran broke the silence as they were crossing Via Santa Cecilia, northbound, swept along by humming traffic. "The ferries we want dock along Piazzale Don Blasco," he said. "From there, they sail to Villa San Giovanni in Reggio Calabria."

"We may still be in time," Bolan said, but he wasn't hopeful. Thousands of passengers and hundreds of vehicles rode those ferries each day, back and forth. So far, he knew only that they were looking for a van, and perhaps one or more escort cars, occupied by men they'd never seen or even heard described. All armed, of course, and ready for a fight if they were challenged on the crowded docks, or even on the ship at sea.

Piazzale Don Blasco, Messina

FERRIES DEPARTED FROM Messina to Villa San Giovanni every twenty minutes, on average, between 12:30 a.m. and 10:30 p.m. Overnight, the gap between sailings extended to forty minutes. Those schedules precluded any serious screening of passengers or vehicles as they boarded the large ships, and since Sicily was an autonomous region of Italy, no customs searches were conducted without warrants or probable cause to suspect contraband in transit.

Waiting to board was the hardest part for Claudio Branca. He had brought the Ark this far, all the way from East Africa, and now only a twenty-minute ferry ride stood between him and the Italian mainland. Granted, a long drive still remained from Villa San Giovanni northward, to Rome and Branca's final destiny, but the Strait of Messina was fixed in mind as his personal Rubicon.

The point of no return.

Sitting in line, boxed in by other vehicles around him that would block escape if anything went wrong, made Branca nervous. An ambush here, by the police or *camorristi,* would be fatal, since he couldn't leave the Ark or carry it away by hand. It would mean fighting to the death, unless...

He wondered what would happen if he crawled back to the van's cargo compartment, stripped the gray tarpaulin from the Ark and battered through the wooden case surrounding it. Would he be stricken dead for blasphemy, or would the blinding light of God's pure wrath surround him, reaching out to smite his enemies before they had a chance to harm him?

And if so…what then?

Branca could hardly picture driving all the way from Reggio Calabria to Rome with a divine light beaming through the windows of his van. The mental image was bizarre; it nearly made him laugh out loud. He wondered—not for the first time—if it mattered *where* the power was unleashed, and once again decided that the best bet was to reach his primary intended target. Strike directly at the heart of the corruption he was striving to obliterate.

A fisherman could tell you that, to defeat an octopus, you crushed the nerve center between its eyes and thus rendered its grasping suckers impotent. Without the death-blow, each separate tentacle was deadly in its own right.

Branca had no reason to believe the Scarlet Whore of Babylon would wither overnight after the Vatican was razed. The Book of Revelation promised tribulation and famine, with battles between great massed armies. Victory was promised to the righteous, but not without losses. Scripture painted the battlegrounds in graphic terms, complete with carrion birds gorged to bursting on ripe human flesh.

Hell on earth, for a while, before paradise reigned.

"They're moving, up ahead," Arieti said, drumming nervous fingers on the steering wheel.

And so they were. Once movement had begun, the line advanced more quickly than Branca expected, with ferry attendants directing each vehicle in turn to its assigned parking place, while dull recorded voices gave directions to the upper decks and snack bars. Twenty minutes barely gave them time to go upstairs and come back down, but there were toilets on the ferry that would save them stopping later on.

Two men remained below while Branca and the rest went off to find the lavatories. They would all be back and seated, ready to depart, before the ferry docked, prepared for trouble on arrival if it found them, quick to hit the A3 north to Naples if their way was clear.

The final lap, to victory or death.

TWO FERRIES, FROM different lines, were pulling away from their docks at Piazzale Don Blasco when Halloran steered the Alfa Romeo Giulietta into the large waterfront parking lot. Bolan tried counting vans waiting to board the next ships out, but gave up when he passed two dozen.

Impossible. Without authority, they couldn't possibly check all the vans in sight before another ferry sailed, and if they tried it as a pair of armed civilians, they'd incite a panic at the very least. To make things worse, another blue-and-white Alfa Romeo with Polizia emblazoned on its side in matching two-tone paint sat near the ramp, well beyond the boarding traffic's flow.

"It's too much," Halloran declared, sounding defeated for the first time since Bolan had met him. "They could be right here and we would never know it."

"Someone else might," the soldier said, and raised his sat phone, pressed a button to connect with Stony Man and waited for the hookup half a world away.

Two rings, preliminary clearance through the farm's secure switchboard and Kurtzman said, "Striker, your timing's eerie."

"Tell me."

"There's a call going, scrambled, to the same number in Rome. It looks like… Damn! They just broke off again."

"It looks like what?" Bolan asked.

"They're still moving, and the GPS puts them…halfway across the Strait of Messina, bound for the mainland. Looks like they're traveling due east, which makes their destination…Villa San Giovanni."

"Thanks. I've got a boat to catch," Bolan replied, and cut the link.

"They've sailed," Halloran said, not asking.

"It doesn't mean we've lost them," Bolan replied. "In fact, we're closer to them than we have been since we started."

"You're an optimist."

"And you're the guy with faith. So break it down," Bolan told him.

"Do you know where they'll be landing?"

Bolan gave the city's name.

"Of course," Halloran said. "The shortest route by sea. Also, the boat to Naples travels only once a week and takes eight hours. They'll shave at least two hours off that time on the autostrada, at eighty miles per hour."

"Meaning we can catch them," Bolan answered.

"We can try." Halloran steered their vehicle into line for boarding on the next boat out.

It would be close, in terms of timing and the ferry's maximum capacity, another twenty minutes lag time if they missed the first departure. Bolan glanced at Halloran and thought he might be offering another silent prayer.

For what? Help getting on the ferry? Taking out the Keepers and the Ark? If God existed, would He welcome prayers for aid in pulling off a more efficient homicide?

It wasn't Bolan's problem, and he left the cleric to it. At this point, he thought anything that soothed Halloran's nerves could only help when push came to shove. They'd been through the preliminary rounds, survived them all so far, and with a little luck—or maybe with a helping hand from Providence—their next engagement would turn out to be the title match. Winner take all.

CHAPTER TWENTY

Villa San Giovanni, Italy

The ferry was on time, another minor miracle, but waiting for the vehicles ahead of him to disembark did nothing to improve Claudio Branca's frame of mind. He'd spoken to Ugo Troisi in transit, reporting his progress and receiving Dextera Dei's personal assurance that all was prepared for their triumph in Rome. To Branca, that just meant that Troisi and the rest were standing by, waiting for him and his surviving troops to do the work, but what else could a soldier in the field expect?

He had the secret weapon, after all. Janus Marcellus, Mania Justina and the rest could do no more than pray for his success. The Scarlet Whore of Babylon, meanwhile, would likely be preparing her defenses, calling on the full machinery of a corrupted state for aid.

All wasted effort.

Who could stand before the mighty wrath of God Himself?

But getting there was still a problem, even with Troisi's blithe assurance that the way was clear. When pressed, Troisi knew nothing of the hunters who'd been dogging Branca's tracks from Africa, through Turkey, Greece and Sicily. He couldn't say if they'd been caught up in the fighting between the Camorra and the Mafia, but hoped some news would be forthcoming from a contact with the police. Until then, anything was possible.

The line was moving now, disgorging cars, vans, trucks and pedestrians onto the docks, where others waited to reverse the process. Branca watched out for police, saw two cars waiting, but the officers inside them all looked bored and half-asleep. Nothing out of the ordinary there.

"Follow the signs to Naples," he told Arieti needlessly. "And make sure that the other car's behind us."

"Okay, okay." Franco sounded slightly irritated, but too professional and dedicated to protest at being treated like a simpleton.

"Sorry," Branca said. "I know we've covered all this."

"No problem," Arieti answered. "Better to be safe than sorry, eh?"

And they were friends again, comrades in arms. Keeping their weapons close at hand as they rolled off the ferry, with the backup car trailing behind them, every man alert to any hint of danger. The police ignored them, watching out for girls in skimpy clothing or for nervous-looking hikers who might have a kilo of marijuana or something stronger in their backpacks.

After he'd dismissed the police, Branca watched for mobsters. It was possible the problems they'd encountered on Sicilian soil might trail them here, the Mafia expecting higher pay to compensate for losses it had suffered, or the Camorra trying one more time to snatch whatever contraband they thought might be inside the van. Branca didn't believe they'd jump his party here, in such a crowded public place, but stranger things had happened.

As it was, they cleared the ferry and the waterfront without incident. Large overhead signs directed them to the Autostrada A3. They'd travel to downtown Naples, then transfer to the A1, at which point about a hundred thirty miles would remain until Rome. Two gasoline stops along the way, at most, and if they kept the pedal down, the last leg of their odyssey should last another six or seven hours, maximum.

How many men could time the hour of their death or triumph so precisely?

Branca was satisfied, in either case, to know that he had done his best for God and for Custodes Foederis. His reward would be assured, whatever happened at the Vatican, but it still pained him to imagine that the whole thing might have been in vain.

Crossing the Strait of Messina

THE SOLEMN VOICE of Cardinal Luis Bouchet greeted Brother Halloran without preamble or enthusiasm. "Have you a report to make, Brother?" he asked.

"I have, Prefect."

"Does it concern the recent incidents in Sicily?"

"It does, in part."

"You've failed to stop the Ark, I take it?" Bouchet asked.

"For the moment. Yes, sir."

"For the moment?" There was just a hint of mockery in the voice. "Is there some prospect for improving your performance, Brother?"

"We are closer, Prefect. Crossing as we speak to Villa San Giovanni in—"

"Reggio Calabria," the prefect interrupted. "Yes. I am acquainted with the territory. And the object of your quest?"

"Crossed just ahead of us. We were delayed by the... unpleasantness."

"Another, what? Two dozen dead by now?"

"None of the latest were our doing, Prefect. As you may have gleaned from media reports, there is a feud between the Mafia and the Camorra. It appears that mafiosi were engaged as escorts for the Ark, and—"

"The cardinal bishop is concerned by your alliance with the stranger. *Unapproved* alliance, as I was compelled to tell him."

"And did you explain the circumstances, Prefect?"

"To the best of my ability, but he wasn't consoled. You understand the risk it poses to the Church, Brother? We take great care to keep the inner workings of the CDF from prying eyes."

"I understand, sir. But—"

"And now we have been compromised. *Imperiled,* I believe, was the cardinal bishop's word."

"I don't believe that Matthew Cooper would—"

"What? Report in full to his superiors? You've already described him as professional. That indicates responsibility and discipline. Or should, ideally."

Halloran absorbed the jab. Replied, "I was about to say, Prefect, that I don't believe he would do anything to harm the CDF, much less the Church."

"His knowledge of us is, by definition, harmful. His report of what's occurred may lead to scrutiny of us, our operations and our influence on various events. That is, *if* he reports."

Halloran caught the tone, said nothing, and waited for the rest of it.

"Of course," the prefect said, "if some unfortunate event befalls him in the meantime, there's at least a possibility that we may not be drawn into the circus that is bound to follow."

"I imagine he's already mentioned me to his superiors, Prefect."

"No doubt. But you might be relocated. Sequestered. Finding one brother out of thousands, when the Vatican doesn't desire him to be found, could prove impossible. Remove the witness and there is no case."

"You want me to eliminate him, Prefect?"

"I've given no such order, and I never would. We all trust you to use your own best judgment, Brother. On a perilous assignment such as this, where your companion has assumed the risk, no one could blame you if he fell along the way."

"And would I be absolved, Your Eminence?"

"For what, Brother?"

"I understand."

"You have our every confidence," Bouchet said. And then the line went dead.

Halloran looked around the ferry's deck and found Cooper at the rail, eyeing the mainland as they closed the gap. Villa San Giovanni lay before them, home to fourteen thousand year-round residents who made their living chiefly from the tourist trade or from the sea. They would regard incoming tourists with the same disdain as citizens of any other busy seaport in the world, masked with a smile to keep the euros flowing through their hands.

Cooper saw him, nodded and began the trek back to their car, belowdecks. Halloran fell into step beside him, wondering if he possessed the skill and nerve required to kill this man.

And whether it would damn his soul to hell.

Washington, D.C.

"I'LL HAVE TO call you back," Brognola told Kurtzman. "I've got a sat phone call incoming."

Switching one phone for another, he picked up before

the second buzzing tone had cycled through, and said, "Brognola here."

"Heads up," the deep, familiar voice replied. "We missed them on the island, so we're going for another ferry ride."

"I got that from the Farm, just now," Brognola said. "Cutting it close."

"We've still got time," Bolan replied.

"Sounds like you mixed it up with the brotherhoods at their busy time of year."

"None of the mess back there was ours," Bolan said. "Call it Family dysfunction."

"Any more of that ahead, you think?" Brognola asked.

"I gave up fortune-telling," Bolan answered, "but I hope they're smart enough to let it go."

"Well, hope in one hand…"

"Right. I hear you. But it's all we've got right now."

"If you want me to, I'll call a guy I know who works with the Financial Guard. See if he can distract them for a day or so, stir up the pot and cramp their action."

"Couldn't hurt," Bolan replied, "unless it puts you too far in the hole on favors."

"I don't know if anybody's keeping score these days," Brognola lied.

Bolan let that one go and said, "It wouldn't be a bad idea to have somebody on alert in Rome."

"No problem there. They've kept it quiet, on the Ark deal, but the other incidents are splashed all over TV and the papers. No one's taking any chances at the Vatican."

"Okay. Just thought I'd mention it, you know. In case."

"Your sidekick holding up all right?"

"Seems like," Bolan replied. "He's praying overtime."

"Whatever gets you though."

Brognola had been raised a Catholic, in a traditional

Italian-American home, and he still believed in something, at some level, after all the horrors life had shown him—or, perhaps, because of them. He rarely thought about it, and if asked wouldn't have said it helped him do his job, but if it comforted another soldier on the line or helped a dying man cross over...well, he couldn't see the harm.

As for the scandals, frauds and sexual abuse, the so-called ministers who lived in splendor like medieval kings, he'd always thought that if there *was* a hell, its lowest, hottest pits were reserved for those who preyed on others in the name of faith.

And dimwits texting while they drove.

"Looks like we're docking," Bolan said. "I'll keep you posted."

"If there's anything you need..."

"I've got your number. Later."

He was gone, just like that, and Brognola replaced the sat phone in its cradle on his desk. Leaned back in his swivel chair and wished that he could be there with the warrior, give his desk the slip for once and work it old-school, as he'd done when he and Bolan met. That was another time, of course; another war.

But in his mind and heart, their enemies were much the same.

Brognola called back to the Farm, got Kurtzman on the line again. "You're staying on that phone, right?" he demanded.

"When they use it," Kurtzman said. "They're not big into chatting on the road."

"Okay. But keep me in the loop, regardless of the time. I'll be here, at the office."

Pulling a double shift and eating out of paper bags. Why not?

When Bolan's life and so much more was riding on the line, it seemed the least he could do.

Custodes Foederis Headquarters, Rome

"THEY'VE REACHED THE mainland," Janus Marcellus said. "It won't be long now."

If it works, Ugo Troisi thought, immediately troubled by his lapse in faith. Aloud, he said, "We'll be victorious, Your Grace."

"What are your plans for paradise?" Marcellus asked.

"Plans, Your Grace?"

He'd thought about it, certainly. Pictured the earth made fresh and new by God's own hand, with no end of rewards for those who persevered. But plans? Who planned a day in heaven, much less all eternity?

"I plan to be sitting at the right hand of our Lord as he completes the judgment," Janus said, apparently with total confidence. "I'm sure He would agree I've earned the place, for helping him depose the Scarlet Whore."

Troisi smiled and nodded, knew he should agree wholeheartedly. Why was he having difficulty with the basic tenets of their doctrine now, when victory was almost there, within his grasp? Why did the man he'd followed through travails and persecution to achieve this moment sound almost…deranged?

Forgive me, Father!

It had to be Marco Gianotti's scheming that was twisting him inside, Troisi decided. This rank suspicion and dissension came at the worst of all possible times, detracting from what ought to be a day of joyous celebration. Premature, perhaps, until the Ark arrived in Rome and did its awesome work.

"A fair reward indeed, Your Grace," he managed to reply, nearly choking in the process.

Marcellus frowned thoughtfully—or was it something more? "I wish that everyone agreed with you, my son. Mania, I'm afraid…well, she may doubt me."

Troisi felt himself begin to blink at that, but interrupted the reflexive action. This could be some kind of test. If Gianotti had discovered something with his snooping and eavesdropping, Marcellus might have thought it best to bait a trap.

"Your Grace," Troisi ventured, hoping that he hadn't stalled too long, "I don't know what to say."

"Imagine how *I* feel," Marcellus replied. "We've traveled all this way together, risked and built so much, only to find… But never mind. Perhaps it's all a figment of my own imagination, eh?"

How far could Troisi press the matter, seeking information to protect himself?

"If I knew what you meant, Your Grace, it's possible I could advise you."

Marcellus frowned, considering how much to share. "We've both been so immersed in our crusade, our duties," he replied. "It's only natural that we should feel a certain…separation. Don't you think so?"

Troisi nodded, hoping that he didn't seem too eager to agree. "Even predictable, Your Grace. When all this is behind you, and the victory attained, I dare say the reunion of your spirits will be all the sweeter." He thought even as he spoke, of lying nude beside Mania Justina in her bed.

"I hope so," Marcellus said. "If I believed that anyone had tried to steal her from me, much less someone I had trusted as a brother in the covenant, you can imagine my reaction."

Yes, I can, Troisi thought. Keeping in mind a certain

member of the inner circle who'd been caught embezzling funds. He'd lingered on the brink of death, praying for mercy, over three full days and nights.

"Your Grace," Troisi said, "if such a Judas did exist, I'd strike him down on your behalf."

Now Marcellus smiled. "Thank you, my son," he said. "I'll keep your offer foremost in my mind."

Villa San Giovanni

HALLORAN INSISTED HE was good to drive another lap after the ferry ride, so Bolan took the Giulietta's shotgun seat again. He didn't need to navigate, leaving the docks, as even a myopic driver could have seen the large blue sign directing them to Napoli via the A3 Motorway. He translated kilometers to miles and settled back to watch the countryside unfold, no end of cities, towns and villages to pass before they reached mainland Italy's third-largest city.

"You think your friend can help us?" Halloran inquired. "Distract the Mafia, I mean?"

"Could be," Bolan replied. "But if I had to guess, I'd say they've lost enough already on a babysitting job. If they're inclined toward payback, I'd expect them to go after the Camorra."

"I admit, it's not my area of expertise," Halloran said.

"Real experts on the Mob will tell you that they're unpredictable, to some extent. All that talk about their honor and the rest of it is mostly nineteenth century," Bolan explained. "They trot it out to justify their actions or enhance their own mystique, but when the chips are down, they're just like any other weasels in a corner. They'll bite you if they can, or cut and run for cover if you give them half a chance."

"And the Camorra?"

"Older, deeper roots," Bolan replied, "but it's the same game with another name."

"You know them well?"

"Too well."

"And understand the feud mentality," Halloran said.

"Old stories for another time," Bolan allowed. "Assuming that there is one."

The A3's posted speed was 130 kilometers per hour, translating to 81 mph. Six hours on a straight shot up to Rome, but there'd be at least two stops for fuel, with the Giulietta guzzling gas en route, and they'd be forced to slow down through various settlements along the way, keeping a sharp eye out for the highway patrol if Halloran tried making up time on the open stretches. Traffic enforcement didn't seem to be a high priority in Italy, but any close encounter with police could end their game before the final hand was dealt.

And if they overtook the convoy carrying the Ark... then what?

It would depend upon the circumstances, Bolan knew. He wouldn't start a firefight in the middle of a populated area unless the Keepers left him no alternative. A lonely rural highway suited him the best, but crazy zealots might desire an audience, at least, if they were intercepted short of Rome. In that case, Bolan was prepared to do whatever might be necessary to resolve the issue, minimizing collateral damage, while keeping the action out of downtown Rome.

In fact, there might be no desirable alternatives. But one thing was already settled in his mind. No matter how the game played out, there'd be more blood.

And if he went down in the fight, he wouldn't be alone.

Gioia Tauro, Italy

AFTER MOUNTAIN ROADS and ferry rides, driving on the A3 almost felt like flying. It ran beside the Tyrrhenian Sea, with Gioia Tauro the latest town in line on Claudio Branca's race up the coast toward Naples. He knew the community was an important seaport, with docks extending some five thousand yards out to sea, and that 'Ndrangheta mobsters controlled local shipping, importing eighty percent of Europe's cocaine through Gioia Tauro, together with thousands of illegal arms. None of that concerned Branca in the least.

After he had unveiled the Ark in Rome and triggered the Apocalypse, all such corruption would be swept away forever.

In the interim, however, he was watching for police, gangsters and any other obstacle that might prevent him from delivering his holy payload to the Vatican. Their speed wasn't a problem, holding to a steady eighty-five miles per hour on the Autostrada's open stretches, slowing as required to pass through towns and villages without incident. Branca supposed a van trailing a lone sedan was easier to overlook than three vehicles, much less six.

He saw the folly now of their Sicilian convoy and soliciting assistance from the Mafia. What seemed to be a good idea had very nearly killed them all, and might have put a vengeful *camorristi* hunting party on their trail. They likely could have passed as tourists on a holiday or bound for some convention, shrugged off by the peasants on their route, but he had listened to Ugo Troisi, self-styled expert in such things, and made the arrangement without consulting Janus Marcellus.

Ugo Troisi.

He was Sicilian himself, Branca knew—and what, if

anything, did that suggest? Could he be a Mafia plant inside Custodes Foederis? If so, to what end? Mafiosi were nominal Catholics, and yet…

A sudden thought struck Branca like a rabbit punch. It sickened and revolted him, but he couldn't escape it. What if Troisi was a secret servant of the Scarlet Whore, who'd used his Mafia connections in an ultimately vain attempt to keep the Ark from reaching Rome? His "help" had almost doomed their mission, and in hindsight, that could hardly be coincidence.

Or could it?

Branca had the sat phone in his hand, and sat there clutching it, watching the port of Gioia Tauro slip away while he considered what to do. Someone had to be alerted if there was a traitor in the church's inner circle, but his normal contact *was* the very traitor he suspected. Neither could he speak directly to the Pontifex. One reason: Marcellus had an iron-clad rule that comments and complaints had to pass through channels, following the chain of command, with only the most serious reserved for his ears. And the second: Troisi was a longtime friend and confidant of Marcellus, who might well persuade the Pontifex that Branca was insane.

What then?

The only person he could think of who might help him was the sect's chief of security. Branca had spoken to him only once or twice—barely knew him, really—but if he could reach the man, explain his fear coherently, and press the urgent need for an investigation…

Would it help at all? Or had the stress of his assignment finally unhinged his mind?

No, there was something out of place, and Branca knew the problem didn't stem entirely from his own imagination. Scowling at the sat phone in his hand, he pressed the speed-dial button to connect with headquarters in Rome—almost a local call, this day—and waited for the switchboard operator to respond. When he'd identified himself, she said, "I'll put you through to the Dextera Dei, sir."

"Not this time," Branca said, stopping her short. "I need to speak with Marco Gianotti, please."

CHAPTER TWENTY-ONE

Castellammare di Stabia, Italy

Mack Bolan was encouraged by their progress so far. Already within the Province of Naples, closing rapidly on that teeming metropolis of three million souls, he hoped they might overtake the Ark well short of Rome. The latest sat phone bulletin from Stony Man confirmed their target still remained ahead of them, but they had closed the gap, their Giulietta's speed eclipsing that of a larger, slower cargo van.

How close? According to Kurtzman, about fifty miles and change.

Good news, when they had started out so far behind, but it wasn't a guarantee of victory by any means. That came only after the last shots had been fired.

And history was written by the designated winners.

This close to their quarry, it was time to eyeball every van they passed along the A3 Motorway, particularly those that seemed to have an escort standing watch and running interference. There would be no further warnings from Virginia if the Keepers managed to refrain from talking on the sat phone Stony Man had marked and registered. It would come down to instinct and experience, maybe something as simple as a passing glance before battle was joined.

Within a few short seconds, between recognition and engagement, it would all come down to life or death.

Bolan had done all that he could to be prepared. His guns were locked and loaded, each one with a live round in the chamber and a full fresh magazine. He had removed the sound suppressors from his Uzi and Beretta, since stealth was superfluous in a running firefight, while suppressors reduced muzzle velocity along with noise. If shooting at vehicles in motion, Bolan wanted all the penetration he could get.

"You have a plan for stopping them?" Halloran asked, as if in tune with Bolan's thoughts.

"Identify, engage, eradicate," he replied. "The usual."

"You make it sound so…simple."

"Hardly. Figure on at least one escort vehicle, and maybe two. They'll try to block us, run or gun us off the road, whatever. I don't see us getting through it without taking hits."

"Of course. We must hold nothing back."

"You're good to keep the wheel?" Bolan asked.

"Certainly. If only one of us can shoot, it should be you."

"Take any shot you can when the time comes. But whatever else you do, we need to keep the rubber on the road."

Halloran nodded. "Yes. We can't afford to let them get away."

"Don't think defeat," Bolan advised. "Focus on winning, but be ready if we have to improvise."

"In what way, improvise?"

"I'm giving that some thought," he replied.

Worst-case scenario, aside from being killed outright, would be losing the Giulietta while their quarry pulled away. He knew that it could happen in a heartbeat, with a single well-placed bullet to the engine or a tire—and then what would they do? Flag down the first civilian who drove past and steal the car? Maybe. But if they didn't snag one soon enough, or if the new car was a clunker, they were bound to lose the race.

Unless…

Turning to Halloran, Bolan inquired, "Do you know anyone in Naples?"

Custodes Foederis Headquarters, Rome

MARCO GIANOTTI FELT as if his head was spinning as he paced an agitated circuit from his desk to his office door and back again. The call he'd just received from Naples had taken him off guard and left him feeling lost amid the intrigue that pervaded the Sedem Illustratio.

His dalliance with Mania Justina had been risky, but a calculated risk. The threat to Gianotti had increased exponentially when Janus Marcellus ordered surveillance on Ugo Troisi and his fellow Concilium members. Now, he had Claudio Branca interrupting transport of the Holy Ark to Rome with a warning that Troisi might be a traitor. A servant of the Scarlet Whore, no less.

Based on what? A suggestion that Branca's team hire mafiosi as their escorts for the run through Sicily. A plan that had backfired with nearly disastrous results for Branca and the church's master plan. Except that Branca now believed the scheme—Troisi's plan—was *meant* to backfire from the moment it had been conceived. An act of sabotage, no less, which could have doomed the mission and the church itself.

Was Branca right? Or had the pressures of his critical assignment sewn the seeds of paranoia, blooming now into delusion? Was there some correlation between Marcellus's suspicion of Troisi and ambushes in Sicily? And if so, was Troisi somehow linked to the *other* attacks that had wiped out Custodes Foederis temples in Africa, Turkey and Greece?

It seemed impossible, but Gianotti was accustomed to thinking in conspiratorial terms. His mortal enemy, the Scarlet Whore of Babylon, circled the globe with grasping tentacles of greed, corruption and unpardonable sin. Was anything beyond the realm of possibility, where agents of the Holy See applied themselves?

The question now, if he accepted Branca's theory, was what he ought to do about it. His surveillance of Troisi, brief as it had been—and limited, to spare Mania—had revealed no contact with the Mafia or the Camorra. That wasn't surprising, in itself, but without proof he couldn't lay a case before the Pontifex for Troisi being taken into custody. Without some kind of evidence, his hands were tied.

Of course, proof could be fabricated. He could rig the phone logs to reflect a conversation between Troisi and some unknown party in Palermo, maybe Corleone. A written transcript could be ready in an hour, though he'd have no audio recording to support it. Mocking up a tape that would convince the Pontifex might well take days, and Gianotti didn't have that kind of time to spare.

Not with the Ark swiftly approaching Rome.

Mania could have helped him, vouching for a conversation with Troisi that exposed his plans, but acting out that part meant she would have to sacrifice herself, baring the details of her sexual exploits with Troisi. Fear of punishment by Marcellus could explain her tardiness in warning him about Troisi's perfidy, but even if she sold the story, it would leave her own neck on the chopping block.

And facing death, she might as well take Gianotti down, for prompting her to lie in the first place.

No good.

One final option came to mind, but it was also perilous. If Gianotti swallowed Branca's story—still an *if*—he could eliminate Troisi personally, stage the scene and claim that the man had attacked him in a rage upon discovering his movements had been shadowed. It was thin, but Gianotti's voice would be the only one remaining to be heard, Troisi in no position to defend himself. If he was dead, with certain evidence concocted in advance, the story just might fly.

But if he planned to take that leap, then Gianotti had no time to lose.

Torre del Greco, Italy

CLAUDIO BRANCA HEARD and felt the tire blow, ducking for the Spectre M-4 submachine gun in its bag between his feet before he recognized the blowout as a highway mishap, rather than the onset of another ambush. Franco Arieti, at the wheel, let out a growl in lieu of cursing and steered the tilting, rumbling van toward the motorway's shoulder.

"Do we have a jack and spare?" someone inquired hesitantly from the rear compartment.

"Look and see," Branca commanded. "And be careful with the Ark."

He shouldn't have to warn them at this point. Excessive caution should be second nature.

"Spare's bolted underneath on vans like this," another of his soldiers said. "Next to the axle."

And they'd still require a jack to change it, if the spare was in its proper place, hadn't been damaged or allowed to simply lose air over time. And time was Branca's problem. They were losing too much of it with this damned delay. Perhaps the hand of Satan reaching out to ruin everything?

Don't think that way! he admonished himself.

How many tires blew out each day, around the world? A million? More? Branca couldn't match strength or wits with Lucifer. He had to deal with earthly problems as they came, remain true to his mission and press on.

"I found the jack!" one of his men called out, to brief applause.

The van was parked now, with the escort car behind it on the berm, more traffic flowing past. The vehicles together were conspicuous, Branca decided. Coupled with his hard-faced soldiers, they might draw attention from police if any passed. He stepped out of the van and walked back to the idling four-door. Elio Fontana saw him coming, powered down the driver's window and sat waiting for instructions.

"We'll need some time here," Branca said. "Ten minutes, minimum, and likely more. Instead of sitting here, drive on to Napoli. It's only nine kilometers. Before the A1 junction, turn around and come back here to join us, eh? We should be done by then."

"You're sure?" Fontana asked.

"Better to break this up and keep the police away," Branca replied.

"Okay. See you soon," Fontana said, putting the car in gear. Branca stepped back and watched it leave before returning to the van.

"How long?" he asked Michele Sansovino, who was just assembling the complicated jack.

"Not long."

"I asked *how* long?"

"Fifteen or twenty minutes, I suppose."

"Make it fifteen," Branca commanded, feeling slightly foolish even as he spoke the words. And feeling troubled, too, as if his time was running out. Sand through an hour-glass.

He eyed his other soldiers, standing idly on the side-lines, watching Sansovino and Gian Verdone doing the work. "Don't be conspicuous," he told them. "Go and sit behind the van, eh? Out of sight until we're ready."

They obeyed, while Branca stayed behind to supervise, as if his glaring helped. At intervals, he turned to eye the northbound traffic moving toward him, worried by a grim sense of impending dread he couldn't shake.

When Sansovino said, "It's done," and started break-ing down the jack, Branca discovered that his shirt was damp with sweat in spite of a refreshing breeze along the motorway.

Cold sweat. A sign of fear.

Ercolano, Italy

LOCATED AT THE western foot of Mount Vesuvius, beside the Bay of Naples and southeast of Napoli itself, Ercolano stood atop volcanic rubble from the great eruption that had destroyed its predecessor, Herculaneum. Aside from serving tourists, its inhabitants make leather goods, some glassware and a wine called Lacryma Christi—"Tears of Christ."

Bolan knew all this because his driver-cum-tour guide had briefed him. Advancing to an anecdote of the Vesu-vian eruption, Halloran stopped dead and blurted, "There! A van and car together. Aren't they? Could it be?"

"We'll need to pass and take a look," Bolan replied.

Italian drivers, like Americans, drove on the right. That placed him on the near side of the Giulietta toward his tar-gets—or *potential* targets—as the brother pulled out to pass. Six miles or less outside of Naples. Could the Ark be tucked away inside that van? And if so, how well was it guarded? If the four-door sedan riding close behind it was an escort, had they already been spotted and identified as dangerous?

Only one way to find out.

They overtook the trailing car, a Volvo S80 sedan jampacked with six passengers in what looked like an awkward arrangement. All men, Bolan saw, as they pulled abreast, at least three of them turning to meet his gaze. The others might be watching him as well, but with the tinted windows Bolan couldn't say.

"A little farther," he instructed, as they caught up with the van. It was a Fiat Doblò, silver-gray, a standard cargo van, its windows blacked out on the sides to mask whoever or whatever lay within. In the wing mirror its driver saw their Giulietta closing up the distance, and treated Bolan to a scowl as they pulled level.

A heartbeat to decide, and the soldier said, "It's them."

He reached down for the AKMS resting at his feet, and later thought that movement may have saved his life. A bullet from the Volvo drilled the Giulietta's hatchback window, cracked through space where Bolan's head had been an instant earlier, and spiderwebbed the windshield as it exited.

Halloran hit the brakes and swerved, just as a burst of automatic fire ripped through the Giulietta's left-rear quarter panel, sending bullets rattling around inside the rear cargo compartment. Bolan heard the gunfire now, echoes of shots coming behind the impact of the slugs striking their car, and lifted his Kalashnikov while elbowing the button that would take his window down.

The Giulietta's swerve and sudden slowdown let the Fiat Doblò van roll out of range and brought the Volvo into frame. Firing left-handed, Bolan marched a burst of

7.62 mm rounds across the four-door's windshield, but the angle was wrong for taking the front-seat gunners. Bolan saw them ducking, shouting, as the safety glass blew inward, mostly landing in their laps, and then the Volvo nosed down, tires squealing as its driver mashed his brake pedal to the floor.

Antilock brakes kept the vehicle from spinning or rolling, but Bolan lost his chance to finish it as Halloran accelerated, following the van. "We have to stop the Ark!" he said, bent forward in the driver's seat as if the angle of his body could persuade the Giulietta to produce another six or seven miles per hour from its racing engine.

He was right. The van was more important—critical, in fact. If they could stop it here, for good, whatever happened next would almost be superfluous.

Bolan was leaning out his window, angling for a clear shot with the AKMS, when a bullet struck the rifle's foregrip with explosive force and sent the weapon spinning from his hands.

HALLORAN HEARD COOPER curse, the first time he had used profanity, and saw him reel back through the open window empty-handed.

"What?" he asked. "You're wounded?"

"Lost the AK," Bolan replied, and came up with his Uzi from the duffel at his feet. "Hold as steady as you can."

More firing then, with Cooper swiveled in his seat to rake the Volvo as it bore down on them, weapons blasting from its open windows. Halloran yearned to engage the enemy, swallowed an urge to crane around and grab his submachine gun from the floor behind the driver's seat. He had to keep the Giulietta on the road and running close behind the Fiat Doblò van until they stopped it, disregarding any danger from the escort vehicle.

Or else die trying.

He was looking for police cars when a bullet clipped his rearview mirror and kept going through the Alfa's windshield, one more near-miss that could either be the hand of providence at work or pure dumb luck. Focused on driving to the exclusion of all else, he didn't have the wherewithal to offer up even the shortest prayer, but keenly felt the lack of one as bullets struck their speeding car like hammer blows on sheet metal.

Hot brass from Cooper's Uzi sprayed across the Giulietta's backseat, whipped around by wind from windows opened voluntarily or shattered by incoming fire. Halloran felt one graze his nape, and managed to ignore the sudden wasp sting of it as it fell away behind him. He would be fortunate indeed if that was all the pain he felt, with bullets ripping through the hatchback, in one side and out the other, some deflecting through the roof.

They were gaining on the van, but Cooper was still distracted, dueling with the gunmen in the chase car who were peppering their vehicle with automatic fire. Determined not to let the Ark escape this time, Halloran reached inside his jacket for his SIG-Sauer P-226. The perforated windshield granted him a field of fire, albeit limited. If he could hit the driver, or at least one of the Fiat Doblò's tires—

A bullet creased his right biceps as Halloran was tugging at his holstered pistol. Just a superficial wound, he knew immediately, but it burned like fury all the same. He lurched away from it, as if he could escape the pain that way, and tugged the steering wheel involuntarily. The Giulietta followed orders, swinging sharply left before he caught it, corrected and overcorrected, veering back into the chase car's path.

Their bumpers kissed at something close to eighty miles

per hour, Cooper still firing at their enemies from what had narrowed down to point-blank range. Halloran's right-front tire exploded, either from the impact or a stray round shredding rubber, and he lost track of their adversaries while he fought the Giulietta's skid.

"They're going over!" Bolan called out, and in his left wing mirror, like a short clip from an action film, Halloran saw the chase car rolling, bits and pieces of it flying free, the arms of scarecrows flailing from its open windows. Seconds later, they were on the highway's shoulder, dust clouds settling around them, northbound traffic either stopped or racing past them to get out of range.

The Fiat Doblò van was gone.

"We need to get away from here," Bolan told him. "And it's time to call that guy."

Casoria, Italy

FIVE MILES NORTH of Naples, when he'd satisfied himself that the pursuit was over, Branca ordered Franco Arieti to park the van at a rest stop while he checked it for visible damage. His men were still on edge, keeping their weapons close at hand, frustrated by their inability to join the recent fight, and angered by the loss of friends.

Branca supposed his six men in the Volvo had to be dead, or critically injured and under police guard by now. Eight of the original fifteen remained, enough to pack the van and make it challenging to give the Ark its designated space, but that was barely half the number he'd expected to be leading into Rome.

It's still enough, he thought. And would be if he had to drive the van alone, with no one to support him when he reached the Holy See. He could unveil the Ark before his enemies—had planned to do it personally all along, in fact—but hoped there would be others to prevent the police from killing him before he managed it.

The van was marked by two small bullet holes, not terribly conspicuous, but Branca had his soldiers patch and cover them with roadside mud as camouflage. It might not stand a close inspection, but he doubted that highway patrolmen passing on the motorway would notice. Most of them from the immediate vicinity were likely on their way to Ercolano, anyway, rushing with lights and sirens to become a tiny part of local history.

They couldn't know that Branca would be making epic history in Rome, sometime within the next two hours, three at most.

His long, grim trek was nearly done.

Back on the motorway, he watched for blue-and-white police cars and motorcycles, just in case. There was a chance, despite the bloody chaos back in Ercolano, that a passing witness may have linked his van to the firefight and reported it. The odds against a frightened driver jotting down his license number were extreme, but anything was possible.

Salvation lay in speed now, putting distance between Ercolano and the Ark before authorities had time to gather witnesses and question them. Their exit to Rome lay 180 kilometers north of Casoria, then it would be crushing city traffic, unavoidable, no opportunity for breaking out, and vastly greater odds of being stopped by the police if they behaved in any way abnormally.

And what would happen, in that case?

A last stand in the street. If given any chance at all, Branca would bare the Ark and set God's power free. Whether it worked, whether he was deemed worthy in the end to be Christ's warrior, was a secret that would be resolved only in mortal combat.

He took a break from staring at the mirror to his right, leaned back and closed his eyes. Not sleeping—he was too keyed-up for that—but gathering his strength for what might be the final act of his unique, extraordinary life. The humming of the van's engine, the steady hiss of tires on asphalt, lulled his nerves after the latest battle he'd survived.

Branca was good to go: straight through the gates of hell, to meet the Scarlet Whore of Babylon.

CHAPTER TWENTY-TWO

Naples

Halloran's guy in Naples turned out to be Brother Gianni Borelli, another member of the Congregation for the Doctrine of the Faith, whose skills included flying helicopters. He'd been standing by since Halloran's first call, prepared to offer aid in an emergency, and Bolan thought their present situation qualified.

No ride. Their last one shot to hell and traceable, albeit to a fictional identity, through rental records. Their primary target was running free and on its way to Rome, within a couple hours of touchdown at the Vatican.

An airlift seemed to be the only answer, and Borelli fit the bill.

His bird was an AgustaWestland AW119 Koala, an eight-seat utility chopper. Its wide-body fuselage sat three abreast in the passenger cabin, with one pilot up front, cruising at a top speed of 166 miles per hour, powered by a Pratt & Whitney Canada PT6B-37A turboshaft engine.

The world looked different from fifteen thousand feet.

It had been touch-and-go there, for a little while, until Borelli swooped in to retrieve them. Running on the open motorway was pointless, so they'd gone off-road to miss the first police arriving at the battle site, and kept moving north on foot while Halloran directed their impending rescue via cell phone. They had been two miles and change north of the Ercolano killing ground before the chopper swooped in to retrieve them for a hasty hop to Rome.

Borelli estimated 117 miles to their destination, say, seventy minutes by air. They should be touching down about an hour prior to the fleeing van's arrival, but the downside was locating it. Rome, with its famous seven hills and 2.8 million year-round inhabitants, covered some five hundred square miles. The only place they could predict the van would go was to the Vatican itself.

Ground zero, right, which Bolan had been hoping to avoid.

But it was too late for finessing any action now. Halloran had already called ahead, reporting late events to his superiors, and had the go-ahead to act on their behalf if he saw any last-ditch opportunity to stop the Keepers and their cargo. Running interference with police was problematic, given recent rifts between the Vatican and Italy's secular state. Prime Minister Romano Prodi had blamed a Vatican "plot" for the collapse of his coalition government in 2008, and the Holy See had "divorced" itself from Italian law a year later. Even more recently, investigators had renewed inquiries into the Vatican Bank—formally known as the Institute for Works of Religion—in 2012.

All in all, it was a bad time for the church to be asking the police for a favor.

Halloran keyed the microphone built into matching headphones both men wore to spare their ears the droning noise of the Koala's engine. "We'll be landing soon," he said. "I want to tell you that it's been…well, not a pleasure, but…"

"A new experience?" Bolan suggested.

"Yes, indeed. A new experience to work with you."

"We aren't done yet, you know."

"Of course. I just wanted to thank you," Halloran replied. "For everything."

Another new experience, Bolan thought, as he set his eyes toward Rome.

Custodes Foederis Headquarters

MARCO GIANOTTI EASED back the slide of his Beretta Px4 Storm Compact semiautomatic pistol, confirming that a .40 S&W round was chambered and ready to fire. Twelve more were loaded in the magazine, but if he had to fire the gun at all, Gianotti supposed he should call it a failure. The plan, after all, was to make an arrest, not carry out an execution.

That, if Claudio Branca's suspicions proved out, would come later.

Gianotti still hadn't consulted Janus Marcellus concerning Branca's call about Ugo Troisi. With the Ark so close to Rome and tension running high at headquarters, he had decided that the very worst thing he could do was introduce another problem to the mix. Better by far, for all concerned, if he could simply take Troisi into custody and hold him while the main event played out at Vatican City. If all went according to plan there, perhaps Troisi would confess his sins against the church—or even die spontaneously, when the power of God's wrath had been released against all infidels.

And if the Ark didn't perform as prophesied…well, then, it might not matter what he did with Ugo. All of them would have worse problems than Troisi's wounded pride. In that event, if they had failed, Gianotti could release him or dispose of the man as he pleased, share Branca's warning with the Pontifex and blame Troisi for the scuttling of their dream.

All hypothetical, of course.

His faith compelled Gianotti to believe the Ark *would* function as predicted and deliver victory into their hands. How could he think that scripture could be wrong, or God denied His triumph?

Standing outside Troisi's office, Gianotti took a moment to compose himself, then knocked and entered without waiting to be summoned. He wasn't a supplicant today, but rather an avenger.

Troisi seemed distracted as he looked up from the ledger he was reading. Numbers ranked in columns, adding up to…what? It made no difference.

"What is it, Marco?" he inquired.

"I have a question," Gianotti said, dispensing with the normal courtesy.

"And that is…?"

"When you recommended use of mafiosi to escort the Ark through Sicily, did you expect it to be captured or destroyed?"

It seemed to Gianotti that Troisi's face went pale, then flushed with angry color from the neck up.

"How dare you! What are you suggesting?" Troisi challenged.

"It's a question," Gianotti said. "Not a suggestion."

"It's an insult! You'll regret it, I assure you."

"Possibly," Gianotti said. The Beretta filled his hand. "But not, I think, just yet."

Troisi saw the gun, gaped at it. "Have you lost your mind? Are you insane?"

"We'll let the Pontifex decide that," Gianotti said. "Later this afternoon."

Troisi frowned, his features caught somewhere between defiance and uneasiness. "And until then?"

"You'll come with me," Gianotti said. "Quietly. Or I'll be forced to use this."

"Now I see you *have* gone mad," Troisi said. "All right. We'll play this foolish game your way, for now."

Troisi rose and walked around his desk, then hesitated in the center of the room until a waggle of the gun that Gianotti held encouraged him to leave the office.

"Turn right as you go," Gianotti said, "and continue on until we reach the elevator."

"Going down, are we?"

"The basement cells."

"Enjoy this while you can," Troisi said. "You've made a grave mistake."

It wouldn't be the first, Gianotti thought. But he held his tongue and hid the pistol, trailing Troisi toward the elevator that would take them underground.

Vatican City

"You want me to disturb the Holy Father with this news?" Cardinal Bishop Jerome Saldana asked.

Cardinal Luis Bouchet considered that and answered, "No, Your Eminence. I'm simply keeping you informed."

"Of failure on your agent's part," Saldana said.

"Not failure. It's a problem that I hope may be resolved, if time allows."

"If time allows," Saldana echoed, not quite mocking him. "And therein lies the difficulty, does it not? A normal drive from Rome to Naples should require...how long? Two hours? Three at most?"

"That is correct, Your Eminence."

"And how long is it since your man lost track of those who wish us harm?"

Bouchet wore no watch, and he didn't need one. "Forty minutes now."

"Indeed. So nearly half of our remaining time is gone. That smells like failure."

"I prefer to judge a contest when it is completed," Bouchet said.

"That's fair enough, Luis, bearing in mind that this is *your* contest, not simply…what's his name, again?"

"Brother Halloran."

"Has he served you long?"

"Long and well, Your Eminence."

"Oh, I'm sure. The trouble and this American he picked up in his travels have accomplished nothing."

"I must disagree respectfully, Your Eminence."

"Perhaps I should have said, 'Besides a glut of corpses scattered from Messina to East Africa.' They have not kept our enemies out of striking range of Rome, you must agree. As for the savagery our followers have suffered in attacks around the world—"

"Those incidents don't reflect on anything that Brother Halloran has done or failed to do," Bouchet retorted. "He can't defy the laws of time and space. I gave him one job to perform—"

"And he has yet to finish it! It may already be too late."

"Your Eminence, he has reduced the hostile force by half its starting number. With the Swiss Guard and Gendarmerie on full alert around us, and the Carabinieri outside, a dozen men or less will never penetrate the Holy See."

"They have no need to penetrate it, if their weapon is as advertised," Saldana said.

"You think they have the Ark? That even if they did, our Lord would let its power be employed against His church?"

Saldana turned cold eyes on his subordinate. "What I

believe—and this, I'm authorized to tell you, is a view the Holy Father shares—is that our enemies wouldn't travel so far and risk so much without believing they possessed a weapon that can ruin us. Whether that proves to be a bomb, some sort of pestilence or just a figment of diseased imaginations, it is dangerous."

"But—"

"Dangerous because our enemies believe. Because if they inflict some catastrophic damage on the Holy See, it damages our credibility. It undermines the Holy Father's mandate from our Lord, the very right to speak for Him. You understand? Taken to the extreme, it could inaugurate a new age of apostasy."

"Your Eminence—"

"Luis," Saldana interrupted him. "It's critical that no disaster be permitted. *You* must not permit it." With a finger-jab to Bouchet's chest, he said, "As Brother Halloran's American might say, the buck stops here. With you. We still have leper colonies in need of pastors, eh?"

"I understand, Your Eminence."

"I knew you would."

"You'll be relieved to know that Brother Halloran and his American are on their way to Rome," Bouchet replied. "In fact, they should be landing any moment now."

Washington, D.C.

"No other traces on that phone?" Hal Brognola asked.

"Nothing since Naples," Aaron Kurtzman answered. "They're approaching Rome by now. Nothing to talk about, unless their poobah tries to call them off."

"That isn't happening," Brognola said, with grim conviction. "No one jams through all this interference just to sit down on the five-yard line."

"I'd say it's down to Striker and his buddy, then," Kurtz-man replied.

Or the thousands of police and soldiers on alert in Rome, Brognola thought, knowing that Bolan wouldn't lift a hand to save himself from them, if he was trapped.

"At least they got an airlift," he acknowledged. "Should be on the ground by now, or nearly there."

"Cutting it close," Kurtzman observed. "How's that supposed to work?"

"I wish to hell I knew."

"No way to put a word in for him with the locals?"

"I've been on the line," Brognola said. "They naturally don't appreciate the meddling."

"Did you let them know about the church connection?"

"I considered it. Decided that it's not my place to blow an ally's cover."

"Hmm."

"I know, okay? It was a judgment call. I wouldn't want somebody from the CDF telling the world what Striker's up to, either."

"Right."

"You think I blew it?"

"No, no," Kurtzman said. "Making hard decisions is the reason you keep getting giant paychecks every week."

"Yeah, right. At least I know you haven't hacked my bank account."

"Well, if I ever need a burger in a hurry…"

"No one likes a smart-ass, Bear."

"So everyone keeps telling me."

Brognola didn't want to say the last bit, but he had to get it out. "Listen, if anything goes wrong—"

"It won't."

"But if it does…"

"Deniability's preserved," Kurtzman assured him.

"And you've got Phoenix Force on standby?"

"With Jack Grimaldi. He's already pissed that no one brought him in at the beginning. Says he would've sunk the Ark, day one."

"Guy needs to brush up on his Bible," Brognola replied. "If it turns out we need them—"

"They were ready yesterday," Kurtzman said.

"And it's scorched earth. The home team goes, no matter where they try to hide, however long it takes."

"And after that?" He was asking about the so-called bishops of Custodes Foederis, tending their temples worldwide.

"Some of them obviously knew about the other hits," Brognola said. "No reason they should skate for free."

"Okay. We've got a list."

"Hang on to it."

Some of the cult's midlevel leaders were already under lock and key, awaiting trial on charges ranging from conspiracy to murder. Where the law could do its job, Brognola was content to let procedures run their course. But if he thought the guilty parties had a prayer of ducking punishment, he wouldn't hesitate to use the mandate he'd been given when the White House had established Stony Man. There'd be no amnesty for zealots whose doctrine included mass murder of innocents.

And walk away from taking out Brognola's oldest living friend? No way.

No way at all.

Valmontone, Italy

Twenty minutes south of Rome, with Franco Arieti at the wheel, still eating up the miles, Claudio Branca finally began to think that they might make it after all. From the beginning, although steeped in faith and dedicated to the grand crusade with every fiber of his being, he had harbored doubts, had begged forgiveness from his Savior for the weakness that is part of every human born in sin. Each step along the way, he'd dealt with fear of failure and disgrace. But now, with Rome nearly in view, Branca began to think once more in terms of triumph.

Were they quaking at the Vatican? Did each news bulletin arriving via satellite increase anxiety among the servants of the Scarlet Whore? Branca devoutly hoped so, since a frightened, anxious enemy was less efficient than an adversary who maintained his confidence.

And he'd begun to think about the Ark.

His problem: no one knew exactly how it worked—or *if* it worked, for that matter. Descriptions found in holy writ were vague, at best. God ordered his disciples not to touch or look upon the Ark, and those who disobeyed were stricken down. As for the rest, it was obscure. A mystery.

Branca had brought no trumpets made from ram's horns with him, to repeat the tactic used by Joshua at Jericho. And even if he had, the Scarlet Whore's police weren't about to let him march around the Vatican for seven days, until a shout brought down the walls. He would be lucky if they gave him seven minutes, once he'd reached the Holy See.

What then?

Another tale from scripture told of how Israel had lost the Ark in battle to the Philistines, which led Branca to wonder if the weapon was infallible, or simply fickle. It had been constantly in motion, plaguing with tumors the residents of each town where it stopped, until it was finally surrendered after seven months. It had been lost again when Babylonians destroyed Jerusalem, in 586 BC, then finally surfaced at Axum seven centuries later.

But how did it work?

There'd been no opportunity to test it, for two reasons. First, they had been on the run since snatching it from Ethiopia. And more importantly, perhaps, Branca had feared that any premature attempt to prime the Ark for battle might produce disastrous results. Suppose he and his team were wiped out on the spot? Or what if one exposure vented all the Ark's reputed power at some point along their journey through the hinterlands, leaving Branca empty-handed when he got to Rome?

And worst of all: what if the Ark did nothing? How could he proceed, asking his men to sacrifice themselves without a hope of victory, knowing the superweapon that they carried with them was a dud?

It was unthinkable.

Turning to his soldiers in the van's cargo bay, he cautioned, "Everyone be ready when we cross the city limits into Rome. Expect the opposition to be anywhere and everywhere. We'll be making our final approach on Viale Vaticano. Anything can happen there. Be ready when it does."

Branca supposed the lecture was unnecessary, since they'd covered it a hundred times before. The handpicked members of his team had all accepted the inherent risks involved in their crusade, had made their peace with God and were prepared to die if necessary. But Branca needed them prepared to *live,* to fight and kill with overwhelming odds against them, in the name of Christ their Lord and Custodes Foederis.

This day, he had no fear that they would let him down.

As for the Ark…well, he would have to wait and see. If God abandoned them, Branca was powerless to stop it, but he wouldn't lie down and surrender like a coward. He preferred to go down fighting and to be transformed at death. March on into the golden streets of paradise.

Amen.

Rome Ciampino Airport

EN ROUTE TO Rome, Brother Borelli explained that he couldn't access the heliport within Vatican City. The CDF's prefect had warned him of dissension in the church's upper ranks, specifically a fear of being linked to any action that Bolan and Halloran might engage in after touchdown. Meanwhile, Leonardo da Vinci-Fiumicino Airport was located twenty-two miles from their target, with a risk of getting stalled in downtown traffic.

The solution was Rome Ciampino, aka Giovan Battista Pastine Airport, seven and a half miles from the city's center, just outside the Greater Ring Road that circled downtown Rome. Five million passengers per year used Rome Ciampino Airport, compared to some thirty-eight million passing through Leonardo da Vinci-Fiumicino. But enough daily flights would cover the arrival of one private chopper coming in from Naples.

Bolan assumed the airport had security in place, but no one bothered coming out to check on the Koala's passengers as they deplaned. Two cars were waiting near the helipad, a red compact beside a snow-white limousine. The limo's wheelman didn't bother stepping out or taking off his sunglasses. The compact's driver stood with dark hair whipping in the chopper's rotor wash, a tight smile on his face, and handed its key to Borelli. He passed the key to Halloran in turn, while its deliverer retreated to the limo's shotgun seat. Without a parting wave from either man, the big vehicle pulled away.

"Your car," Borelli said. "Untraceable. I won't delay you further."

"About that other item," Bolan said.

"Of course. On the rear floorboard, I believe. You'll want to check it?"

Bolan did. A duffel bag was lying in the borrowed car, as advertised. Unzipping it revealed a rifle with a telescopic sight and folding stock, plus half a dozen loaded magazines.

"Not quite the easiest to find," Borelli said.

"But worth the effort," Bolan said.

"It pleases you?"

He checked the weapon's action, keeping it below the line of sight for anyone outside the car, and said, "It should be fine."

"In that case," Borelli said, "I will say goodbye and wish you good luck."

"We could use it," Bolan answered, engrossed in preparing his weapon.

The rifle was a venerable Beretta BM59 Mark III, based on the American M-1 Garand but chambered for 7.62 mm NATO rounds, fed from detachable 20-round box magazines. The Mark III was designed initially for mountain troops, with a pistol grip and folding metal stock, together with a folding bipod and a combination flash suppressor-grenade launcher at the business end. Removed from military service in 1990, the BM59 was still a formidable weapon, with selective fire and a full-auto cyclic rate of 750 rounds per minute. The addition of a Schmidt & Bender 5-25x56 PM II LP telescopic sight with a stadiametric range-finding reticle made the "obsolete" weapon a crack sniper's rifle.

The alternative had been Accuracy International's Arctic Warfare Precision Marksman, present standard-issue for Italian military snipers, chambered in the same caliber and equipped with the same Schmidt & Bender telescope. Its drawbacks, for the present mission, were the rifle's bolt action and its magazine capacity of ten rounds maximum.

No good in this case, when the Executioner had no idea how many targets he'd be spotting, and a rapid rate of fire might make the difference between success and a catastrophe.

"Ready?" Halloran asked.

"I will be, by the time we get there," Bolan said. He closed the compact's door behind him, settling in the backseat with his new best friend.

CHAPTER TWENTY-THREE

The trick was finding somewhere to set up and wait. Halloran was quick to find an exit from the airport, tooling north on Via Appia Nuova into Rome. They crossed the Tiber River and continued on northwestward toward Vatican City, with the numbers running down to doomsday inside Bolan's head.

Two points of entry to the Vatican were available to tourists. On the north, pedestrians had access to the Vatican Museum. On the southeast, they could stroll into Saint Peter's Square and visit the Papal Basilica of Saint Peter, arguably the most famous cathedral on earth. Neither approach was open to outside motorized traffic, however, which meant Bolan's adversaries either had to crash the Holy See headlong or park outside and haul the Ark by hand through one gate or the other.

His problem: while Vatican City was the world's smallest sovereign city-state, covering only 110 acres, no external vantage point granted equal coverage of the two public entryways. He had to choose one or the other, and decided that his best bet was Saint Peter's Square, picking a sniper's nest somewhere along the east-west straightaway of Via della Conciliazione. A drive-by showed him that his best shot, literally, would be from the rooftop of a hotel on Via Rusticucci, fronting on Piazza Pio XII.

Dressed once again—and for the last time, he devoutly hoped—in priestly garb, Bolan stepped out of the car, shouldered his duffel bag and ducked his head for a fare-well as Halloran lowered the driver's window.

"I'll be just inside," the brother said, "covering the ground approach."

"Don't try to stop them by yourself," Bolan advised, for all the good that it would do. "If I don't see you after-ward—"

"Then go with God," Halloran said, and pulled away without waiting for a reply.

Bolan passed through a service entrance into the hotel and caught an elevator to the fourth floor, where a door marked Privata—Persone Autorizzate! barred access to unauthorized personnel. He ignored it, passed on through and climbed a flight of concrete steps to reach another door, then opened that in turn to reach the roof.

The hotel's southwest corner was his vantage point, granting a long view of Saint Peter's Square past its obelisk, the hub of rail traffic inside the Holy See, to the looming columns of the great basilica. Tourists roamed freely over the width and breadth of the piazza, with nearly tame pigeons milling around their feet, spinning occasionally into whirlwind flights that rose and fell without apparent rhyme or reason, like a form of living artwork.

Ready for the long hunt to be over, Bolan made a last check of his BM59 and settled down to wait.

"I'M TELLING YOU we *can* drive in, as far the facade of the hotel," Claudio Branca said. "The barricades are farther back, inside the square."

"That's for official cars, from the hotel or Vatican," Franco Arieti replied. "You may recall I checked the place myself."

"And if someone complains, we'll reason with them,"

Branca said, patting the Spectre submachine gun resting in his lap.

They were rolling northwestward on Corso Vittorio Emmanuele III, crossing the Tiber's green water to reach Via della Conciliazione: Conciliation Street. But there would be no conciliation this day. No appeasement. Only bloody reckoning.

Via della Conciliazione ran one-way from east to west, spanning four hundred meters between Piazza Pia and Saint Peter's Square. Within the next few minutes, Branca knew, it was slated to become the world's most famous avenue. The place where God Himself—with Branca's help, of course—fired the opening shot in a war to purify the planet.

Arieti signaled for the left-hand turn, leaving the flow of traffic that continued north on Via di Porta Castello. A white hotel shuttle bus made the turn in front of them, showing Franco the way if he'd had any doubts.

"An escort," Branca said, smiling. "How thoughtful." Then, to his tense soldiers riding in the back, around the Ark, "Be ready!"

None of them responded, but he knew they would be peering past him, through the van's windshield, or out through its tinted windows in back. They would alert him to the first hint of a hostile tail, but it was already too late to stop them short of their objective now.

Branca had half expected ranks of armored vehicles— or at the very least, police cars—to be blocking Via della Conciliazione. He was surprised to find the way wide-open, with nothing to obstruct them but the shuttle bus, and even it was hastening as if to clear their path. A few more seconds and the Ark would yield its secret: blazing power to eradicate the Scarlet Whore, or else a dud that left his team to fight and die alone against all odds.

The shuttle bus turned off to Branca's right, following a line of arrows painted on the pavement to the hotel's entrance. Arieti kept on going straight, as ordered, toward a line of concrete barriers beyond Via Paolo VI, where they would have to stop or crash. At last, he tapped the van's brake and they decelerated to a stop, front tires against the curb, crosswise to southbound traffic on Via Paolo VI.

"End of the line," Branca announced. "God's blessing to you all!"

BROTHER HALLORAN STOOD in the hotel's shadow, with his back against its stucco wall, watching workmen unload groceries and linens onto rolling carts and trundle them inside. He kept his right hand in the pocket of his knee-length raincoat, where he'd slit the lining, fingers wrapped around the pistol grip of his Beretta M12S. The little SMG was cocked, its safety set to "Fire," Halloran's grasp keeping the grip safety depressed and ready for action. He had two magazines taped end-to-end for swift reloading, and if that wasn't enough, he still had the SIG-Sauer P-226 tucked underneath his belt, for backup.

If he couldn't do his part with eighty rounds, Halloran thought that he deserved to fail.

Vans came and went while he stood waiting, including a couple of Fiat Doblòs, but none was the van he expected. It took a moment for his agitated mind to realize that all the service vehicles collected in the hotel's parking lot were white, devoid of anything resembling commercial logos. Now that he thought of it, all of the church's cars and vans were white.

Just like the airport limousine.

He waited, shifting nervously from foot to foot, then caught himself and realized that he had to look suspicious—or like someone with a fierce need to relieve himself. Taking a deep breath and holding it until he heard his own pulse echo in his ears, Halloran finally exhaled when he felt calm enough to stand at ease. He had to be a fixture of the landscape now, until his enemies arrived.

If they arrived. If Matt Cooper was correct about the angle of attack they would choose.

But Halloran agreed with him. It *had* to be Saint Peter's Square and the basilica. There was no other point where vehicles could penetrate the Holy See without encountering immediate resistance. Terrorism's constant threat had altered life around the Vatican, as everywhere, compelling an already insular community to double-lock its doors and guard its walls. The trick, of course, was keeping up free access for the visitors and pilgrims who arrived each day, bearing their cameras, their prayers, their cash.

This day, Halloran guessed, would tighten the security still further. Would it mean more barricades? Armed guards patrolling the piazza? Metal detectors on every exterior doorway? A kennel of bomb-sniffing dogs?

Devoted as he was to his religion, Halloran despised and mourned the countless ways that clashing faiths had stained the course of human history with blood. Sometimes he wondered if the murdered songwriter from Liverpool was right, about a world free of religion being happier, more peaceful. Then he thought about the other motives for atrocity, ranging from gender, race and politics to simple greed, and he despaired of ever seeing peace on earth.

But he could strike a blow this day, if not for peace exactly, then at least in the defense of freedom to believe, to worship, without fear of being murdered or assaulted. There would always be more enemies, Halloran realized, but if he did his job correctly this time, there would be a few less when the sun went down.

A van loaded with flowers parked a few yards to his

right, its driver stepping out and rolling back its side door
to unleash a heady wave of fragrance. For a second, Halloran imagined that he'd wandered into Eden by mistake,
but the chattering of workmen and the steady stream of
tourists passing by dissolved that beatific image.

A Fiat Dobló rolled into view, its silver-gray paint as
peculiar among the white ranks as if it had been sprayed
shocking pink.

Halloran watched the van roll forward to the barricades
across Via Paolo VII, before he stepped out of the shade.

MACK BOLAN SAW the van approaching, could have nailed
its driver with a clean shot through the windshield, but held
his fire and waited. He had weighed the risks between his
two alternatives—to watch or to fire at once—and knew
that if the Ark turned out to be a dirty bomb instead, it
made no difference.

Even the smallest "briefcase" nuke, one kiloton, would
kill half the people exposed to its blast within 350 meters,
rupturing eardrums at double that distance, and producing
penetrating wounds out to almost three kilometers from
ground zero. Flash-blindness might be suffered at about six
kilometers. As for radiation from a dirty bomb, he hadn't
memorized the tables but knew tens of thousands would
die as the breeze wafted poison aloft.

Bolan had the van scoped as it rolled along Via della
Cinciliazione and entered the bottleneck for Saint Peter's
Square. He tracked it across Via Rusticucci and past the
hotel's parking lot, across Piazza Pio XII and Via Paolo
VI, until it nosed into the barricades and halted, blocking
traffic. While he couldn't hear the engine switching off,
there came a moment when the van *felt* still.

Would it explode now? Was a weapon being primed inside it? Should he fire into the roof, the tinted windows, or sit back and wait?

He waited, watching through the scope, until the doors all at once sprang open. Armed men were spilling from the van through both front doors, the rear access and the left-side cargo door. Bolan counted nine in all, a full load for the Fiat Doblò's size. Their sudden appearance caused a ripple in the flow of foot traffic toward Saint Peter's Square, from pedestrians spotting the weapons and instantly changing their minds about staying to shop, gawk or pray. A woman's scream rose up to Bolan's ears, then people down below were bolting off in all directions, rushing to find cover in a zone where none existed.

One of the Keepers raised his weapon to his shoulder, aiming generally toward the frightened crowd, and Bolan shot him in the face. The 150-grain FMJ round struck his target traveling at 2,800 feet per second, delivering 2,500 foot-pounds of destructive energy on impact. It drilled a neat hole through the shooter's cheek, but vaporized the right-rear quadrant of his skull, causing a puff of blood and mangled tissue to burst outward like a ruddy halo as the dead man fell.

One down, and as his gunshot echoed from the beige hotel facade across Saint Peter's Square, the other raiders started firing. None knew who or where their adversary was, as yet, but firing back at something, someone, was an automatic reflex. At the same time, one of them ducked inside the van, leaving the others to it while he scrambled to do—what?

Unleash a taste of hell, perhaps.

CLAUDIO BRANCA HADN'T seen the sniper, only knew his first shot had beheaded Franco Arieti, spraying blood and brains across the nearby traffic barricades. Seven survivors from his team had opened fire instinctively, responding in the knowledge that they might not tag the enemy, but they could still protect Branca in the final moments of their lives, while wreaking havoc on adherents of the Scarlet Whore.

Deafened by gunfire and the pounding of his own heart, bass-drum loud inside the echo chamber of his skull, Branca lunged back inside the van, expecting to be shot at any instant, grateful when he gained the meager sanctuary and was crouched beside the Ark.

He had imagined this climactic moment differently, saw himself in daydreams facing down a phalanx of Swiss Guards as he unveiled the Ark in daylight, visible to every person in Saint Peter's Square. What happened next varied from one fantasy to the next. In some, he was incinerated with the infidels and welcomed it; in others, God's unearthly fire swept past him, seeking out the nonbelievers who had given up their souls, and any claim on paradise, to serve the Antichrist. Sometimes the flames he pictured were a blinding white; at other times, they stung his optic nerves with rippling, ever-changing shades of gold.

Impatient for it to be finished now, he shoved at a cardboard carton filled with hand grenades he'd brought along as a precaution, but had found no opportunity to use. They rattled in their box as Branca pushed them to one side, then set his Spectre SMG beside the carton, reaching out with both hands for the tarp that masked the Ark. His hands were trembling as he clutched it and started tugging it aside, his lips moving as he mouthed a silent prayer.

Our Father who art in heaven...

The tarp snagged on something, resisting, then yielded as Branca redoubled his effort.

A corner of the Ark was now revealed, a wooden chest with brass bindings. Atop its lid—perhaps the object that had snagged the tarp—was an angel, one of several sculpted in a kneeling posture, facing one another with their wings outstretched and touching at the very tips.

Could he raise the lid? Was it sealed or fastened down somehow? There was a toolbox in the van, but in his panic he'd forgotten to retrieve it.

He would try the lid bare-handed, see what happened if he wasn't stricken dead immediately. If it simply jammed, then he could find the toolbox, use its pry bar.

The lid shifted, began to rise, but it was heavy. Branca put his back into it, hissing through clenched teeth. He almost had it, when a voice cried out behind him, "Stop!"

HALLORAN RAN INTO the killing zone, heedless of danger to himself. Tourists and workmen jostled past him, running for their lives, veering away in panic when they saw that he, too, was armed. The vision of a priest wielding a submachine gun may have shocked them more than anything they'd seen or heard since the arrival of the death van in their midst.

Halloran moved among them, heedless of their fear, marking his targets as he closed in on them, firing from the hip. Spitting bullets at 550 rounds per minute, his Beretta SMG could empty its magazine in less than four seconds of steady firing. One man could take all thirty-two rounds before falling if Halloran let himself fire without restraint, and there were so many to kill yet, before he secured the van.

Matt Cooper had dropped the first one from his rooftop sniper's nest, but it was each man for himself after that. Halloran jogged toward the van through the fleeing tourists, dodging them like a broken-field runner in football, milking short bursts from his M12S when a target was clear. One fell, and then another, two of the survivors on the left side of the van turning with their automatic weapons to confront him, covering the open cargo bay.

Halloran felt a bullet crease his left thigh, throwing him off stride and balancing the pain he still felt from the graze he'd suffered to his right arm, back in Ercolano. Fearing that he might fall, he dropped to his knees instead, returning fire, stitching the Keeper who had wounded him with half a dozen Parabellum rounds.

The other made a critical mistake by pausing long enough to aim. Halloran gutted him and left him writhing on the pavement, then lurched upright and pressed on toward the van. As he approached, a scuttling movement in the shadowed cargo space warned Halloran that someone was inside. Not watching him, but doing something with the Ark.

Pain lanced into his stomach as another bullet found him. Whirling, Halloran brought down the shooter with the last rounds from his SMG's first magazine. Time to reload, but he discarded the weapon instead, used every ounce of his remaining strength to reach the van and leap inside.

One of the Keepers was crouched beside the Ark, struggling to raise its lid. Halloran shouted, "Stop!" and lunged to grab the man as he was turning, something close to madness in his eyes. They grappled, fell, sharp objects gouging Halloran's back while waves of pain spread from his wounds, leaving him weak. He lashed out with a fist, connected with his adversary's jaw and somehow found himself atop the other man, hands groping for his throat.

The next pain that he felt was different, a gliding bolt of agony. Halloran glanced down toward his stomach, saw the knife protruding from his body, ripping upward. As he bellowed, coughing blood, the next thing he beheld confused him for an instant. Then he recognized an open carton of grenades. Collapsing forward, he released his adversary's throat, fumbling for one of the metallic eggs. Found it.

And pulled the pin.

BOLAN SAW HALLORAN advancing toward the van and taking hits along the way, dropping the gunmen who were in his path, leaving the rest. The BM59 reached out to nail them, one by one, in semiauto rapid-fire, thinning the pack before the last of them finally spotted Bolan's rooftop nest and turned his piece in that direction, emptying his magazine.

Too late.

A final NATO round tore through the panicked shooter's throat and nearly took his head off when it clipped his spine. The dead man toppled backward, instantly forgotten, Bolan tracking toward the van with his scope.

He was in time to see his comrade crawl inside, and then the van was rocking from a struggle going on in its interior. He couldn't help by firing through the roof, couldn't descend from where he was in time to be of any use. A rising wail of sirens told him that police were on the way, and Swiss Guards in their garish costumes—plumed medieval helmets, blue-and-orange striped uniforms with puffy sleeves and pantaloons—were running through Saint Peter's Square to join the fight with halberds, while their reinforcements scrambled to the armory.

Again, too late.

The Executioner was scoped in on the van when it exploded, one blast followed swiftly by a string of echoing explosions from the cargo bay, and then a rising fireball as the fuel tank detonated. A portion of the vehicle's roof spun off, whirling like a twisted flying disk, falling back at last to grate across the plaza's cobblestones and lines of travertine that radiated from the central obelisk.

Bolan stood waiting for another moment, half expecting more. But from the smoke and flames there rose no mushroom cloud; no lightning bolts descended from the cloudless sky; no wave of blinding brilliance swept across Saint Peter's Square toward the basilica. Below him, there was just the Fiat Doblò's burning hulk—and somewhere in the heart of that inferno, Brother Joseph Halloran.

The soldier set down his rifle, not bothering to wipe it for fingerprints since his had been erased from law-enforcement files. He retraced his steps to the hotel's ground-floor exit at a steady, almost plodding pace, since running was the quickest way to draw attention at a crime scene. He was simply one more priest among the hundreds passing through the Holy See on any given day, appropriately stunned and saddened by the scene of carnage laid before him. No one seemed to notice him as he retreated in the flow of massacre survivors surging from the battleground. Police cars passed him, headed in the opposite direction, none of those inside the cruisers sparing him a second glance.

Halloran had parked their borrowed car behind a restaurant on Via Scossacavalli, two long blocks east of Saint Peter's Square and one block to the south. He'd risked leaving the car unlocked, its key behind the driver's sun visor, and Bolan found it still in place, ready to roll when he arrived on foot.

High time to leave the Holy See behind.

But he was still not done in Rome.

EPILOGUE

Custodes Foederis Headquarters

"What do you mean, we've failed?" Mania Justina asked, a tremor in her voice.

"I think it's self-explanatory," Janus Marcellus answered. "Failure. The antithesis of triumph."

"And we're leaving, now?"

"It seems the better part of valor, wouldn't you agree?"

"Where will we go? Won't they be watching for us everywhere?"

"Not quite," Marcellus replied. "You may not be aware of our investments in Bhutan."

"Bhutan? What's that?"

"Not *what,* my simple darling. *Where.*"

"All right, where is it?" she demanded.

"At the east end of the Himalayas, bordered on the west by India, and on the east by China."

"Are you mad? You want to hide out in a frozen wasteland?"

"We don't have time to talk about the climate now," Marcellus said. "Suffice it to say that Bhutan has cell phone networks, internet access and daily flights to Bangkok and New Delhi. We'll live like royalty on what I've banked there, until we can start again."

"But what about…the others?"

Marcellus lost his smile as he replied, "Your close friend

Ugo won't be coming with us, I'm afraid. Marco arrested him for treason and was forced to kill him during an escape attempt."

"And Marco?"

"Sadly, it appears that he was so grief-stricken that he took his own life afterward. It's just the two of us again, my dear."

He loved the stricken look that crossed her face, but had no time to savor it. Taking Mania by one arm, he steered her toward the exit.

"But…my things!"

"No time to pack, love. If we don't make haste, I fear that we may never leave this blighted city."

On the street outside, their limousine stood waiting for the drive to Naples. Rather than attempt a flight from one of Rome's airports, where they might be expected and detained, Marcellus had a charter jet on standby at Naples International, fueled up and ready to go. They could be in the air within two hours, if their luck held and they weren't stopped on the southbound motorway.

He heard his wife weeping softly as they got into the car. For which of her late lovers? Marcellus neither knew nor cared. When they were safely settled in Bhutan, he reckoned she might have a mountain-climbing accident, or might simply disappear. It was a time for new beginnings, and he didn't need the bitch who had betrayed him getting in his way.

"Leave quickly!" Marcellus snapped to their driver, and the limo started rolling. He was just beginning to relax when something altogether startling happened.

From the sky—or was it from a rooftop just ahead?—a blazing comet raced to meet them, smashed into the limousine's windshield and filled the car with scorching flames before Marcellus could muster a scream.

MACK BOLAN HELD the empty rocket launcher for another moment, watching as the limo creaked and shuddered to a halt downrange, bright flames and oily smoke pouring from shattered windows. Nothing could survive inside that oven, any more than Halloran had managed to escape the van he'd detonated at the Vatican.

Job done? For Bolan's part, at least.

He'd leave the scattered outposts of the cult to someone else, whether the powers that be opted to prosecute their leaders, simply make them disappear, or leave them fuming over dissolution of their sect in scandal and disgrace. The serpent's head was severed. He could do no more in Rome—except, perhaps, to stop and light a candle for a fallen comrade.

Would it make a difference?

He doubted it, but sometimes gestures were enough. Sometimes they were the best that anyone could do.

The following day, or the next, there would be another crisis. He would face another predator who hid behind religion, race or patriotic zeal to victimize the innocent. The adversary might be white, black, brown or yellow, but the constant would be odious corruption of his soul.

Or hers.

For now, this time and place, the Executioner had done enough.

* * * * *

TAKE 'EM FREE

2 action-packed novels plus a mystery bonus

NO RISK

NO OBLIGATION TO BUY

The Executioner®
Don Pendleton's

EXTRACTION

The ransom clock counts down....

When the U.S. Secretary of State is kidnapped in Madagascar by a terrorist organization, Bolan must partner with an operative from his past to help him track the captors. But the lines between traitor and rogue are not only blurred, they make a deadly combination. Hunted by an assassin as dangerous as he is, the Executioner will need to employ every stealth move he knows to get the secretary—and himself—out of the island nation alive.

GOLD EAGLE®

Available in July wherever books are sold.

GEX416